1/12

Praise for *What a Goddess Wants*:

"This is one hot book! Plent[y] ~~~
ing, fast-paced story."

"Julian's world building is uniqu[e] ~ rich, and her characters are intriguing."

—*Night Owl Romance*

"Fast-paced action, hot romance, fascinating mythology, and fantastic secondary characters all make *What a Goddess Wants* a must read."

—*A Bookworm's Haven*

"Julian has a gift for tossing in intriguing twists and turns in the plot."

—*Fresh Fiction*

"The chemistry... comes alive for the reader. It sizzles right off the pages."

—*Sizzling Hot Books*

"*What a Goddess Wants* provides a thrilling and unique spin on the gods and goddesses of old while giving readers spice, passion, and action all the way through."

—*Long and Short Reviews*

"Stephanie's world building is amazing... fast, exciting, and sizzling hot."

—*Anna's Book Blog*

HOW TO WORSHIP A GODDESS

STEPHANIE JULIAN

sourcebooks
casablanca

Copyright © 2011 by Stephanie Julian
Cover series design by Lesley Worrell
Cover and internal design © Sourcebooks, Inc.
Cover image © MaxFX/Shutterstock.com

Published by Sourcebooks Casablanca, an imprint of Sourcebooks, Inc.
P.O. Box 4410, Naperville, Illinois 60567-4410
(630) 961-3900
FAX: (630) 961-2168
www.sourcebooks.com

Library of Congress Cataloging-in-Publication Data

Julian, Stephanie.
  What a goddess wants / by Stephanie Julian.
    p. cm.
  1. Goddesses—Fiction. I. Title.
PS3610.U5346W47 2011
813'.6—dc22
                    2011015763

Printed and bound in the United States of America
        VP 10 9 8 7 6 5 4 3 2 1

This one's for Judi, because even when she has her own deadlines,
she's more than willing to read for me. And reread. And talk about it.
And talk about it some more.

Glossary

Aguane—Etruscan elemental water spirits, always female

Aitás—Etruscan Underworld

Arus—Magical power inherent in the races of Etruscan descent

Berserkir—Shapeshifters who take on characteristics of bears

Cimmerians—Warriors from Cimmeria with legendary strength and bravery.

Enu—Humans of magical Etruscan descent

Eteri—Etruscan for foreigner, used to describe regular humans

Fata—Elemental beings of magical Etruscan descent

Fauni—shape-changing Etruscan elemental beings with an affinity for animals

Involuti—Founding gods of the Etruscans, those from whom all other Etruscan deities were descended

Linchetto (pl. linchetti)—Etruscan Fata, a night elf

Lucani—Etruscan werewolves

Salbinelli—Etruscan satyr

Silvani—One of the Etruscan elemental races

Strega/stregone (pl. streghe)—Etruscan witch

Versipellis—Literally "skin shifter;" shapeshifters including Etruscan Lucani (wolves), Norse Berserkir (bears), and French loup garou (wolves)

Chapter 1

SOME DAYS IT DIDN'T pay to get out of bed.

Especially if you happened to be a once-powerful goddess and you'd just spent the last half hour on your hands and knees cleaning the clogged drain in your bar.

Lucy Aster, still known to an ever-decreasing circle of followers as Lusna, Etruscan Goddess of the Moon, had filthy hands, stains on her shirt, and at least one streak of grease on her face.

So, of course, the door to Howling Wolf opened and a young voice called to her.

"Lady Lucy, are you here?"

The girl knew she was. Catene Rossini Ferrante was *lucani*, an Etruscan wolf shifter whose sense of smell was ten times better than any human's. Catene had been able to scent her from outside.

But Catene was nothing if not polite and respectful. A beautiful young woman in every way.

Stifling a sigh that Catene would also detect because of her enhanced hearing, Lucy straightened from her crouch, pasting on a pleasant expression for the girl who had the brightest smile this side of Thesan, Etruscan Goddess of the Sun.

"Hello, Catene. How are you, sweetheart?"

The girl dropped into a curtsy when she caught sight of Lucy.

Catene's lustrous copper-colored hair dipped over her shoulders as her blue eyes lowered in deference. "I'm fine, Lady. I just... I was in the area so I thought I'd stop to say hello."

The girl was an absolute doll. Too bad she couldn't lie worth a damn.

"It's nice to see you, sweetheart. It's been too long."

Of course, Lucy could lie. She'd had *so* much more practice.

Lucy hated that she had to lie, but she wasn't happy to see her. She adored the girl but Catene represented Lucy's worst nightmare.

"I'm so sorry, Lady. I've been so busy—"

"That wasn't a rebuke, dear." Damn it, Lucy felt like she'd kicked a puppy. "Only an observation. Now, what can I do for you?"

Catene blinked and Lucy knew exactly why she was here. Sympathy made her stomach twist into knots. Young love really did suck.

"Tivr's not here." Lucy said it as gently as she could. "And I don't know where he is."

Catene tried to hide her disappointment, tried to keep her smile from faltering. She managed, for the most part. She might have fooled someone else.

But she couldn't fool Lucy. The *lucani* were hers. More than two thousand years ago, she'd given a small village of Etruscans the power to transform their bodies from human to wolf. And for that, they continued to worship her. Even if she no longer deserved it.

Life was too damn complicated.

"Oh." Catene bit her lip and nodded. "I'm sorry, Lady. I didn't mean to bother you."

At least in this she could respond honestly. "You're never a bother."

Only a reminder of my obsolescence.

The girl's smile rebounded and Lucy felt her black mood lift, even if it was only a little.

"Thank you, Lady. I just… Thanks."

With a wave, the girl headed back out the door, bright hair flowing behind her.

Lucy stared at that door for several seconds, making sure she heard the girl start the bright yellow muscle car she and her father Kyle had rebuilt from the tires up, and peel out down the lane away from the bar.

Then, with a muffled screech, Lucy grabbed the first thing within reach.

The wooden bowl of peanuts on the bar didn't stand a chance. She flung the bowl across the room, where it hit the wall and shattered, peanuts and splinters falling to the floor in a pile of debris. She reached for a second bowl but forced herself to stop.

Great Mother Goddess, she needed to get a grip. She'd been losing control more often and—

Well, damn. She was an idiot. The full moon approached. No wonder her mood swings were worse than a teenaged girl's.

She really needed to get laid. Sex would go a long way to soothing her mood. But like everything else in her life, sex would have to wait. At least for now. She had a business to run.

With a huff, she got the broom from behind the counter and cleaned up the mess she'd made.

Too bad she couldn't sweep her mistakes away as easily.

"Hey, Mom, everything okay?"

Tivr stuck his head out the door from the back room, sharp gray eyes narrowed in concern, short dark hair spiked in every direction.

Her child looked as though he'd just stepped off the stage of a metal concert in his sleeveless black T-shirt and ragged skintight jeans. With muscles any bodybuilder would be proud of, Ty appeared to be only twenty or so in human years.

In reality, he'd been born more than two millennia ago.

Which, yes, made her even older, but she'd stopped counting birthdays long ago.

"I'm fine." She forced a smile. "Just dropped a bowl. And covered your ass with Catene."

His lips quirked in a smart-ass grin she loved with every fiber of her being, but his eyes… oh, those eyes held their own secrets. "Yeah, uh, thanks. How's she look?"

"Beautiful, of course." She let Ty drift in the breeze for a few minutes before she took pity on him and switched the subject. "Are you here to go to the game with me tonight?"

Thank the Blessed Mother, there was a Railers game tonight. The minor-league hockey team filled her winter nights with hot guy-on-guy action. She loved hockey. Loved the speed, the agility. The fights. The men.

Brawny, sweaty, messy. They let their hair grow, though no one would ever accuse them of being feminine, not with perpetual five o'clock shadow and bulging muscles. They skated with the grace of ballet dancers and fought at the drop of a glove.

Who didn't love hockey? Especially these past two seasons—

Ty shook his head. "Can't go tonight, sorry. Told Caeles I'd cover for him in here. The band has an early gig but he'll be here later for your set. I'm sure you'll find someone to take."

As Ty ducked back into the kitchen, Lucy knew he was right. Every night, she surrounded herself with people. Men, women. Mostly her *lucani*. They brightened her nights and helped keep the loneliness at bay.

After so many millennia, the nights could become interminable. Yet, for the past two seasons, she'd looked forward to each game.

Because of him. Her chest tightened and she had to work to draw in a breath.

How ridiculous was it that just the thought of him could make her sex clench and her lungs tighten with desire.

Brandon Stevenson. Six foot two, two hundred. Born 6/10/76. She could recite his stats in her sleep, which was a pitiful thing to admit, she realized.

Brown eyes the color of dark chocolate. A crooked smile that could taunt another player into throwing down his gloves or make a woman's heart race. Dark blonde hair cut short enough to be conventional but long enough to run fingers through.

She entertained dreams of stripping his sweaty uniform from his body, piece by bulky piece, exposing broad shoulders, ripped abs and strong thighs, and every other piece of gorgeous flesh in between.

Railers Number seventeen ignited something inside her that she hadn't felt in… well, never.

It confused and confounded her. *Vaffanculo*, she'd never even met the man. Truth be told, she'd been reluctant to approach him. Didn't want to discover how truly deep her attraction to this *eteri*, this regular human, was.

Coward.

Yes. With good reason.

Her powers had steadily declined over the centuries, as had all of the Forgotten Goddesses. They were still immortal. But now they were useless.

Case in point: five months ago, Charun, the Etruscan God of the Underworld, had begun to terrorize Sun Goddess Tessa in her dreams. Her sister goddesses had been unable to help her. Now bright, sweet Tessa had been missing for weeks. Lucy sincerely hoped Tessa and her Cimmerian bodyguard, Caligo, had holed up somewhere safe. With a bed. Tessa needed someone to take care of her.

Lucy had been taking care of herself for years. She wasn't frightened of Charun. Bullies tended to pick on weaker prey and Lucy had never been weak. But she was obsolete.

Her wolves no longer worshipped her, not as they once had. And both of her sons were of an age where they didn't need her. Ty hadn't for longer than she cared to remember. Caeles, adopted when he'd been only a few days old, hadn't truly needed her for almost two decades, the blink of an eye in an eternal lifetime. And even though her boys still paid lip service to her maternal instincts, she knew the truth.

She had become obsolete in more than one way. Sighing, she checked the clock. Only an hour until she could leave for the game. And watch the man who made her hot and wet between the thighs for the first time in a very long time.

~~~

"Hey, old man, you get that bump checked out last night? You got knocked into the boards pretty hard. Your old brittle bones can't take a beating like they used to."

"Stevie, you need to take more care. We wouldn't want to lose you now, not when you're actually playing better than you have been in years."

Brandon Stevenson tossed his bag in his locker and gave a finger to the twins. Jason and Thomas Fransechetti were barely twenty-one years old. Baby-faced bruisers who weighed more than two hundred pounds, stood six feet tall, and had blazing wrist shots from opposite wrists.

The Terrible Twosome, as they'd been dubbed by the Railers, were identical except for the length of their wavy brown hair—Jase's cut short and Tommy's to his shoulders. The only other way to tell them apart was by their scars. But they had to be naked to see them.

The puck bunnies made a habit of cataloging those scars.

"Fuck off, children, and let the adults get ready for the game." Brand swallowed a smile as the boys followed him anyway. "Or do you need me to tie your skates for you?"

"Fuck you." Jase's fist shot out to Brand's shoulder. The kid didn't pull his punches but Brand shrugged off the hit like it was a fly. At thirty-five, twenty-five of those years spent on the ice, his body had sustained more damage than a professional boxer's. He knew how to control pain.

"Maybe Grandpa Stevenson needs his nap," Tommy chimed in. "Or maybe you just need to get laid. Christ, how long has it been, anyway? Why don't you come out with us after the game? We'll hook you up good."

Brand rolled his eyes and shoved his elbow in Tommy's chest. "The girls you pick up can barely spell their names. Why the fuck—"

"They don't need to be able to spell. They only need to—"

"Jesus fucking hell, don't you two ever get tired of fucking? You're like little fucking machines." Goaltender Shane Conrad walked into the locker room and smacked Tommy on the back of his head. "Have some respect for your elders. At least get Stevenson a woman his own age. 'Course, that'd mean you'd need to hit the early bird specials."

"Hey, who you calling little?"

Brand shook his head as the guys continued to ride each other with increasingly obscene gestures and suggestions as they geared up for warm-ups before the game.

But he couldn't hide his smile.

For the past two seasons, this locker room in the bowels of the Reading arena had been home. Unlike a lot of the younger guys who moved up and down from this league to the American Hockey League and, if they were really good, to the NHL, Brand had become a fixture here with the Railers.

But not for much longer.

Pulling his practice jersey over his head, he shoved away the depression that wanted to pick and poke at his brain. He couldn't allow it to fuck with him, not before a game.

At thirty-five, this was his last stop as a player. He'd been playing professional hockey since he was eighteen years old. He'd played for the ECHL, the AHL and, for one season, the NHL, first for the Washington Capitals then the Toronto Maple Leafs.

He'd had a good run, but he was getting too old to play. He didn't recover from injuries as fast as he had. Some mornings, his entire body ached for no reason.

All good things must end.

But what the hell would he do? No wife, no kids. No skills beyond the ice, except those behind a bar. He could go home to Maine, take over the family business from his parents, but…

Hell, you've never even met the woman.

Didn't mean he hadn't been fantasizing about her for months. From the first moment he'd seen her in her seat at the arena, he'd wanted her. And not just for some wimpy date where they had dinner and drinks and he kissed her good night before going home to jack off.

No, he was talking down-and-dirty, do-me-in-the-backseat, up-against-a-wall, inferno-hot sex. She looked like she could handle it. She wasn't some twenty-year-old puck bunny who hung out at the bars after the game, hoping to snag a player for the night. No, she looked to be thirty-something, at least. A real woman with a decent career, if her clothes and her bearing were any indication.

She wore jeans, sleek and sexy and perfectly fitted to her gorgeous female curves. The woman had a rack to die for and an ass he wanted to get his hands on, preferably while she was naked.

She always wore sweaters that were feminine and pretty, not bulky and concealing. Or slutty. She never slouched and her attention was always focused on the game.

The only part of her that hinted at a wild side was her midnight black hair that waved over her shoulders and down her back like a rough ocean. She never had it pulled back in a tail. He wanted to sink his hands into it, drape it over his naked body and feel it caress his thighs as she— He shook his head, trying to dislodge the image of her going down on him that he now had stuck in his head.

Her name was Lucy Aster. He'd asked the ticket guys who she was and, after they'd busted his chops for at least five minutes, they'd come up with a name. And an address that had turned out to be bogus. Which had intrigued the hell out of him. Why—

"Hey, Stevenson, let's go."

With a start, he realized the guys were heading out for warm ups. Shit, he needed to focus. Or he'd find himself checked headfirst into the boards tonight. A few more hits like the one he'd taken the day before and he could kiss his career good-bye. For good.

Chapter 2

Now that he was here, Brand felt pretty frickin' stupid sitting in front of her house, like some damn stray dog that had followed her home.

Or, worse yet, a stalker. Christ, just what he needed—a woman calling the police to say some stupid-ass hockey player followed her home. And just what the hell did he think he was going to say to her if he actually got out of the car and knocked on her door?

Hey, I noticed you never miss a home game and always manage to be in your seat for the pregame warm-up. Wanna have sex?

Yeah, he really was an idiot. A woman like that, she had a husband or, at the very least, a boyfriend. Still, even though she usually came to the games with a man, sometimes the same man, it wasn't usually the same guy two nights in a row. The men rotated, as if she had a wide group of friends and they shared the extra season ticket.

He'd never seen her kiss or hug or hold hands with any of them—which just meant he spent way too much time watching the woman when he was supposed to be concentrating on warm-ups. During the game, he'd learned not to accidentally catch sight of her or he'd wind up checked into the boards.

Tonight…

He sighed. Tonight he'd been distracted from the moment he set foot on the ice. He automatically flexed his shoulder and let himself wince because no one could see him do it. That hit into the boards had rattled him and the team doctor was still debating treatment.

Which was why he sat here, outside the address it'd taken him a month to track down, because the one on her season ticket application wasn't hers. Oh, it was a real address. She just didn't live there.

About a month ago, he'd actually gotten up the nerve to introduce himself. He'd knocked on the door of the house in Wyomissing that was listed as hers. And ended up looking like a jackass when the homeowner recognized him as one of the players. Turned out the guy was a season ticket holder. Just not the one he was looking for.

So he'd had to dig a little deeper into Lucy Aster's life before he'd come up with a real estate deed with her name on it. His mother had sold real estate once upon a time. When he'd made his weekly call home Sunday, he'd asked her how to find an address for someone who might not want to be found. Mom had come through.

Now, staring out the window of his truck, he studied the stone farmhouse that had to be at least two hundred years old and in perfect condition. It'd been built at a time when the second and third floors had housed the humans and the first floor had held the animals.

Today, the ground floor housed a bar. Not that the sign hanging outside actually said *bar* on it. It didn't need to. The figure of the wolf sitting on a stool holding a mug pretty much made that clear.

Though there were no open windows, music filtered out into the cold January air. He'd opened his window so he could hear it. Something from the seventies. Boston, "More Than a Feeling." Good song.

There were three cars parked in the gravel lot where he now sat several hundred yards from the house. Estimating two people per car and a few locals who might have walked, there might be ten people in there.

He'd only found this place because he'd taken the time to get a longitude and latitude for the property to plug into his car's GPS system. The property literally didn't have an address, though how the hell that oversight had happened, he had no idea.

Farm roads and unmarked lanes crisscrossed Oley Township and meandered all the hell over the place. The map of the area he'd bought hadn't been much good, so he'd needed every bit of help he could get.

Her home sat at the very end of a dirt lane that had started as a two lane road that ran straight through the most picturesque country village he'd ever seen. A village with no name that wasn't listed on his map.

It sat in a small valley, surrounded by old-growth woods, not farmland, like most of the rest of the township. He'd passed through the little town of Oley on his way here. The houses along Main Street looked like they'd been transplanted straight from a German travel brochure. Wood, stone and plaster buildings with shingled roofs and old-fashioned shutters on the windows lined a narrow street, with many of the houses boasting placards with the year of their construction—a seventeen started most of the numbers.

Quaint.

This village's buildings looked German, but not completely. Almost as if they wanted you to think they were built by German immigrants. The edges here were softer, the windows and doors arched. The houses were nearly all plastered, their walls smooth, except for a few made of stone. Those actually looked like something out of a fairy tale. A place hobbits or elves might feel right at home.

He hadn't intended to end up here tonight. He'd only planned on taking a drive, clearing his head. He'd driven for an hour before he'd pulled to the side of the road and plugged in these coordinates.

Yeah, he probably should've thought this through a little more, thought about how he'd look, showing up unannounced on her doorstep. But now… now that he had a legitimate excuse to walk into the bar and talk to her… now he just sat here.

"Christ Almighty," he muttered. "You're thirty-five years old. Act your fucking age."

He got out of the car and walked to the door, gravel crunching beneath his feet, his breath visible in the night air.

The building had no windows on the ground floor, so he had no idea what to expect. But he'd practically been raised in his parents' bar. Nothing here should surprise him.

Reaching for the doorknob, he had a moment of what-the-fuck when it felt warm to the touch. Almost hot. Weird. Shaking his head, he turned the knob and pushed against the door which was heavy and huge. Solid wood and beautifully decorated with intricate carvings that looked like random squiggles and lines. He had to give it a good shove to open far enough for him to walk in. It almost felt like someone was leaning against it from the inside. Which couldn't be right because when he crossed the threshold, there was no one within ten feet of him.

As he closed the door behind him, he realized he'd been wrong about the number of people. There had to be at least thirty, spread out around the handful of tables on the floor or at the long bar opposite the door.

And they all stared at him.

Good thing he wasn't shy because the combined weight of those gazes was worse than the home audience at a losing playoff game. Walking up to the bar, he took an empty stool. The bartender, who looked like a teenager with short, spiked dark hair, heavy-duty tats covering his arms, and a serious addiction to his Nautilus machine, came right over.

The kid's sharp gray eyes took in everything about him in seconds. "What can I get you?"

"Draft, whatever's on tap."

The guy nodded and moved down to the taps to fill his order. "Haven't seen you here before." He set the mug in front of Brand. "How'd you find us?"

Brand took a swallow, trying to figure out why the guy sounded like he was trespassing. If this was a private club, why had he let Brand order?

"Heard about the place from a friend," not quite true but good enough for now, "thought I'd check it out."

The guy nodded and Brand found himself staring into the guy's eyes. He couldn't be sure, because the lighting was so dim, but the bartender's eyes looked silver, not just gray. And they glowed. Whoa.

Blinking, he forced his gaze to drop.

"Is your friend here tonight?" the bartender with the freaky eyes asked. "What's his name? Maybe I know him."

"Lucy Aster."

The guy's eyebrows shot up. "Then you're in luck. She'll be on in just a few. I'll be back to see if you need anything else."

On? What the hell did that mean? Brand settled in to find out.

———

Lucy stood at the door separating the kitchen and office from the bar, her lips parted in surprise.

Her hockey player was out there. Brandon Stevenson was in her bar. Dumbfounded, she watched him drink a beer, taking in everything around him, looking as comfortable as if he were a regular. She flashed cold then hot, her body shaking with conflicting emotions. He'd found her. How the hell had he found her?

She didn't know whether to be flattered or terrified. The full moon was only a few days away and more than three-quarters of her patrons were *versipelli*. He had absolutely no idea of the danger he was in from a room full of skin-shifters this close to the full moon.

Of course, the man had been knocking heads on the ice for the past sixteen years. He could take care of himself. To a point. Lucy let her gaze trip over the rest of the crowd. They had a good house tonight and she saw no one who might cause a problem.

Actually, some of the male *versipelli* eyed Brand warily. He easily stood inches over the tallest of them and probably had at least twenty pounds on the biggest guy out there.

The women, on the other hand… They stared at him like, well, probably just like she was. Like they wanted to throw him on the nearest bed.

No matter who was staring, Brandon Stevenson was a man to watch. And she had been, for the past two seasons. How had he found her? And why?

It couldn't be coincidence. He couldn't have just walked in here off the street. There were no signs, no arrows pointing the way. The village was listed on no map in existence. The only way he could have known to look for her here was if he'd seen the most recent deed to the property, which was more than a hundred years old. Had he really gone to that much trouble? Her breasts tightened and her thighs quivered just thinking about it. "Mother, are you ready? It's time." Caeles walked up behind her, guitar in hand.

She turned to smile at the young *fauni* she'd adopted after he'd been dropped on her doorstep as an infant.

Now thirty-two, he had the face of a young man just out of his teens. His golden-brown hair curled in ringlets to just above his shoulders, and his golden eyes gleamed in the low light. When he walked among the *eteri*, he had to hide those eyes. They attracted unwanted attention.

Caeles would much rather be known for his music than his looks. The boy had a gift and she'd often wondered if whoever had placed him on her doorstep that night had known exactly what they were doing when they'd given him to her. He'd brought music back to her life.

And she'd never tried to find out who had abandoned him because she hadn't wanted to lose him to them.

Selfish? Yes. She didn't care. He was hers and she protected what was hers.

"I am. Is the playlist okay, sweetheart? I tried to include a few new songs for you."

The boy's smile lit the entire room, just as it had from the moment she'd held him in her arms. "You know it is."

"Good." She grasped his hand and squeezed. "Now, let's go knock 'em dead, kid."

Pushing through the door, she deliberately ignored Brandon, though she wanted to seek him out. Instead, she pinned her gaze to her stool on the small stage in the west corner of the room and walked toward it with a determination she hoped no one else noticed.

The room went silent as she sat, the heavy weight of anticipation settling over her. Taking a deep breath, she closed her eyes. And swore she felt his gaze like a physical caress. Curious and hot and… No, not just hot. Blindingly passionate. The man wanted her with a physicality that made her stomach clench in reaction.

His presence energized the room to a degree she hadn't thought possible with an *eteri*. And she sensed no trace of *Fata* or *Enu*, the Etruscan magical races, in him.

Of course, that didn't mean he couldn't be a descendent of the *Sidhe* or any of the other magical races of the world. Egyptian, Sumerian, or… *Berserkir*. Yes, with his dark-blond hair and stormy gray eyes, she wouldn't be surprised to find a little Norse magic in his blood.

The click of Caeles's guitar being plugged into the amp drew her out of her thoughts to the task at hand. They had a set of music to perform, one she hoped her guests liked. What would Brandon think?

For just a second, she let her gaze connect with his and had to suppress the jolt of heat that shot through her veins like quicksilver. Blessed Mother Goddess, she wanted him. Could she let herself have him? Knowing she'd have to give him up tomorrow?

Maybe the question should be, could she let him walk out of

here *without* having him? That might require more willpower than she'd possessed in millennia.

<hr>

For the next forty-five minutes Brand sat at the bar, barely remembering to drink his beer or hide his raging hard-on.

Not that anybody was looking at him. All eyes were glued on Lucy Aster. The woman had the voice of a fallen angel, a smoky tenor that blew through a set of jazz and R&B and standards any cabaret singer would be proud of. A little Janice Joplin, a little Billie Holiday, a whole lot of Lucy. Sexy without being in-your-face flagrant. Smooth and rich but undeniably hers.

Brand swore he felt sex waft through the room. Every man wanted her and every woman wanted to be her. Hell, the once or twice he tore his gaze away from her and looked around, the expression on every single face in the crowd was rapturous.

The audience felt every emotion with her, a roller-coaster ride of unrequited love, heartbreak, and finally, redemption. It was almost eerie, how he felt every breath she took, felt the deep sadness that made her voice so husky, without ever making eye contact.

Instead, he watched her every move. And he meant *every* move. The deep, scoop neck of her purple velvet dress bared the tops of her breasts, the flesh quivering with every breath. The high waist emphasized the length of her body and molded the luscious curves of her hips and ass. He wished it bared her legs but he wasn't complaining.

He did wish she'd look at him, though. Except for that one glance before she'd started singing, she hadn't acknowledged his presence during the entire forty-five-minute set. He didn't know if that was deliberate or because he was on the other side of the room, but he was beginning to think she was ignoring him.

And it pissed him off.

He wanted her to acknowledge him, which made absolutely no

sense, considering they'd never met. He wanted to stalk up there, throw her over his shoulder, and head for the nearest bedroom. Christ, he needed to get a grip.

"Thank you all for coming tonight." Lucy's voice snapped Brand's attention back to the stage as the object of his desire stood and addressed the crowd. "Caeles and I are going to take a break but we'll be back a little later."

Her adoring fans stood and applauded. Reverently. No foot stomping or whooping, just a wall-shaking applause that made her smile from ear to ear. A heart-stopping, earth-shattering smile that made his knees weak and his gut clench.

Christ, what was it about this woman that made him hot, horny, and hard in seconds?

Stepping off the stage, she walked through the crowd, stopping to shake hands or touch shoulders, say a few words. She didn't stop for long, though, and it became clear she was making her way across the room to the bar. To him.

His palms sweaty, he waited for what seemed like forever for her to get to him. Just before she reached him, his mother's manners kicked in and he slid off the stool to stand.

She was smaller than he'd thought, the top of her head not reaching his shoulders. And her eyes were a beautiful light blue, so pale they looked gray. The color of clouds at night.

"Hello, Brandon. Welcome to Howling Moon. I'm Lucy Aster."

He held out his hand and felt hers slide into place. Her skin warmed against his as her smile grew. And Brand knew, just from that look, that she wanted him, too. His night was looking up.

"I enjoyed your set. Your voice is phenomenal."

Sliding onto the stool next to his, she nodded to the bartender before turning back to him. Her smile hit him like a ton of bricks in the chest, making him struggle for every breath.

"Thank you." Damned if that sultry voice didn't make him

want to lick her from head to toe. "I'm so pleased when others receive enjoyment from listening to it. I am surprised to see you here tonight, though. You had a game tonight. And another tomorrow with Trenton, don't you?"

He laughed and took a sip of his beer. "Are you trying to tell me I should be home in bed?"

So much heat filled the look she gave him, he swore the beer in his hand would boil over. "I would never presume to do that. You're a grown man. I'm sure you know when bedtime is."

Her smile led him to believe it was her bed he should be in. And not to sleep.

An image of Lucy naked on a moonlit bed popped into his head, arms open, beckoning to him. He had to blink it away before she realized what he was thinking. Of course, if the look on her face was any indication, she already knew. And welcomed it.

"But I am curious how you found my place. It's a little... out of the way."

And there again, he got the sense that she wasn't exactly happy he'd found her. "Would you think I'm a nut job if I told you I went to the courthouse to track down your name?"

Her gaze narrowed as the start of a smile lifted the corners of her beautiful mouth. "You checked out the address on my season ticket application?"

"Yeah, I did. And found out it was bogus. But I wanted to meet you and when I want something, I don't stop till I get it."

Her head cocked to the side. "Why go to so much trouble to track me down?"

Because you invade my dreams and drive me crazy with lust?

Probably not what she wanted to hear. "I think you're beautiful and I wanted to meet you."

There was that smile again, the one that made the bottom fall out of his stomach. The one that grabbed hold of his balls and squeezed.

"Then I guess I can't be mad, can I? Because I must admit I'm glad you're here."

So can we get the hell out of here to somewhere more private? was on the tip of his tongue but he managed not to embarrass himself by blurting that out. He wasn't a real smooth talker, not like some of the guys on the team, but he did have enough sense and years on him to know what *not* to say to a woman.

And this was a woman unlike any he'd ever met. So confident, so in charge.

Sure, they were sitting in a bar, but she was the owner. And this was no dive. The wood floors gleamed, as did the bar, and the glass mugs were clean. It didn't smell of smoke or grease, but there was an underlying scent of something musky, kind of like the forest in spring, woody and fresh.

"Do you sing every night?" He finally managed to form a coherent sentence.

She shook her head. "Not every night, but several times a week."

"I'm glad I got to hear you. You do a decent business." It was Friday and nearly all the seats in the place were taken; decent was an understatement.

"I'm blessed with loyal customers."

"I'm kind of surprised you do so well out here. It was hard to find."

She laughed and he swore everyone in the place stopped what they were doing to listen. He completely understood. That husky, sexy, purring laugh made every part of his body strain toward her. He had his hand on her arm, his thumb stroking the fast-beating pulse at her wrist, before he realized he'd moved.

"Yes, it is hard to find." Her gaze met and held his and the heat began to build into an inferno. If he wasn't careful, he was going to kiss her and he had a feeling every male in the place would jump him for daring to. "But you managed just fine. How is that?"

Her voice held an undercurrent of something he couldn't put his finger on, something a little dangerous. "I have a great sense of direction. And a GPS unit in my truck."

"I suppose that would do it, wouldn't it?" Taking a sip of her beer, Lucy swallowed, and Brand found his gaze drawn to her throat. Her skin was such a pale cream against her dark hair. The sight mesmerized him. Damn, he wanted to grab her and pull her close so he could lick her neck.

"So, Brandon, how late are you allowed to stay out and play tonight before you have to get home to bed?"

He cleared his throat and took a sip. The only bed he wanted to be in right now was hers. "I've got a few hours yet. I'm not *that* old."

She laughed, a quiet exhalation of air. "I didn't mean to imply that you were. I guess that was my sloppy way of asking if you can stay for a while. I have another set to perform but I'd love to talk to you some more afterward."

Hot damn. That was exactly what he wanted to hear. "I can stay however long you want me to."

"Good." She wasn't smiling now but her eyes glowed with promise. "Because I might want you to stay all night."

Chapter 3

BRANDON'S EXPRESSION MADE LUCY light up inside.

He looked pole-axed and lust-struck at the same time.

She hadn't meant to be so blatant, hadn't planned to lay her cards on the table so fast. But she'd been lusting after this man for almost two years, since the first time she'd seen him skate onto the ice.

She'd denied her need of him for what seemed like forever but she'd been denying other, darker needs for so much longer. Decades. Centuries. She'd denied them to take care of her sons and her *lucani*. So worried that the mistakes of the past would bite her on the ass.

But even a goddess deserved to reward herself every now and then, didn't she? And Brandon looked like the kind of man who could give her what she needed.

"I'll stay as long as you want," he said, his gaze warming to molten hot. Then he blinked, as if realizing the implication of what he'd said, and he turned the conversation back to safe ground. "So, where are you from, Lucy?"

Well, not really safe. The question was one she couldn't answer truthfully. But she gave him as much of the truth as she could. "I'm originally from Italy but moved to the States several"—*hundred*— "years ago. I never really settled in one place until I bought this property about ten years ago."

"Was the bar already here?"

"No, I converted the first floor myself. Took about a year, but I did most of the work with the help of friends."

His gaze left hers to travel around the room. "You've got talented friends. It's beautiful. The acoustics are perfect. You don't need a sound system."

She smiled. "Yes, my friends are rather remarkable." More so than he would ever know. "What about you, Brandon? Do you like playing in Reading?"

"Yeah, actually, I do." He eased back a little, as if getting comfortable. His smile... Blessed Goddess, that smile. "I get along well with the coach and the team. And the fans are great. We're having a good year and that always helps."

"You've played all your life, haven't you?"

He nodded. "Yeah, I've been to the NHL a few times, played AHL mostly. Got hurt year before last and decided to take the assistant coach position here so I could play, too."

"You're very good."

His smile broadened, setting off a firestorm of lust in her blood. "If I were really good, I would've had a career in the NHL instead of bouncing all the hell over the place." He shrugged, not looking like he had any regrets. "But I like to play and it leaves my summers open to help my parents with their place in Maine."

"What do they do?"

"They run a bar."

She let out a little laugh. "Really?" Sometimes the world worked in mysterious ways. "Something else we have in common. Besides hockey, of course."

"Have you always been a fan?"

"Oh, yes. I was thrilled when they built the arena. I love the game. The men are big and brawny. They swear, they sweat, and they don't back down from a fight. What's not to love?"

His smile set sparks glowing in her blood. "A woman who gets it. Where have you been all my life?"

If he only knew. "I guess I've been waiting." She may actually have been waiting for him. The thought made her pause for a brief second. "I have another set to perform. Will you be here when I'm through?"

His gaze never left hers. "Absolutely."

⸻

By the time the bar cleared out around 1:00 a.m., Brand thought maybe he'd regressed back to his teenage years.

He'd had a hard-on all night. His throat felt like sandpaper and his heart pounded like he'd just finished a half hour of sprints.

Her last set had been in Italian. Well, he was pretty sure it was Italian, though there were a few times he was pretty sure it wasn't. But it might have been Latin. Whatever language it was, she sang it beautifully. And the kid accompanying her on guitar should've been playing arenas to sold-out crowds. Brand didn't move the entire forty-five minutes of the last set.

When she finished the last note, the crowd got to their feet and gave her a several-minute standing ovation.

So did he.

With a smile, she stepped off the stage and made the rounds again, this time as everyone in the bar made their way out the front door. She acknowledged everyone by name as they approached her to say how much they'd enjoyed the show and to say good night.

And he could have sworn some of them bowed or curtsied. Weird.

When all the guests but Brand had gone, she walked to the opposite end of the bar and spoke to the bartender for a minute. Brand couldn't hear a word and his hearing was pretty damn good.

After a few seconds, the guy nodded but the look he shot Brand was a warning. The woman obviously inspired loyalty from her employees. Brand returned the guy's gaze until the bartender disappeared into the back room.

Then he looked at Lucy and found her watching him with a sexy half grin that made his blood flow like lava through his veins.

"Did you enjoy the second set?"

She accompanied the question with a little tilt of her head and he watched, spellbound, as one midnight-silk curl slipped over her shoulder to curve around her full breast.

Damn, he was going to spontaneously combust if he didn't watch out. Not that that would be a bad thing, but he didn't want to come off as too eager and scare her away.

He was sorry to say it'd happened before. He weighed over two hundred pounds and was built to take more than a few hits. Luckily, he still had all his teeth but his nose had been broken a few times and showed it.

His hands were chapped and rough and he knew his shoulder had probably turned about five shades of purple by now. Still, he'd never had much trouble picking up a woman when he wanted one. And he wanted this one.

"I did, though I couldn't understand most of it. Italian?"

Her lips curved a little higher. "Some, yes. And a little Latin."

He expected her to go on but she stopped, as if waiting for him. To what? He felt like he was missing something.

"Do you have classical training?"

Now her smile broadened into a full-blown grin. "Yes, you could say that. Would you like another drink?"

He glanced down at the tumbler on the bar in front of him and realized he couldn't remember finishing it. He'd been that engrossed in her performance. "Yeah, sure. It's a—"

"Seven and Seven." She moved behind the bar, mixing his drink with deft hands. She placed it on the bar. "A good bartender always knows what her customers are drinking."

He smiled and he swore he could smell her arousal. "My dad has the same saying."

"Your dad sounds like a smart man."

"He is. The bar's been in the family for almost sixty years."

"So, Brandon, would you like to come upstairs?"

Oh, hell, yeah. I will follow you anywhere.

Instead he nodded, swallowed and said, "Sure, I'd love to."

Motioning for him to come around the bar, she led him through the spotless kitchen to a narrow staircase.

As he followed her up, he was damn lucky he didn't trip and fall back down the stairs. The ceiling was so close to his head, he felt he had to hunch. Which meant he was staring right at her ass.

She had a great ass. Hell, she had a great body. Even a step above him she was shorter, but she packed a lot of curves into so little real estate.

By the time they reached the second floor, the erection he thought he'd controlled returned with a vengeance. Luckily, she didn't turn to look at him but continued across the room.

It took him a second to notice his surroundings, but when he did, the sight made him stop and gape. Moonlight poured in through the two solid walls of windows, illuminating the room.

Lucy flicked a switch on the wall, and the faint light from recessed fixtures in the ceiling made the other two pale gray walls shimmer with the opalescent sheen of mother-of-pearl. Nothing hung on the walls, no art, no photos. Thick crown molding that reminded him of waves was the only decoration.

In the center of the room, six chaise lounges upholstered in a pale gray material formed a loose circle. In the center of the circle sat a pair of low, bleached wood tables elaborately carved with trees and flowers and animals.

No, not animals. Wolves. Howling with their snouts pointed upward or running, long and sleek. Beautiful.

Lucy moved to stand before a huge, ornately decorated buffet that matched the tables. Opening the doors on the front of the piece, she pulled out an old-fashioned bottle of Coke and twisted the metal cap off.

He watched as she lifted the bottle to her mouth, then followed the line of her throat. He drew closer without realizing he'd done it and, when she turned, he was only inches away.

Not startled at all, she smiled into his eyes. He was damn lucky he didn't drop the heavy crystal glass in his own hand. That look fried the synapses between his brain and his mouth, rendering him mute. And really, what did he have to say? Probably would've embarrassed himself, anyway.

So he took a sip of his drink and let her lead him back to the chaises. She sat on one, lifting her legs and draping her body on the thing like she was setting up for a photo op. He would have thought she was trying to pose for him, but she looked completely comfortable, as if this was how she sat all the time. And considering it was her house, she probably did.

He debated sitting next to her, but she hadn't asked, and his mother hadn't raised a fool. He took the chaise opposite so he could stare at her.

And damn, she made terrific eye candy.

But they couldn't just sit there and stare at each other all night. "You've really got a great voice."

She smiled. "I've been singing for… more years than I care to admit. I'm fortunate enough to be able to indulge myself at the bar."

"You never wanted to make a career of it? 'Cause you certainly have the talent."

"Thank you, Brandon, but no, that path wasn't in the cards for me. I enjoy singing but I can't give it my full attention. The bar takes up much of my time."

He got the sense there was more to the story. "Just the bar? No family?" He didn't ask about another man.

Her pale gaze grew intense. "Many good friends. But no mate or lover at the moment."

His brain stumbled over her use of the word mate instead of

husband but his body only recognized the fact that no man had a claim on her. It was all he needed to hear. Leaning forward, he set his glass on the table in front of him and stood. She tilted her head back, her gaze following his every move as she, too, set her glass aside. He watched her draw in a deep breath, her lips parting as if she was having trouble getting enough air.

Good. He was having a damn hard time breathing through the lust. He hoped like hell she was having the same reaction to him.

When he reached for her, she moved into his arms and he lifted her easily against his body. He swore she weighed less than his gear bag.

Her hands threaded through his hair a second before his mouth covered hers, sending a jolt of lust through his body as they molded together from knee to chest. Free of a bra, her breasts flattened, nipples already tight and pointed. Her slim hips tilted into his body, catching the tip of his cock as she rubbed against him with maddening pressure.

She opened immediately to the thrust of his tongue, and he slid into her warm mouth, flicking at her tongue, encouraging her to tangle with him. Slanting her head to the side, she opened farther for him.

Damn, she tasted great, like hot, sweet honey. He wanted to consume her, to mark her. Make her his. His inner caveman pounded his chest, wanting to take her to the ground and fuck her senseless.

His knees actually bent in preparation, but he came to his senses a second later. Christ, he wasn't a green kid anymore. Somewhere in this house was a bed. But first, he needed to slow down. Enjoy the moment. He hoped like hell that he wound up in her bed soon enough. And if she didn't let it go that far, no problem. He'd deal.

But he'd probably have a better damn chance of making it all the way to her bedroom if he made her beg for it first.

Fuck it all, he wanted her to beg.

Concentrating on their kiss, he indulged in the silky feel of her lips, warm and clingy as they moved against his. He pulled his tongue back and let her play with him, moving one arm under her ass to hold her so he had one hand free to do… whatever.

For now, he let it rest on her hip as she licked at him with delicate flicks of her tongue, fanning an already red-hot lust.

That delicate little tongue stroked until he was panting and he couldn't remain passive any longer. He let his hand drift up her back then down again, the smooth velvet of her dress warming to his touch. So soft, but he knew her skin would be even softer.

Shifting against him, she moaned as she rocked her hips in a motion that made his cock stiffen in anticipation. More. He needed to touch her, to feel her skin against his.

His hand slid under her hair until he felt the warmth of her nape bared by her dress. Softer than the dress, her skin forced a groan from him.

Tearing his mouth from hers, he strung a line of kisses from her cheek to her neck, where he couldn't help himself. He opened his mouth on the pulse beating furiously at the base of her throat.

Her scent made him want to lick her, so he did. A long swipe of his tongue that coaxed a shiver from her. Her hands tightened in his hair, the slight pain cranking his lust into high gear.

He felt his body heat rising, burning, searing. He wanted to devour her right here. Throw her on the floor and ravage her. Hell, the chaise lounges were too civilized for what he wanted to do to her.

And that should be a warning, he realized.

Slow down.

How could he when her every motion made him drunk with lust? He wanted to bite her and he meant really fucking bite her until he left a mark on her skin to show everyone whose she was. Christ, when the hell had he turned into an animal?

With an indrawn breath he pulled back, though she wouldn't let him go far. She kept her hands locked around his neck, allowing him only a few inches of breathing space. Not that he wanted more. What he really wanted was her naked and under him.

Lucy stared at him, her gaze as warm as her kiss had been. Inferno hot.

"Would you like to continue this somewhere more comfortable?" she asked.

He caught back the *Hell, yeah* on the tip of his tongue.

So he nodded. "Just show me the way."

Her lips tilted in a seductive curve. Damn, the woman's mouth made him think dirty thoughts. Then she inclined her head toward the doorway across the room. "Through the kitchen to the stairs at the back."

Yes, ma'am. He didn't have to be told twice. Making sure he held her securely, he headed out of the room, through the kitchen he barely took notice of, and up the darkened staircase. When he reached the top, he stopped, mesmerized by the sight.

"Holy shit, Lucy. This is amazing."

The entire third floor was completely open. Moonlight poured in through three huge skylights, bathing the large bed in the center of the room in silver. Four white-marble columns held up the ceiling, and painted murals covered every square inch of wall.

The murals depicted woodland scenes, satyrs and fairies eating and sleeping, dancing and fucking. The pictures were so incredibly lifelike, Brand thought he could pet the fur on the wolves and run his fingers through the hair on the fairies. Lucy smiled at his reaction. "They are beautiful, aren't they?"

She said it with so much pride, he asked, "Did you do this?"

She shook her head. "No. A friend painted them for me."

Shit, that really shouldn't matter but his back straightened. "You've got a lot of those."

Her smile broadened, as if she were amused. "Yes, I do. But not many have seen this."

He got the message. "Then I'm honored."

"I'm glad, but I think I'd also like you to be naked."

Heat hit him square in the gut as he grinned. "I think I can accommodate that."

"Then you'll have to put me down."

He let her body slide down his, absorbing the feel of her lush breasts against his chest before he took a step back. Goddamn, he couldn't wait to get his hands on her, to taste her nipples and slip his fingers inside her pussy.

Naked, he needed to be naked. And so did she.

—⁓—

Lucy's gaze followed Brandon's hands as he unbuttoned his shirt and toed off his sneakers.

The man had huge hands, scarred and tough. She couldn't wait to feel them against her naked skin. Her skin fairly vibrated with her desire and she took a deep breath, trying to calm her racing heart. She couldn't remember ever being this nervous with a man before.

She was a Goddess. She didn't do nerves.

But this man, this *eteri*, made her knees weak and her breasts ache in anticipation. And he hadn't even taken off his shirt yet. His big fingers eased the buttons through the holes, making her wonder if maybe Brandon had done some stripping on the side because he made taking off his clothes an art. His fingers worked the buttons, making her long to have them on her nipples, pinching and caressing. She went wet just thinking about it.

Each button revealed a tiny slice more of his golden skin, and when he finally got to the bottom and pulled the tails of his blue, button-down shirt out of his brown cargo pants, her gaze locked onto the masterpiece that was his body.

He had broad, strong shoulders, one that bore the scars of a long-ago operation. And his chest begged for her hands to run over the light mat of dark hair, to pet him. From his chest, her gaze dipped to six-pack abs so defined she wanted to follow each rise and valley with her tongue. But the prominent bruise that covered most of his left side forced her to reconsider her desire to throw him on the bed and fuck him until they both collapsed.

Blessed Goddess, that must be painful. How could he even bear to move his arm without flinching? Yet he did.

She stepped closer and lifted her hand but stopped just short of touching him. She wanted to make that bruise go away. It made her angry to see how it marred his gorgeous skin.

She had enough power to heal that injury. But what would she tell him when it miraculously disappeared?

I'm an ancient Etruscan Goddess who has just enough power to heal bruises.

Yeah, that would go over real well.

"You're hurt."

He shrugged, those broad shoulders moving so beautifully. "No, not really."

He was lying. She could tell by his nonchalant tone. And when she looked into his eyes, she saw he was worried about the injury. And that made her worry about it, too.

What was wrong with her tonight? It wasn't like this man was her mate. He was *eteri*. He was a fling for an evening, a man who had no idea who she really was. A man who wanted her simply because he thought she was desirable.

Not because she was Lusna, Etruscan Goddess of the Moon.

What would he say if she told him who she really was?

His hands moved to his pants and her thoughts fractured as he popped the button. They hung so low on his hips, the tip of his erection emerged as soon as he started to unzip them.

And, oh, Sweet Mother Goddess, his sex was just as gorgeous as the rest of him. His thick cock stood straight out from his body from a nest of dark curls, full and ruddy red, his balls heavy beneath. She wanted to go down on her knees and take him in her mouth. Something she'd never been able to do with any of her *Fata* or *Enu* lovers. They would've been scandalized.

She'd never had an *eteri* in her bed, had never met one who evoked this heated response from her. Was it hormonal, something to do with the moon cycle? The full moon would rise in only two days. No, she couldn't blame her reaction on the moon. She simply wanted *him*.

Stepping closer until she could feel his heated breath against her cheek, she reached for his waistband and helped him push the pants down his legs. Her fingers stroked against his thighs, the light coating of hair soft against her skin. And now bared for her pleasure. She went to her knees on the plush rug then, dragging his pants to his ankles as she went.

His hands settled on her shoulders, not drawing her closer, just resting there, kneading, stroking.

She let herself stare at him for a least a minute, watching how he pulsed and grew harder before her eyes. The thick vein on the side of his shaft throbbed at a faster pace and the head deepened to the shade of ruby.

She heard his breathing shallow out, rasping in his throat as she pursed her lips and blew on the tip. He groaned, his cock flexing and moving as his fingers tightened. But he didn't try to draw her closer. He didn't have to.

She closed the distance and opened her mouth over the silky, hot tip. The taste of musky male exploded on her tongue, and she gripped his hips and took him deep as he groaned out her name.

She stroked her tongue along his length before she sucked hard. Then she drew back, allowing her teeth to scrape along the skin until only the fat tip remained inside her mouth.

She repeated this motion several times, each time taking him deeper than the last. She lost herself in the taste and feel of him, his skin so soft on her tongue, the shaft hard and hot, the scent of his body intoxicating.

His groans lit a fire in her blood that made her fingers dig deeper into his skin, hold him tighter. She felt one of his hands brush along her cheek and around her lips, where they were wrapped around his cock. He stroked at the corner of her mouth before cupping her jaw.

Gently. Almost too tentatively. She didn't want tentative. She wanted him out of control.

She sucked on him harder, continuing to work him as his hand fell back to her shoulder and he pushed his fingers under the stretchy material of her dress, tunneling straight for her breasts.

She moaned around his cock when his fingers pinched at the puckered tips of her nipples. Her humming motion made his shaft throb.

He pulled back with a groan, and Lucy released his cock slowly, enjoying the tease.

Looking up, she saw his eyes closed tight and his mouth parted to draw in unsteady breaths.

"Give me a minute, babe. I don't wanna come yet." His voice, a husky rumble like thunder in the night air, sent an erotic shiver down her back, inching her that much closer to the orgasm gathering low in her body.

She moved her leg a fraction of an inch, in preparation for standing, and Brand had his hands under arms and her on her feet in seconds. Again, his strength and the ease with which he moved her struck a deep chord in her.

She was no weakling. She could more than take care of herself if the situation arose. But she liked feeling small and protected with him.

She also liked how he took charge. A second after she found her feet, he pulled her dress down her shoulders. Her breasts popped out of the springy fabric, full and taut and high. No sagging. One of the perks of being an immortal female.

The look on Brand's face said he approved.

"Christ, you're gorgeous." His calloused hands palmed her breasts and kneaded them, her womb clenching at the sensation and the rough need in his voice. He leaned down to lay his lips against her neck before stringing kisses along her jaw to her ear. "I want to devour you."

"I have no problem with that." She turned her head to lay her own kiss along his jaw. "But you'd better hurry before I go up in flames."

She felt him smile against her cheek. "No way. I don't want to rush. Now that I'm here, I want to make this last all night. I want you so wrung out you can't move by the morning."

His words made her moan, made her stomach clench with desire. Just the thought of what they could do to each other with the hours ahead of them, how they could pleasure each other, made her long to stop time, to halt the passage of the moon across the sky and indulge for as long as she wanted.

Turning her head, she whispered into his ear, "Then you'd better prepare for a workout, because I've got a lot of stamina."

He pulled back long enough to stare into her eyes with a gaze hot enough to melt diamonds. "Honey, I can take whatever you dish out."

Yes, he could. To a point. Just the thought of what she could let herself do with Brandon made her wetter than she'd ever been with anyone else.

"Then get on the bed, Number Seventeen. On your back and don't move."

His eyes flared and a muscle in his jaw jumped. Letting her gaze travel down his body, she saw his cock twitch in response. She couldn't wait to feel him moving inside her.

Brandon didn't speak, his chest rising and falling as if he'd just done a set of wind sprints. Then he took a step backward and turned, letting her watch his absolutely perfect ass flex and hollow as he took the few steps to the bed.

Tinia's teat, the man's body—scars and all—should be classified a work of art. One that needed hands-on attention.

Her hands. On every part of him.

But first, she needed to get rid of her own clothes.

She waited until he'd climbed onto the bed and propped his hand under his head before she hooked her thumbs into the velvet and began to ease it down. She went slowly, the elastic material clinging to her skin, battling to stay in place while she tugged it off.

Brandon watched her every move with an intensity that made her wish she had more clothes to remove. Unfortunately—or fortunately, depending on how you looked at the situation—she was commando under the dress. Anything she wore would show through the velvet and completely ruin the line of the dress.

Of course, the look on his face made it obvious he appreciated the fact that she was now naked.

As she stared, he crooked his finger at her. Putting her hands on her hips, she smiled and tossed her hair over her shoulder. "Are you trying to entice me to come over there, Mr. Stevenson?"

"Do you need to be enticed?"

She shrugged, watching his eyes dip for a few seconds to her breasts. "You could give it a try."

His mouth curved in a grin so charming, she felt her knees actually wobble before he lowered his hand to his waist and flattened it against his defined abs.

As her mouth dried, she watched as he eased that hand down until he ringed the base of his cock with his thumb and forefinger. His big hand barely fit about the base. Oh my.

She'd known he was big from having him in her mouth, but

seeing his hands demonstrate his size made her want to fall to her knees and sing his praises. Right before she crawled onto the bed and ravished him.

Instead, she stood mesmerized as he used his hand to stroke his erection. He pumped from root to tip, slow and steady. She watched him handle his cock with a tight grip, so tight she thought it had to hurt. Then again, this man had his body slammed into the boards three and sometimes four nights a week. He obviously knew what his body could take.

As he worked, she watched the ruddy red tip burn even darker as it appeared and disappeared in his fist. She took a step forward, then another, drawn by an erotic pull deep in her gut.

She had to touch his skin, feel his heat. Moisture drenched her sex and began to seep out of her body. She could smell her own arousal, mixed with Brandon's heat, and the combined scents made her body tense on the very tip of orgasm.

Great Mother Goddess, she felt her body clench, wanting to fall into ecstasy but not wanting to go without him.

By the time she reached the bed, Brandon had rolled onto his back, the motion of his hand increasing.

She couldn't decide if she wanted to watch him come all over himself or if she wanted him to release in her body.

Brandon made the decision for her by grabbing her hand and pulling her onto the bed next to him. In the next second, he covered her body, spreading her legs with his knees and holding her hands outstretched.

He held himself above her, the dominant position keeping his erection from touching her but pretty much enveloping her body with his.

She felt caged, overpowered.

And she loved it. Loved having the decision taken from her. Loved being conquered.

So many people depended on her, so many decisions to make. So much—

Brandon dropped his head and sealed his mouth over hers, his kiss wrenching her back into the moment. He made her sigh in relief even as her body tightened in anticipation. He tasted so good, so *right*. His tongue rough against hers, his lips demanded a response she wanted to withhold only so he'd continue to kiss her just like this.

Her hands clenched into fists as she kissed him back with equal desire. His hands loosened on her wrists and she moaned, trying to tell him without words that she liked to be held down. He understood exactly what she wanted. He moved his hands onto hers, laced their fingers together and stretched her arms out straighter.

She didn't know how long he kissed her, but it built a charge between them.

Lucy felt her *arus*, her magic, rise so close to the surface of her skin, goose bumps coated her arms. Her magic wanted to come out and play, to wind around him like a cat and rub against him until it exploded.

But she couldn't let it get away from her. He wouldn't understand the intensity of her reaction. Didn't want to frighten him with it.

Then again, her hockey player didn't scare easily.

With his mouth still locked on hers, he drew her hands over her head and secured them in one of his. Then he drew his now-free hand down her body in a light caress. He grazed down her side, missing all the important parts, yet still managing to make her feel as if he had touched them.

Her hips tilted up, trying to brush against his cock. She felt the heat of his erection but couldn't quite touch him.

He broke contact with her mouth but remained close enough that she could feel breath on her cheek. "Did you want something, Lucy?"

She opened her eyes and looked directly into his. "Touch me."

His hand stroked along the curve of her hip. "Here?"

"Higher."

He brushed just under her breast. "Here?"

"My breast. Touch my breast."

"Oh, I'm not sure you're ready for that yet."

His lips curved in a hard, masculine grin and he ran one finger along the curve of her nose, so far from where she wanted him to be touching.

Her gaze narrowed as she thought of ways to make him pay for his insolence.

"And what makes you think you know what I'm ready for?"

"I want you to beg."

She caught back the immediate demand that he obey her. Didn't want him to think she was a demanding bitch in bed. Still, she was used to getting her own way and there was no way she would beg.

Two could play this game.

With a quick twist of her wrist, she got him to release one of her hands. Starting at his throat, she let the nail of her index finger scrape down his chest to just above his nipple. His chest expanded on an indrawn breath then froze as he waited for her to continue.

With a lift of her eyebrows, she let her hand fall back above her head.

And waited.

As his mouth slowly lost that stomach-gripping grin, he moved until he sat back on his heels. With her legs spread around his knees, she was bared to him completely. And he took full advantage of the position to let his gaze stroke down her body.

"You know," he reached out with his left hand and cupped her breast, as casually as if he'd reached for a melon on the shelf, "I don't think you understand the rules of the game."

He only held her, didn't fondle her or stroke her but her body responded with a surge of lust, arching her back and pressing her breast more fully into his palm.

After a brief squeeze, he released her again, causing her hands to clench into fists before she forced them to relax.

"And what are the rules?"

"The rules are... you have to ask for what you want."

"I thought you wanted me to beg."

"Maybe I just want to hear you talk. You have the faintest hint of an accent but I can't place it. It's driving me crazy."

"In a good way, I hope."

"Baby, everything about you drives me crazy in a good way."

Blessed Goddess, the man would make her orgasm solely using words.

"Then I'll say whatever you want me to say."

Those beautiful brown eyes narrowed down to slits. "Tell me to touch your breasts, Lucy."

"Please touch my breasts, Brandon."

"I love the way you say my name." Reaching for her, he cupped her breasts, his warm hands molding to her curves, plumping them. As she arched again, he let his thumbs and forefingers bracket her nipples then pinched them with a hard twist.

A moan on her lips, she lifted her hands to cover his, forcing him to tighten on her.

"You have such gorgeous ti—breasts." He let her guide his movements for a little while, let her work herself harder. "And your skin is like silk."

"And your hands are magic. Don't stop."

With a sleek move, he flipped their hand position, wrapping her hands around her breasts.

"I won't stop. But I want to see you touch yourself." His voice sounded like he had gravel in his throat, a low growl, another sensation that stroked against her *arus*. "I want to watch you touch yourself. Christ, woman, you are fucking beautiful."

Her eyes fluttered closed as she followed his directions, massaged her breasts, working her desire higher. Pushing the mounds together, she pinched her nipples, flicking them into hard, aching points. She felt her orgasm build, felt the tightening in her womb.

She wanted to come, needed the release. She could lose herself in this, could make herself come and—

As if he'd read her mind, Brandon grabbed her hands and pulled them away from her body, making her cry out in denied need.

"Wait just a minute. I think you're having too good a time. I don't want you to get too far ahead."

She opened her eyes and looked into his. "Then you need to catch up."

His lopsided smile made her legs want to tighten, to rub together and ease the ache there. "Trust me, babe. I'm right here with you."

With easy strength, he slid his hands behind her back and lifted her off the bed and against him. He held her high enough that he could get his mouth on her breasts.

Sucking her nipples into his mouth, he rolled and licked and nipped, working her into a frenzy. Her muscles tightened to an almost painful ache.

And then, in the blink of an eye, she combusted.

A sharp orgasm ripped through her, shooting up her spine, making her body bow in his hands and a moan fall from her lips.

Without losing his grip on her, he drew it out, tonguing her nipples. Made her body burn for him.

An inferno of repressed need consumed her and she lost herself in the vicious heat of release.

When she came back to herself, she realized Brandon had laid her back on the bed. His hands gripped her hips and he'd lost the smile. His expression had sharpened into determined lines, his desire for her stamped plainly on his face.

On his knees between her legs, he lifted her hips until her sex aligned with his. She felt the heat pouring off his body, branding her, making her wet and leaving her aching.

Then he leaned forward and let her wet lower lips brush against his cock, painting her juices all over his shaft.

The eroticism of the moment left her breathless. She barely dared to move, afraid it would break the spell he was weaving. A spell not magic, but completely sensual.

His gaze burned with it as he finally released one hip so he could push his cock down until she felt the wide head breach her sex.

She drew in a deep, shuddering breath and lifted her hands to grab his wrists. She had to touch him, had to anchor herself to him in some way.

He slipped inside with little resistance because she was already so wet for him, her sheath contracting around the invader, trying to draw him deeper. He wouldn't be rushed, though, biceps bulging as he held her still.

His expression tightened, determination so clear on his face. And she knew exactly how determined he was. She'd seen him go into a corner with three opposition players and come out with the puck after a fierce battle. He could take a hard hit into the boards and still manage to get the puck out of the zone. He'd gone one on one with the best fighters in the league and was the last man standing.

If he wanted to wring every last ounce of pleasure from her before he came, she had no doubt he could do it. But that didn't mean she couldn't get in a few shots of her own.

She tilted her hips, his cock moving just enough to get a little friction. She drew in a deep breath, eyes closing as the motion sent ripples through her sex and deep into her womb.

She heard him groan, felt his fingers tighten and finally... finally, the man lost his tight control.

In one fluid motion, he fell over her, covering her completely as he crushed her into the bed.

His body bathed hers in heat as his hips began a punishing rhythm, nailing her hips into the bed as he drove inside her. Wrapping her arms and legs around him, she let him pound away, loving the heat, the power... Hell, she loved everything about him.

The rough sound of his breath panting in her ear made her sex clench around him. Her fingers dug into his back, nails surely drawing blood. It only spurred him to move faster.

He was so much bigger than her, her head fit under his chin. Tilting back, she angled so she could lick the galloping pulse at the base of his throat, the scent of his skin intoxicating her.

Her blood pumped through her veins, warm with *arus*, that certain tingle letting her know she was about to lose control.

Blessed Goddess, she couldn't lose control. Not completely. Not with him.

She shuddered, trying to reach for some measure of sanity, but Brandon wouldn't let her have it.

He tightened his arms around her, the one behind her hips lifting her into him, letting him go even deeper.

Then he punched his other hand into the bed beside her head and lifted his upper body off hers. His hips dipped and the angle hit that sweet spot deep inside.

In a flash of fire, she convulsed around him, crying out his name.

And losing her hold on her *arus*.

It burst around them, tearing into Brandon and pushing him into the orgasm he'd been holding back so desperately. His moan sounded like it was dragged out of him and his body bucked, trying to fight it. He couldn't. He pulsed his seed deep into her body before collapsing onto her with a deep sigh.

Lucy pulled him in even tighter and closed her eyes.

—◦◦◦—

Hours later, Lucy lay with her head on the pillow, watching Brandon.

He'd fallen asleep almost immediately after he'd come, his bulk pinning her to the bed.

Though she could barely breathe, she hadn't wanted to move and disturb him. But with each passing moment, she knew she'd have to send him away. This night had been amazing. Utterly and completely thrilling. And absolutely the last thing she should have allowed. She had to get him home. It would be dawn soon and, if she was going to erase his memory of last night and have him transported back to his own bed, she needed to do it before the sun rose above the horizon and her power waned with the day.

Still… She hesitated.

Last night… Last night, she'd experienced something she'd never experienced. Something special. Something amazing.

For all of her very long life, she'd secretly wished for a man she could love and who would adore her for the person she'd become. Not the goddess she'd been. Not the obsolete object of power who no longer held much of a role in today's world.

Not even her *lucani* needed her aid as much as they had, what little she could give them anyway.

But Brandon…

She shook her head, fighting back the anger that wanted to rise up. She'd been accused by her sister goddess, Tessa, of having anger-management issues.

After she'd told Tessa where she could stick her opinion, which had only made Tessa laugh, she'd secretly had to agree. But when you were a moon goddess, your moods were ruled by the waxing and waning of the beautiful silver orb in the sky.

It could almost be said she was in a nearly constant state of PMS.

Which had been getting worse these past few centuries. Loneliness could do that to a person. Even to a goddess. She wanted to keep him. But she really didn't have a choice. Tears welled and she leaned over to kiss his cheek before closing her eyes and wishing him away.

Chapter 4

DAMN, WHAT THE HELL did he drink last night?

Brand woke with the entire cast of *Stomp* doing their first act inside his head. Fucking hell, his head fucking hurt. Sitting up in his bed, he rubbed his fingers against his throbbing temples, waiting for the rest of the hangover to kick in. But he didn't have the typically shitty taste in his mouth. And his eyes weren't dry.

Wait, *had* he been drinking last night?

No, he didn't think he had.

So what the hell *did* he do last night? Where the hell had he been?

He'd had a game last night. He'd taken a pretty hard hit. Maybe that had fucked up his head.

No, it couldn't have been that bad. If he'd had a concussion, he would've been in the hospital overnight. Where the hell had he gone after the game? Vague memories of him having a few beers as he watched a West Coast hockey game on TV bubbled up in his brain. Then bed. It sounded right. It sounded like what he did most nights after a game.

Then why did he have the feeling he was missing something? Something important. Something to do with a certain brunette he had the serious hots for. Now why the hell would he even think that? The feeling stayed with him all day. By the time he got to the arena for the game, he'd almost convinced himself he was imagining things.

Until he got on the ice for the pregame warm-up.

And *she* wasn't there.

Lucy Aster. The woman he'd been lusting after all season. Some guy sat in her usual seat and she was nowhere to be found.

He was so dumbfounded, he nearly tripped over another player stretching by the boards. *Shit*. Where was she? She hadn't missed a game yet. And why the hell did it matter so much?

He shook his head as he skated toward the net. This obsession with a woman he'd never even met was getting out of hand. Time to do something about it.

———

On the opposite side of the rink from where she normally sat and way the hell up near the top row, Lucy watched the game with an increasing sense of dismay.

Brandon was off his game. So much so, he was a danger to himself. As she watched, he raced to the corner, head down, oblivious to the guy at his back who checked him, head first, into the boards.

Brandon went down hard. And didn't get back up. The referee blew his whistle and play stopped as the team trainer hustled onto the ice on the arm of one of the players.

Sweet Mother Goddess. Lucy's breath stuck in her throat, and she gasped so loudly, the people on either side of her looked to see if she was okay.

She forced herself to control her reaction, to wipe her expression free of the breath-stealing fear before she made a spectacle of herself. How well she managed, she couldn't tell because fear made her weak.

Was he unconscious? He didn't seem to be moving. She didn't see any blood but he was at the opposite end of the ice.

Tinia's teat, this was her fault. She needed to fix this. She started to rise—and then sat back down again.

What the hell was she going to do? Go to the locker room? As far as he knew, they'd never met. She could get past the guards. A few simple spells and she'd have the run of the place. She still had enough power to control the minds of a few *eteri*.

Still… Brandon wouldn't remember what had happened last night. She'd made sure of that when she'd wiped his memories. And she knew it would cut her heart out to see the blank expression on his face when he looked at her.

Muttering apologies as she climbed awkwardly over two couples as she made her way to the aisle, she barely managed to hold back her tears until she got out of the building.

~~~

Brand sat in his truck in the parking lot of the arena, staring out the window at the moon.

He'd started the engine, intending to go straight home, take a shower until he'd drained the hot water tank, then fall into bed with a couple of the painkillers the team doctor had given him to ease him into dreamland.

Where maybe he could ignore the fact that his body felt like he'd been hit by a semi rather than the Elmira team's resident goon.

Instead, here he sat, seemingly mesmerized by the round gray rock that hung in the sky. He didn't want to go home. He wanted… What? What the hell did he want more than painkillers and a bed right now? Her. He wanted her. Lucy Aster.

And damn it, tonight he was going to—What? He was going to track down the address he had for her. And—Whoa. Wicked déjà vu.

Brand shook his head, then winced at the pounding headache in his temples. He didn't have a concussion from that check into the boards earlier tonight, which had been a lucky break. There was nothing lucky about the shoulder injury.

He tried to flex it but he could barely move it without being in pain. And for him, that meant he was in bad shape.

Goddamn it.

He hadn't yet taken the pain meds the doctor had given him because they would've impaired his ability to drive. He wasn't going home.

The vision of an old stone farmhouse drifted through his head. No, not a vision, a memory. One so clear, it had to be recent. A memory associated with Lucy Aster.

Fuck it. Turning on the GPS unit, he called up the address he'd programmed in earlier tonight—No, not tonight. He remembered doing it yesterday. And last night… More images, disjointed but completely real, flashed through his head.

Images that became clearer the closer he drew to his destination. That sense of déjà vu hit him again as he drove through Oley, a town he would've sworn he'd never seen before tonight but that he recognized.

From when?

Last night.

He shook his head again then winced as a sharp pain shot through his bruised body. That just didn't make any sense. Still, when he parked in the lot at the house owned by Lucy Aster, he knew he'd been here last night.

Trying to keep his shoulder as immobile as possible, he slid out of the car. And swore a blue streak when the fucking seat belt caught on his hand and made him pull back.

"Sonofabitch."

"Hey, dude. You okay?"

Brand took a second to take a deep breath before turning to nod at the guy who'd appeared behind him. A guy who looked so damn familiar. "Yeah. Thanks. Just twisted my shoulder."

"That was one big hit you took tonight, man. Thought maybe you dislocated it."

The guy couldn't have been older than twenty-two or twenty-three years old with wavy brown hair to his shoulders, long features to go with his long arms and legs and the bluest eyes Brand had ever seen.

"Caught the game tonight, huh?"

They started to walk toward the door, the guy falling into step beside him.

"Good one till you got creamed. Then it kinda went downhill."

Yeah, the guys had needed him tonight and he'd let them down. "Bad night."

They reached the door and the guy opened it for him.

"Hey, we all have 'em. I'm Casey, by the way. Guess you liked this place enough to come back, huh?"

Brand froze for a second before he whipped around to nail Casey with narrowed eyes.

Casey went pale as a sheet of paper. "Oh shit. Hey, man—"

"Casey, my love, why don't you go get a drink? I'll take care of Brandon."

Brand's head whipped the other way. That voice belonged to Lucy Aster.

Goddamn, that voice, husky and sultry. He couldn't wait to hear her sing again. Disjointed memories pushed and shoved to the front of his brain. Lucy naked and under him. Lucy singing, offering him a drink, inviting him upstairs.

"Hello, Brandon. Welcome to Howling Moon. I'm Lucy."

His name spoken by her made his cock begin to harden. With a force of will, he cooled the lust creeping into his gut. And tried to force back the anger, as well.

He held out his hand, knowing before they touched that she'd fit perfectly against him.

"Hello, Lucy. I'd say it's nice to meet you but that'd be a lie, wouldn't it? Because we've already met, haven't we?"

She blinked, just barely, and tried to pull her hand away but Brand refused to release her, his hand tightening around hers.

Careful not to hurt. He didn't want to hurt her. But he needed her to know he knew something had happened last night. Even if he didn't know what that was exactly.

"I'm glad to see you here. Why don't you have a seat at the bar, and we can talk after my set."

Okay, he could take a hint. She didn't want to talk about the fact that he'd spent the night with her last night and somehow his memories had gotten fucked up.

Drugs, hypnosis… Hell, he didn't know how. He only knew she had the answers and he wasn't leaving until he got them.

He wanted to demand she tell him now but there were an awful lot of eyes on them right now. And none of them would have his back. Biting back the confused anger that wanted to consume him, he nodded. He'd wait until after her set.

His gaze turned to the corner where he knew a kid with a guitar was waiting. For her.

Not waiting for him to respond, she turned and walked toward the stage.

The déjà vu he'd experienced earlier was nothing compared to what he felt when he sat at the bar. The bartender came over immediately and Brand looked into his eyes. He knew those copper-colored eyes. He'd looked into them last night and thought how strange they were.

And when the guy put a Seven and Seven in front of him without asking… Brand had to take a deep breath because he felt like he was suffocating.

How much weirder could this get? And why did he still want Lucy with a lust bordering on obsession?

The first notes of "My Funny Valentine" echoed through the suddenly silent room, and he turned to watch Lucy without taking a sip of his drink.

Beautiful. Absolutely beautiful. And so damn familiar, he felt he knew her voice as well as he knew his own. What the hell was going on?

———— ∼∼∼ ————

Lucy let the last note of the ancient Etruscan lament hang for a few seconds before cutting it off.

As one, the audience inhaled, as if they'd been holding their breath, then began to applaud. Usually when she'd had a bad day, that sound lifted her spirits. Tonight, the adulation fell on deaf ears. She couldn't hear, couldn't see anything but Brandon.

She felt his intense gaze from across the room. He hadn't taken his eyes off of her for the entire set.

He waited impatiently for her to come talk to him, watched as she greeted the *lucani* and a few *linchetto* as they made their way out the door. He sat on the same stool as last night. She knew he'd regained his memories. And the suspicion in his expression bit into her conscience.

What had she done wrong last night?

Well, that's easy. You didn't want *to wipe his memories so you did a shitty job of it.*

No, she didn't believe that.

Come on. You didn't want him to forget you.

That she couldn't deny.

And now you're stalling.

Silently, she told herself to shut up and made her way to the bar, pulling herself onto the stool beside Brandon. She barely had her ass on the cushion before he said, "Tell me why the hell I didn't remember I was here last night until about two hours ago. And don't lie and tell me you don't know what I'm talking about. I *know* I was here."

His brown eyes bored into hers. Anger, determination, and desire made his voice drop almost to a growl.

Behind the bar, Ty tensed and set down the rag he'd been using to wipe bottles. Her son would fight to the death for her. And he'd win.

She shook her head at Ty then watched as he poured her a tumbler of Crown Royal and set it before her. After a healthy sip, she took a deep breath.

"Thank you, sweetheart." She smiled at Ty, though she knew it didn't reach her eyes. "Why don't you get going? I'll lock up tonight."

Ty looked like he wanted to say something but he must have thought better of it. Finally he sighed and nodded. "See you tomorrow. If you need anything…"

It was Brandon's turn to stiffen, as if he was offended by the implication that he might hurt her. But he didn't say anything.

"I'll be fine. Good night, Ty."

Brandon stayed silent as Ty made his way out the door. But his gaze never left hers.

"How badly are you injured, Brandon?"

His mouth drew into a straight line. "It's a deep bruise. I've had worse. What the hell happened last night? Was I drugged? Hypnotized? What?"

She took another sip of her drink and looked him straight in the eyes. "Yes, you were here and no, you weren't drugged."

A muscle in his tight jaw jumped and his hand tightened into a fist. She had no fear that he would hit her but she worried that any excitement would agitate his injuries. "Why do my memories seem messed up, jumbled?"

"Are you really sure you want to know?"

He didn't answer right away, as if he were thinking about it.

"Why wouldn't I?"

She took another sip of her drink, listening as Ty closed and locked the front door. When he'd walked back to the bar, he stopped behind Brandon, staring at her steadily.

Her lips quirked at his frown before she nodded and Ty left through the kitchen, leaving her alone with Brandon. "Because you might not like the answer. You might not *believe* the answer."

And tomorrow morning, he wouldn't remember the answer. She would do a better job of the spell this time. She had to.

His eyes narrowed as if he'd heard her thoughts. Or maybe he'd just read them on her face. "What the hell does that mean?"

Since he wasn't going to remember anything tomorrow, she told him everything.

"I call myself Lucy Aster now, but I was born—well, born might not be the right word. I was first called Lusna and I was worshipped as the Etruscan Goddess of the Moon."

Brandon's mouth dropped open but he could get no sound to emerge. Hell, he'd be lucky if he could just close his mouth. She paused for a brief second, as if waiting for him to say something, her eyebrows slightly lifted. When he didn't speak, she continued.

"For centuries before the year the *eteri* decided to start again at one, I commanded the power of the moon and took care of those Etruscans who worshipped under its light.

"When the Romans assimilated the Etruscan civilization, many of the Etruscan deities found ourselves at loose ends. For centuries we wandered as regular humans, though necessity demanded we move quite often. Some humans have trouble dealing with the very idea of us and, since we never age or die, we need to move so as not to arouse suspicion. Pitchforks and stake-burnings can be painful.

"I arrived in the States several centuries ago. I followed the descendents of the Etruscans who had settled in the Americas, mainly in the northeast; there are also a few pockets in the southeast, mainly in Florida and along the Gulf Coast. I think the water reminds us of home."

She paused and Brandon watched her nibble her full bottom

lip. Amazingly, he found that sexy as hell. Even after that completely unbelievable story. "Brandon, are you okay?"

Good question.

Of course he wasn't okay, though not because of his splitting headache or his shoulder. He wasn't okay because she was nuts.

She had to be. She thought she was the freakin' Etruscan goddess of the moon. Of course she was crazy.

Christ Almighty, he wasn't even sure he knew what the fuck Etruscans were, but he absolutely knew what the hell a goddess was. And there was no such thing.

But... she didn't look crazy. She looked completely sane. She stared straight into his eyes without any of the scary intensity crazy people had, the wild look that would've marked her a few cans short of a case.

No, she looked perfectly rational and pretty damn sincere.

But she couldn't be. There were no such things as gods and goddesses who weren't born and lived forever. No way.

He shook his head. "No. I'm sorry. I can't participate in your delusion."

She smiled, as if she'd known he was going to respond that way.

And raised her hand toward the ceiling.

The room brightened, but not with the bright, harsh glare of the sun or an artificial bulb.

Silver light washed over every surface, every inch of space in the room. It held no warmth, just a cool brilliance that made everything sparkle.

Like moonlight.

He looked up, expecting to see skylights but he knew there were none. Besides, the light appeared to be coming from Lucy, as if... as if she were the moon, absorbing the sunlight and reflecting it back to Earth.

Oh, hell no. He was *not* buying into her delusion. No fucking way. Lights. Stage magic. Had to be.

Again, she seemed to read his mind. "No tricks. It's true, Brandon. Everything I've told you is true. Now I'm sure you can understand our need for discretion. Why I had to erase your memories of last night."

"Erase my…" He shook his head. "No. You must have done something to me last night, slipped me something. That's why I was so out of it during the game tonight, why my memories are all fucked up. Because you did something to me."

His anger increased with every second, a fiery blaze he tried to keep tamped down but wasn't having much luck containing. He needed to leave, to get out of here before he said something he'd regret.

She grimaced, and the light winked out, leaving her standing there in a midnight-blue dress that cupped every curve of her beautiful body in sleek, shiny satin.

"I wiped your memories with a spell before returning you to your apartment. I should have wiped all knowledge of me from your brain but… obviously I couldn't do it." She drew in a deep breath and he couldn't stop his gaze from dropping to her chest for a brief second. "I was selfish. I wanted you to continue to want me because I have lusted after you for so long. That was a mistake. Would you like me to remove it so your memory will be fixed?"

A spell. Right. More like illegal pharmaceuticals. And now she was going to *fix* him? Yeah, like that was going to happen. He needed to leave, go back to his apartment and forget about this crazy obsession for this crazy woman.

He slid off the stool, turned toward the door—and his brain split open. Images, pictures spilled across his mind. No, not pictures. Memories.

The bar. Lucy singing, this time in a purple velvet dress, not blue satin. Following her up the stairs in the kitchen… Oh, hell.

His cock instantly hardened. Lucy on her knees in front of him, sucking him off. Lucy naked, beneath him on the bed.

Oh, fuck. A weight fell on his chest, crushing the air out of his lungs. Jesus, he couldn't breathe. The mess of images he'd been seeing in his mind all night lined themselves up like soldiers in formation. Everything made sense now. The timeline had corrected.

Lucy laid her hand on his good shoulder and he tensed, making his other shoulder radiate pain from his injury. Goddamn, that fucking hurt. She drew her hand back and he immediately wished she hadn't.

Okay, there had to be a rational explanation for all of this.

"Brandon, take a deep breath. I know this is strange—"

He huffed out a laugh but felt no amusement. "No, this isn't strange. Strange is two-headed snakes and crop circles. This is fucking weird."

"Yes, I'm sure it seems that way to you."

Something in her voice made him turn and the expression on her face made his heart hurt.

She looked… lost, sad, without a friend in the world. Why the hell did he have the overwhelming need to comfort her?

He almost gave in to the impulse and wrapped his arms around her. Almost. Instead he stood there staring at her, trying to find a way to make it so she wasn't insane.

But neither of them moved and he didn't have a clue what to say.

"Would you like me to heal your shoulder, Brandon?"

His brain stumbled over her words for several seconds. "Heal my shoulder?"

She nodded. "I can repair your shoulder, if you'd like."

Hope leaped in his chest before he realized she had to be delusional.

His damn shoulder hurt too fucking bad for her to do some Reiki shit or New Age voodoo with her hands, it hurt too bad for her to fool him into believing she'd actually heal him.

But what would it hurt for her to try?

No. No freaking way. It'd be like encouraging the schizophrenic to listen to the voices in his head. But what if he let her? What if he told her to go ahead? And when nothing happened, he could leave knowing he'd proved himself right. That she *was* crazy.

Yeah, so what are you going to think if she actually does it?

"Fine. You think you can fix my shoulder, have at it."

With a curt nod, Lucy stepped closer then lifted her hands to his injured shoulder, placing one palm on his front and the other on his back.

Her hands warmed him through his shirt and, for a few seconds, aggravated the pain. His breath hissed in but then oh, Jesus, that glow started again.

He looked down and saw that the glow was now contained in her hands. They had turned translucent, like someone was shining a flashlight through them.

He had a momentary flash of fear that she was going to burn him to a crisp and the pain flashed into agony. His groan echoed through the bar and his head fell back on his shoulders.

Seconds of pain that felt like an eternity. And then the pain ended. It was just… gone.

Lucy stepped back, her hands falling away from him. She stared at him steadily. "Go ahead. Move it."

Heart pounding, he took a deep breath. And flexed his shoulder.

Holy shit.

No pain.

No fucking way.

He stared at her, trying to figure out if he was going to pass out or fall on his knees in front of her and kiss her feet. He'd never passed out in his life unless he'd gotten his head knocked into the boards. He wasn't starting now.

"How—" His mouth snapped shut, cutting off the rest of his question. She'd told him how. Magic.

"Would you like a drink?" she asked.

"Yeah, I think… Yeah. Whiskey. Just get the bottle."

Lucy turned to grab a bottle and two glasses from behind the bar, then motioned for him to follow her through the kitchen and up the stairs into the living room.

Brand stopped to look at the amazing murals on the walls and realized not only did he recognize them but that now he realized they probably weren't just showing mythological scenes.

He lowered himself to sit on one of the chaises, almost missed the edge and nearly fell on his ass on the floor. He shoved back before he embarrassed the hell out of himself.

Lucy sat next to him, cracked the bottle and poured healthy amounts for both of them.

After a few good pulls, he set his glass, now nearly empty, on the table in front of him.

"Explain the comment about not being born," he asked, lifting his gaze to hers. "Are you human?"

She nodded, her expression solemn. "Yes, I am as much human as you are, except for the aging and… dying. I also have abilities you don't."

He realized she'd sidestepped an explanation for being born and figured maybe he didn't want to know the answer to that one just yet. "Abilities like healing. And glowing."

She smiled and his gut twisted. She was the most beautiful woman he'd ever seen.

"Actually, what I do is harness the power of the moon and manipulate it to my needs."

"How?"

She shrugged. "It's what I do."

"But *how*?"

She frowned. "After you learned how to skate, did you have to think about how you do it every time you go on the ice? No, it's instinctive. It's the same for me. I don't think about how I do it anymore. I just can."

"And when did you learn how?"

She smiled, but it looked almost painful as her gaze sank to the ground for a second. "Long before you could ever imagine."

Okay, he'd let that one go. For now.

"But you weren't born?"

Her gaze dropped for a brief second as she shrugged. "That one's a little more difficult to answer. We came to be because our people had a need for us yet we do have parents, of a sort. We never age. We cannot be killed by conventional means and we don't die of natural causes."

"You're immortal."

"So far, yes."

Holy shit. Just… holy shit. She was dead serious. And he was fucking crazy to believe anything she said.

But he did.

She'd healed his shoulder. And she'd glowed like the fucking moon.

Now, he wasn't the sharpest blade on the ice, but he'd been smart enough to get an academic scholarship as well as a hockey scholarship to his first-choice college, even though he'd decided to go pro out of high school.

What she was telling him shouldn't be possible. Weird didn't begin to describe it.

But he couldn't explain what she'd done through conventional means. Which made her explanation the only rational explanation. Or he'd had a psychotic break with reality and was in a mental hospital somewhere talking to a wall. He let his gaze travel around the room once again.

"So, Etruscan? That's somewhere in Italy, right?"

She blinked, as if surprised by his question. "Yes. Long before Italy became the country it is today, Etruria had a rich history and a fascinating culture. The *Rasenna* formed the basis of much of the Roman civilization."

"*Rasenna*. What does that mean?"

"That's the name the Etruscans called themselves, before the Romans decided to call them Etruscan."

Brand took a deep breath, feeling like he was wading through deep water and the current was starting to drag him under.

"Brandon, I know it's a lot to absorb—"

He laughed, then shook his head at the slightly crazed sound of it. "Uh, yeah. Just a little."

"But I'm not crazy and neither are you."

No, she wasn't crazy. She was beautiful. Sure, he'd noticed the absolute perfection of her features before. But now when he looked at her, he saw the purity of her skin, the clearness of her eyes, the perfect balance of her features.

Ethereal. Otherworldly.

But it wasn't just her beauty that he responded to. It was also the heat in her gaze and the wildness he felt just below the surface of serenity. They called to that core of wildness in him.

The one he had to work so damn hard to keep under control.

"So… you're a moon goddess. What does that mean exactly?"

The corners of her lips curved upward and she released a quick breath, as if she'd realized he wasn't going to run screaming into the night.

"Not as much as it used to. You may have noticed polytheistic religions have gone the way of the dodo."

"But you still have followers, don't you? The people in the bar…"

She nodded. "Yes. Believe it or not, there are some who still follow the old ways. We just don't advertise in the local paper. When the *Rasenna* held sway over much of Italy, I had many more duties. I reigned over the world from the second the sun set to the second it peered over the horizon at dawn. Those who lived their lives in those hours worshipped me, paid fealty to me, begged for my mercy, and pleaded for my aid."

Her tone sounded flippant but her expression showed a fierce yearning. She missed those days. Couldn't say he blamed her.

"I could be a ruthless bitch to those who crossed me." Her smile turned impish, making his body burn with a sudden, fierce heat. "But I was good to those who worshipped me. I had quite a following at one time."

Yeah, he didn't have to stretch his imagination to believe that. Hell, he'd follow her anywhere. And maybe do a little worshiping himself. Which was just so totally fucking weird.

"Brandon?"

He loved the way she always called him by his given name. Hell if he knew why. "Yeah?"

Damn but her smile tied his guts in knots. "Do you have other questions?"

Oh, hell, yeah. He wanted to know everything. He had so many questions, he couldn't begin to formulate just one. They all jumbled together in his head until the noise was too great.

She must have sensed his confusion because she went quiet, still. As if she was afraid to make any sudden movements around him.

Christ, he didn't want to scare her. He'd never hurt her. He didn't want her to worry. He wanted her to— Well, he just wanted her.

Need for her clawed at his guts, made his cock hard and his mouth dry.

"Brandon."

"I don't even know where to start." He shook his head, then couldn't stop. "Jesus, this is fucked up."

Her smile slipped away. "I know it must seem that way to you. I'm sorry. I never meant for this to happen. You were never to know. I screwed up and I'm sorry."

Shit. He heard the implication in her tone. The only reason he'd remember her was because she'd done something wrong with her spell last night, the one that had wiped out his memories. She'd already said she wouldn't make that mistake again.

"You're planning to take away my memories again, aren't you?"

Her chin tilted and she looked him straight in the eyes without answering. He took that for a yes.

Finally she dropped her gaze. "This time you won't remem—"

Cupping her face in his hands, he pressed his mouth on hers and kissed her. The impulse was impossible to control, more like an imperative. One that wiped out every other thought in his brain.

Pushing his tongue into her mouth, he inhaled her.

He remembered her taste from last night, the dark, sweet flavor that flooded his senses and threatened to take him under, make him lose all control.

He tried to rein it in, to repress the base instinct to dominate, but he couldn't. Not when her arms came around his shoulders as she kissed him back, sighing into his mouth. Heat pulsed through his body, his muscles tightening with lust.

He couldn't slow down, could barely think through the firestorm eating him from the inside out.

The fire must have infected Lucy as well, because she came at him just as hard. Her fingers dug into his back, nails pinching into his skin. She pressed as close as she could until her breasts were crushed against his chest.

He cupped one hand around a firm mound and squeezed, a fierce joy lighting through him when she moaned into his mouth.

Goddamn, she tasted so fucking good.

He wanted—

With a groan, he twisted, taking her down onto the chaise. She lay back, staring up at him as he knelt between her legs.

He reached for the hem of her dress. The material felt like mist under his fingers, gauzy soft.

Moonlight.

He wanted to rip it from her body. Barely controlled the urge to just do it.

Instead, he let it slip through his fingers before he pushed his hands under her dress and skimmed up her thighs. Softest fucking skin he'd ever felt. Jesus, he needed to get her naked.

So, you're just gonna fuck the crazy woman?

Shit. *Shit.*

He pulled back, his hands clenched into fists as he stopped, his breath ragged and shallow.

Lucy lay back on the chaise, arms above her head, watching him. She looked almost placid but her eyes… Damn, her eyes. She wanted him but she refused to beg. He admired the hell out of that.

For Christ's sake, the woman thinks she's an ancient goddess.

"Brandon. I think you should let me up."

On the surface, her tone sounded deceptively calm. But underneath, he heard pain. She knew what he was thinking. Damn it. He didn't want to let her up.

"No."

She stared up at him. "You think I'm crazy."

He shook his head. "I don't know what to think. I only know I want you more than I've ever wanted another woman. Did you put me under a spell?"

Her mouth flattened into a thin line. "I don't have to bespell men to make them want me. Besides, you don't believe in magic, do you?"

He rolled his shoulder, feeling no pain at all. "Then how else do I explain why my shoulder doesn't hurt anymore?"

"*I* don't need to be convinced, Brandon."

No, she had absolute faith in who she was. Her expression showed total confidence.

He leaned forward, setting his hands on the chaise above her shoulders and trapping her between his arms. He lowered his head until his lips were only inches from hers and his eyes gazed directly into hers.

She wanted him. He swore he felt the heat of her desire rubbing against his skin.

And he wanted her. What else mattered right now?

"You need to take the dress off." Christ, was that his voice? He sounded like a fucking animal. "Lucy…"

She stared up at him, not moving. "You have to be very sure, Brandon. I am not crazy."

Right now, he believed every word out of her mouth.

He closed a few more inches between them. "I want you."

It took a few seconds, but when her lips curved into a smile that promised so much pleasure, he couldn't stand the distance between them.

He shut everything but her taste out of his mind and let himself fall. Not physically. She might be a goddess but he weighed more than two hundred pounds. He didn't want to crush her.

But he did want her naked.

As he coaxed open her lips with his tongue, he let one hand begin a slow exploration of the skin of her neck. Soft, warm. He wanted to lick her but he didn't want to give up her mouth just yet.

Her taste seeped into him like a drug, making his dick hard and his heart pound against his ribs. Fuck it. Slow wasn't gonna happen. Not this time, at least. He slid his hand into the neckline of her dress, wanting to touch her skin. The material gave way— And a second later, it wasn't there at all.

He opened his eyes and lifted his head just enough to see her now-naked breasts. Her dress had vanished, leaving her completely naked beneath him.

His mouth hung open for a few brief seconds before he lifted his gaze to hers and shook his head. "Now there's a skill you don't see every day."

"It comes in handy." She watched him with deceptively half-lidded eyes. She didn't miss a damn thing. "Would you like me to help you with your clothes?"

She was asking him much more than that. She was asking for his trust. For his belief. She wanted to watch his reaction to her magic. At the moment, he didn't give a flying fuck about her magic. If it got his clothes off faster, he was all for it.

"Please do." The faster he got naked, the better. Naked meant sex. Naked meant no more thinking.

Something brushed against his skin. It felt like electricity but different. He didn't know how to explain it. And he just didn't care.

One second he was dressed. The next his clothes were gone, and he knelt between her legs naked with a hard-on that stood at full mast. As her gaze dipped, his cock throbbed. He swore the damn thing strained toward her.

It took him a few seconds to get past the holy-shit-that-really-happened feeling. But he was a champion compartmentalizer. Lucy lay naked in front of him and he had a massive erection. Everything else could wait.

He thought about simply falling over her and fucking her until they both lost consciousness. Then he figured that might seem a little desperate.

But he couldn't shake the feeling that his time with her was borrowed.

Well, fuck that. Leaning back until he sat on his heels, he inched his knees forward, spreading her legs farther apart. If he let his gaze fall, he'd see her sex spread open, beckoning him. But he kept his eyes on hers, watching her reactions.

She didn't disappoint him. Her lips parted as she drew in a deep breath. Good. She wasn't as composed as she pretended.

"Damn, you have a fucking beautiful body."

He wanted to take the words back as soon as they'd escaped.

Not that he didn't mean them. But, Christ, he could've phrased it better. He wasn't a twenty-year-old horndog anymore. She deserved better from him.

He expected to see another one of her cool smiles and was surprised when her lips curved in a sweet grin that lit his blood on fire.

"I'm glad you think so."

Okay, maybe his beautiful goddess enjoyed things a little dirty. Dirty he could do.

He let his gaze fall to her breasts, the dusky nipples quivering slightly with each increasingly unsteady breath. He lifted a hand and tweaked one. Hard. And watched her skin flush. "Do you want me to suck on your nipples or bite them?"

She didn't answer as he kept up the rough caress, rolling the pebbled tip between his fingers until it had hardened into a firm peak. Then he switched sides. His cock continued to thicken, the blood beating in his veins like an insistent drum.

When he had both nipples as hard as stone, he took a breast in each hand and kneaded them with a firm grasp, loving the feel of her soft flesh. "So fucking soft. I could suck on these all night."

"Then put your mouth on me, Brandon."

"I'm not sure you're ready for that yet. You're not begging for it."

"Goddesses don't beg. For anything."

Did he hear a note of regret under that haughty tone? He leaned forward, almost until their noses touched. He thought about kissing those gorgeous lips but forced himself to hold back. He really wanted her to beg.

Her breath whispered against his cheek, hot and sweet. When she drew in a deep breath, he thought, *Now. Now she'll ask for it.*

But she only leaned forward and nipped at his bottom lip. With her teeth. Hard enough to make a tiny, sharp pain knife through him. It faded immediately but now he could barely breathe. Not with the surging lust in his body.

He wanted her to use those teeth all over him. On his neck, on his nipples, on his thighs. Hell, he'd beg to feel them scraping along his dick.

Not hard. Just enough to catch the skin and make him want more.

"Come on, baby. You can do better than that. I'm not going to break."

He heard her breath stop for a few seconds. Easing back just a little, he caught that hint of yearning in her expression again.

Where the hell was that coming from? What did she want?

"Lucy, baby, I'm gonna fuck you so hard, you're gonna scream. Do you think you can handle it?"

Brand swore a wave of heat rose from her body and covered him. Heat and lust and… Holy hell, he had to get inside her.

His cock so hard it hurt now, he lowered his hips until it brushed against the curls on her mound. Christ Almighty, that felt so fucking good against his cock and balls.

"Brandon."

"What do you want, babe? You gotta tell me."

"You like to torture, don't you?"

Did he? "Actually, no. You're the only one who's brought this out in me."

Her hands cupped his head, her fingers sliding into his hair before she gripped the short strands and yanked. The burst of pain made him growl, fucking *growl*, low in his throat. He didn't think he'd ever heard himself make that sound before.

"Good." She smiled, another one of those sweet grins. "Because I like it."

Jesus. The grip on his control slipped away from him as he dropped his head and covered her mouth with his. He crushed her lips so hard, he felt her teeth grind against them.

Her mouth opened to his marauding tongue and he swallowed her deep moan. He licked and tasted and couldn't get enough so he released her mouth and bit a path to her neck. Her scent invaded him, tormented him.

He realized he was dry-humping her, his cock pressing against her mound, pushing him closer to the edge of orgasm.

Way too soon.

With a groan, he forced himself to ease down her body, his stomach now pressing on the wet heat of her pussy. With his mouth at her breasts, he sucked one nipple between his lips. He sucked hard, as if he could draw her flavor out of her skin and into his mouth. He alternated sucking and biting, harder than he normally would because Lucy seemed to love it.

Her moans sank deep into his gut, clawing at his control. He ground his cock into the bed, trying not to explode. Damn, she pushed him right to the edge.

No other woman had ever done this to him. And, oh *fuck*, he liked it.

When he had both nipples rock hard and rosy red from his teeth, he began to move again, inching down her body. He licked at the undersides of her breasts, scraping his unshaven skin along her soft flesh. He wanted to bite her, to consume her, to—

Christ, what the hell was he, a caveman? Next he'd want to drag her by the hair back to his apartment. He already had one hand wrapped in the midnight-black strands, tugging on them. She moaned each time he did it.

And not in pain. He knew the difference. The first time she gave him even a hint she was in pain or didn't like what he was doing, he'd stop. On a dime.

Right now, she writhed under him, rubbing her mound against him. Enticing him. Teasing him. Destroying him. *No.*

He moved lower, his tongue painting wet streaks along ribs to her belly button. He dipped into the little hollow and felt her shudder. *Good to know.*

With his hands on her hips, he held her steady as he slid even lower until his mouth hung above her mound. His breath ruffled the short dark hair there and her fingers tightened on his head.

"Brandon, do it. Now."

She tried to force him closer but, as strong as she appeared to be, he refused to bend until he was damn good and ready. She was going to beg.

"What do you want, Lucy? You have to beg."

She moaned, a sexy sound that made his cock pulse and pre-cum moisten the tip.

"A goddess never begs."

"Well, this one will, if she wants me to eat her out."

Crude, yes, but effective. He swore he felt her entire body vibrate. Her fingers felt strong enough to crush his skull but he knew she wouldn't hurt him. He knew it in his bones.

Or maybe that was the lust talking. Either way, he didn't care.

"Come on, baby," he coaxed, letting his tongue flick out to wet her curls. "What do you want? Beg me. And remember to say please."

Silence reigned. Shit, had he pushed her too far?

"Lucy—"

"Please, Brandon." Her voice had a breathy quality, almost inaudible. "Please use your mouth on me."

Yes. He wanted to shout out his triumph but he couldn't take the time. By the time she spoke the second please, he'd latched his mouth onto her clit.

The stiff bundle of nerves felt like a little stone against his tongue, hard and hot. He sucked on it with strong pulls before drawing back to flick at it.

Lucy squirmed and cried out beneath him, her hands releasing his head for a brief second before latching onto his shoulders, as if to hold him to her.

Not that he was going anywhere. Hell, the earth could have split open beneath them and he would've continued to feast on her as they fell.

She tasted like the best fucking liquor. It went to his head, drowning him in pleasure so great his muscles tightened as he ached for more.

His cock nearly exploded from the pressure as he rubbed himself against the slick fabric of the chaise.

No way was he coming yet.

With another growl, he pushed himself to his knees, his hands under her ass, lifting her hips off the cushion. *Yes.* Her pussy tilted at the perfect angle for his mouth, he licked her, the flat of his tongue swiping from her perineum to her clit.

Her hands had fallen to her sides when he'd lifted her and he pulled back to see how hard they gripped the sides of the chaise, hard enough to rip through the fabric.

"Play with your nipples, Lucy." He barely recognized his own voice, the sound closer to the rumble of an animal. "Use your hands and keep them stiff."

She didn't hesitate to obey and he felt like a fucking god when she began to pinch and roll her nipples, possibly even harder than he'd done it.

He filed that away for later. Right now, he had pussy to eat. So sleek, so wet. So damn good. She tried to move, but he refused to let her squirm. He held her hips in a ruthless grip as he stiffened his tongue and fucked it into her tight, hot channel. She cried out his name, her moisture overflowing and spilling onto his tongue.

Forcing back his own lust, he worked her with his teeth and his tongue, alternately biting her clit and thrusting his tongue into her channel.

She came with a choked cry, her body seizing and going tight with her orgasm. He lapped it up, her flavor intensifying as she clenched around his tongue.

He teased it out as long as he could but, when her body went limp, he couldn't hold back any longer.

He let her hips drop back onto the cushion, his knees ensuring she kept her legs spread. His gaze dropped as well, taking in the sight of her sex splayed open for him.

Those lower lips had felt like silk against his tongue and her channel had gripped him as tight as a vise. He couldn't wait any longer to feel her wrapped around him. But he needed…

"Open your eyes, Lucy. I want you to watch my cock sink into you."

Drawing in a shuddering breath, she opened those beautiful gray eyes only halfway, as if she didn't have the strength for more. Good enough. He knew she was watching him.

Her gaze dropped when he moved forward, lifting her hips again and sliding her ass up his thighs. Grabbing his cock in one hand, he angled it down, aiming straight for her slit.

Tilting her hips, she rubbed her clit against the head of his cock, forcing a groan out of him. His hand tightened on her hip until he swore he felt her bones. He knew he shouldn't hold her so tightly but that thought got lost in the sensation of her juices coating the head of his cock.

Sweet fucking Christ. He clamped his hand around the base of his dick, forcing back the orgasm that wanted to detonate now. He kept it there, knowing if he released his grip now, he'd blow.

He also knew Lucy wasn't going to make it easy for him.

Despite his hold on her, she managed to move her hips just enough to continue to rub her lower lips against his cock.

Goddamn, it felt great. And when she got the angle just right and he slipped into her, just the head, he sucked in a deep breath. *Fuck, fuck, fuck.*

He thrust once, hard, releasing his hold on his cock, and sank all the way to the root in one smooth motion.

Despite her tightness, she was so wet he had no trouble at all.

Tight, so tight.

"Holy fuck, Lucy."

Her lips curved in a smile so hot, the muscles of his stomach clenched hard. "I think it might be your turn to beg, Brandon."

Then she tightened the muscles of her sex and clenched him in a grip so fierce, he swore his eyes crossed.

He forced his eyes to focus again. When they finally cooperated, he watched her as he pulled out as slowly as he could manage. Each drag of flesh, each centimeter he pulled away sent shafts of pleasure streaking through his body. Pleasure so great he deliberately bit down on the inside of his mouth until the pain drew him away from the edge.

He needed to show her... needed her to see what she'd be missing if she sent him away again.

Pulling free completely, he made her wait as long as he could possibly stand before he shoved back inside.

And this time he used force, so much so, her back bowed and she cried out.

He froze. Shit, had he hurt—

"Blessed Goddess, Brandon, again."

Her words unleashed something primal in him. The instinct to cover her couldn't be denied. He fell over her, crushing her into the chaise as his hips began to piston his cock into her.

His bigger body completely enveloped hers. Planting his elbows into the cushion on either side of her shoulders, he lifted his upper body just enough for her to breathe.

With his hips pounding and his cock spreading her wide, he bent his head to press openmouthed kisses to her neck.

He felt her pulse pounding at the side, ran his tongue over the throbbing vein then bit her. Hard.

Fuck, too hard. He felt out of control, his body reacting without conscious thought. But he couldn't stop. He had to take her. She was his.

He tried to slow down, to lengthen each thrust. To draw this out.

Each inward thrust drew his orgasm closer to the fore. Each retreat made him long to be thrusting back in.

Her arms curled around his back, her fingers digging into his skin before sliding down his back to grab his ass.

Yes. God, yes. He wanted her to reach between his legs and stroke his balls. He widened his legs and moved his mouth to her ear, about to tell her what he wanted. She didn't need to be told. Her fingers slid between his thighs, sending shivers up his spine and making his balls draw up even tighter.

His orgasm gathered in the base of his spine, making him struggle to hold it off. Lucy teased and tormented, her hips moving with his, forcing him into her harder.

Lacing the fingers of one hand through her hair, he pulled her head back, until her throat arched in a slim column and he could reach her mouth. He fitted his lips to hers as he felt his cock pulse wildly, pumping his seed into her. Groaning into her mouth, he kissed her until he could barely breathe.

And when he finally felt his orgasm fade, he slumped over her like he'd taken a crosscheck shot into the boards.

—⁓—

Lucy could barely breathe.

Brandon felt like a ton of bricks but there was no way she would tell him to move. She basked in his body heat like a cat in the sun and reveled in the feel of his cum seeping from her sex.

Blessed Goddess, she'd never thought to have him again. Had told herself she couldn't. It wasn't smart. It didn't matter one damn bit.

Her arms tightened around him and she felt his head turn

toward her, felt his lips caress her cheek. When he made a move to slide to her side, she tightened her arms around him.

"No, don't."

"I must have a hundred pounds on you, babe. I'm gonna crush you."

"No, you won't." She didn't tell him she could withstand much more weight than he could ever put on her. She was stronger than he'd ever know. "Stay."

"Do you mean for the night? Because if I do, I wanna wake up in the morning knowing I was here. Knowing what we did."

How did she answer that? Well, she knew how she *wanted* to answer him. She wanted him to remember, to want, to ache for her. But she knew it was too dangerous. He couldn't leave here with his memories.

"I want you to stay."

He must have understood what she'd left unspoken. With a sigh, he rolled to a seated position, then stood before reaching down for her.

He gathered her in his arms and headed for the kitchen and the stairs he knew would take them up to her bedroom. He eased onto the bed with her and they ended up on their sides, face to face, those dark eyes staring relentlessly into hers.

"Then I'll stay."

He sealed his mouth over hers and kissed her long and deep until she felt like she was about to pass out.

"Go to sleep, Lucy."

And she did, with Brandon wrapped tight around her.

Brand woke with a start, his eyes flashing open to stare at the wall across from the bed.

Lucy's bed.

He knew exactly where he was. He felt none of the brief disorientation he sometimes experienced on a road trip. And he still had his memories.

Yeah, but for how long?

He glanced down at the woman in his arms. Lucy lay with her back to his front, his body curled around hers. Her head lay pillowed on his arm, his other arm wrapped around her waist like a vise, as if he was afraid she'd try to get away. She continued to sleep, out cold.

It was still pitch black in her room and he turned his head to see if she had a clock on the bedside table. He didn't want to wake her but he had the sudden awareness that something wasn't right—

"Holy shit!" Brand sat up, pulling the covers over Lucy's naked body and coming up onto his knees, fists up. "Who the hell are you?"

Two people stood at the bottom of the bed. At least, he saw two human-sized outlines at the bottom of the bed. Damn it, he needed light.

"Oh dear," a female voice said. "I am so sorry to barge in like this. I do apologize, but I need to talk to Lucy."

What the fuck?

"Tessa?" Lucy's sleepy voice sounded beside him as light flicked on from somewhere overhead and her warm hand landed on his shoulder. "Tessa, is that you?"

As his eyes adjusted to the light, he realized a pretty blonde bombshell smiled at him from the bottom of the bed. She winked at him before turning her sky-blue gaze to Lucy. "Yes, it's me. I'm so sorry to arrive unannounced in the middle of the night, but I need to talk to you."

Yawning, Lucy sat up, letting the covers fall away as she stretched. Completely naked.

Brand had the almost uncontrollable urge to throw a sheet over her because the other person at the end of the bed was male. But the hard-ass standing next to the blonde never glanced at Lucy. He was too busy staring at Brand.

Good thing for him or Brand would've had to punch the guy. As it was, the guy looked ready to pound him, so maybe—

Lucy started to slide off the bed, but he grabbed her arm and pulled her back behind him.

"Wow, he's a cutie." The blonde tilted her head and let her smile widen as she gave Lucy a thumbs up. "I highly approve."

Lucy sighed as she laid a hand on Brand's shoulder. But she made no move to leave his side.

"What's wrong, Tess? What's happened?"

The blonde's smiled dimmed as her gaze skated over Brand again. "Maybe you'd like to talk alone?"

Lucy paused, her hand tightening on his shoulder. "Whatever you need to say, you can say in front of Brandon."

Well, damn if that didn't stroke his ego. And since he was naked, he'd better try not to get a hard-on. He glanced over his shoulder and got caught in Lucy's warm smile. The woman lit him up like a firecracker.

Fuck, he really needed to get his mind off sex because he didn't want to be kneeling here on the bed with an erection in front of two other people. So he went back to staring at Hard-Ass.

Dark hair cut military short except for the front fringe that hung nearly to his eyes, the guy's glacial gray gaze bored into his. He wasn't tall, but he was built like a fighter, broad through the chest, lean through the hips and clearly not happy to see him.

Yeah, well, the feeling was mutual.

"Who're you?" Hard-Ass asked.

"Maybe you want to answer that question first," Brand threw back at him.

"Boys, boys." Lucy's tone held a hint of amusement that made Brand's back straighten. "Play nice, please. There's no need for macho posturing, at least not unless Cal's naked too. Tessa, what's going on?"

Tessa giggled, her features becoming even more beautiful as she did, but she stopped after too short a time and sighed. "It's a long story." Tessa glanced at him again, her gaze making a thorough inventory before she glanced up at Hard-Ass. When she reached for him, her hand landing on his forearm, Brand watched the guy relax. And when Hard-Ass looked at Tessa, Brand knew Hard-Ass would do anything for his woman.

Brand lowered his fists and felt Lucy's breast brush against one of them.

Yeah, really not helping keep the dick in line.

Tessa's mouth twitched again. "Maybe you want to, ah, put some clothes on, and we'll meet you downstairs. I really need to talk to you."

Lucy stiffened, her expression screwing into a frown. "What's wrong?"

"I think you're going to want to do this downstairs. I'm Tessa, by the way." She smiled at Brand again before putting her hand on Hard-Ass's shoulder and squeezing. "And this is Cal. We'll wait downstairs. For however long it takes."

Brand caught the blonde's raised eyebrows and bright grin aimed at Lucy before she turned and dragged Cal out of the room.

Lucy's frown worried him as she reached for a silky blue robe lying on a chair in the corner, then tossed his jeans and T-shirt on the bed.

"You okay?" he asked as he pulled on his clothes.

She stood in the doorway, watching him with a look he couldn't decipher.

"Yes, I'm fine." She gave him a smile before she turned and walked through the doors, probably headed for the stairs. "We'll be in the living room when you're dressed."

Throwing on his clothes, he dragged his hands through his hair then flat-out ran for the stairs.

Lucy was worried. What the hell would a goddess have to be worried about? Jesus, did he really believe she was a goddess? He stopped at the top of the stairs, weight settling on his chest.

All the doubts and questions he'd forced himself not to think about last night barreled through his brain now like a runaway train.

Common sense told him there was no such thing as gods or goddesses. He should be running for the nearest exit, not running to her. Not worried that she'd take his memories for good this time.

So how the hell do you explain that?

He couldn't. He didn't have one Goddamn rational explanation for his jumbled memories of the night they'd spent together before last night. Drugs? He'd never heard of a drug that would do that except in TV shows. Electroshock therapy? Hypnosis? What?

Maybe she's just telling you the truth?

Shit.

At this point, he wouldn't be surprised if she told him the sky was falling and that there was a goddess to fix that.

The oceans overflowing? Surely Poseidon—wait, Poseidon was Greek, right? Was there an Etruscan Poseidon? Oh, hell, were there Greek and Roman gods and goddesses?

He forced himself to take a deep breath, bending over until he felt the need to hyperventilate pass.

He'd have to go to college to study ancient mythology just to date this woman. Goddess. Lucy. To him, couldn't she just be Lucy? Because if he continued to think about the rest of it, he might not think about anything else. And that was one fucking awful migraine just waiting to happen.

After a deep breath, he took the stairs to the second floor and followed the sound of voices to that amazing living room.

Tessa sat on a chaise, Hard-Ass standing behind her, one hand stroking through her golden hair.

In here, with the lights shining, he saw how beautiful Tessa was. Her blonde hair was the exact color of the sun and her blue eyes recalled clear fall skies.

"Are you a goddess too?" Tessa's smile broke out again. Shit, he'd said that aloud.

"You're just too darn cute," Tessa said. "And yes, Thesan, Etruscan Goddess of the Sun, at your service. Well, not really, but you get the meaning. But you can call me Tessa. And this is Caligo, but you can call him Cal."

Caligo, huh? Sounded foreign, though he had no discernible accent.

"Brandon, why don't you have a seat?"

His gaze shifted to Lucy, sitting on the chaise opposite Tessa. She stared at him, an inscrutable expression on her face. So fucking beautiful.

She held out her hand and he moved to take it before he realized he'd done so. When she tugged on his hand, he let her pull him down onto the seat beside her.

Lucy's gaze tangled with his for several seconds. She was searching for something… acceptance, fear, confusion. Whatever it was, she finally took a deep breath and turned back to Tessa.

"Alright, Tess. Spill it. What's going on? Where have you been?"

After a quick glance up at Cal, who nodded, his hand squeezing her shoulder, she started. "Lying low. We know Charun is attempting to break free of Aitás by consuming deities. Namely, those of us who no longer serve much of our original purpose. After our meeting at Salvatorus's a few months ago, he nearly caught me. I was this close," she held her hand up, thumb and forefinger pinched together, "to being taken to Aitás by a *tukhulkha* demon."

"Blessed Goddess, Tessa, why am I just hearing about this now?" Shock rasped through Lucy's voice. "What happened? Why didn't you come to me? How did you get away?"

"Well, I had some help getting away." Tessa sent Hard-Ass an adoring smile that actually made the guy's mouth quirk. "Cal and his father killed the demon before it got me into Aitás, but there were… complications and I spent some time, um, recuperating before I could get back to Cal."

"Recuperating from what? Tessa, were you injured?"

"A little, yes, but…" She turned to Hard-Ass, who pulled her back against his thighs. Tessa didn't seem to be able to complete what she was going to say.

"We've been keeping off the radar," Hard-Ass picked up the story, "making sure Tessa isn't targeted again. So far, she hasn't been."

"So we're here to warn you. When I was," Tessa slid a quick glance at Brand, "being healed…"

"Tessa, just say whatever you want to say." Lucy sighed. "Brandon knows what I am, what we are."

"Yeah, but does he know what that means?" Cal shook his head. "*Eteri* don't handle this stuff well, Lady. You know that."

"Brandon's handling himself just fine." Lucy's voice had a note of haughty control Brand had never heard from her before. He liked it. Especially since it made Hard-Ass nod and shut up.

"I bet that's not all he's been handling well." Tessa wiggled her eyebrows at him and Brand felt his lips curve in an answering smile. "How did you and Lucy meet, anyway?"

"I've been watching her all season so I finally decided to track her down." He didn't mention the fact that he'd done it twice.

"Season?" Tessa shook her head. "What do you mean?"

"I play for the Reading Railers. So I asked the ticket office for her address."

Tessa's eyes rounded in shock. "You gave out your real address for season tickets to a hockey team? *Anyone* could track you down. Oh, Lucy—"

"I'm not that stupid, Sister." Lucy sighed. "Brandon tracked me down through the County Recorder of Deeds. Apparently he's resourceful."

"Yeah, well, he's gonna need to be if one of those demons comes after you, Lady." Hard-Ass scrubbed a hand over the back of his neck. "Look, we're not positive, but Tessa thinks she might have overheard something while she was… recuperating that makes her think Charun might be coming after you next."

Tessa nodded. "I would have come sooner but I only had this memory tonight. We came as soon as I woke. You haven't been having any weird dreams lately, or thought about killing yourself? No visits from any *tukhulkha* demons?"

Brand blinked, his mouth dropping open before he could stop it.

Demon? Had she actually used the word demon? He needed a fucking glossary to keep up.

Lucy shook her head. "No. No dreams, no demons."

"Well, maybe you better be on the lookout, Lady." Cal gave him a critical look. "And maybe you want to get yourself some guards. Maybe have a few of your wo—uh, a few friends stay with you. I could arrange for my brother to stay with you for a while. He's not a Sentinel but he's damn handy with a sword."

"You're kidding? A sword?" Brand snorted as the image of Hard-Ass in a kilt swinging a sword around popped into his head. "What the fuck—"

"You have to separate a *tukhulkha* demon's head from its body to kill it." Hard-Ass looked straight into his eyes. "You either rip it off or you slice it off."

Okay. This conversation had just stepped over into the land of Bigfoot and ancient aliens, both of which Brand loved to watch on cheesy TV shows but neither of which he believed to be real.

And yet the woman he'd spent the night having sex with thought she was a goddess.

"So what does that make you? Captain Jack Harkness?"

Did he actually see amusement glint in Hard-Ass's gaze at Brand's reference to *Torchwood*?

"Oh!" Tess clapped her hands, just once. "I love that TV show. That guy is just too cute. But no, Cal is Cimmerian."

Cimmerian. Where the hell had he heard that name before…

Oh, no way. No *fucking* way. "Wait. Are you seriously telling me he's Conan the fucking Barbarian?"

Tessa laughed in a sunny burst of sound, while Lucy's husky chuckle played over his skin like smoke.

Hard-Ass rolled his eyes. "Fuck you, jackwad. Who the hell is this guy, anyway?"

Brand stood, noting that he had at least two or three inches and probably twenty pounds of muscle on the other guy. "Brand Stevenson."

Cal shrugged. "Okay, so who the hell cares?"

"Well, I think Lucy cares." Tessa laid her hand on the guy's arm and squeezed. "No harming the pretty *eteri*, Cal. You're a hockey player, right, Brand?"

"Yeah."

"Ooh, I love athletes." Tessa smiled and raised her eyebrows at Lucy, which made Brand smile at her. And made Hard-Ass the Barbarian scowl that much harder at him.

"Fuck, at least you're not a pansy-ass baseball player." Hard-Ass turned and shook his head at Lucy. "Seriously, my lady, you can't keep him. You gotta throw him back. He's in no way prepared for what's coming. I was barely able to protect Tessa and, yeah," he glared at Brand, "I'm Conan the fucking Barbarian."

"Then I guess it's a good thing I don't need protection." Lucy shook her head. "I don't believe Charun would be so stupid as to attack me. I retain too much power for him or one of his demons to get the jump on me."

"I wouldn't be too sure about that." Tessa gnawed at her bottom lip. "I know over the years I… I lost most of my abilities and that made me vulnerable to attack. But just because you have some of your powers doesn't mean you shouldn't be worried. He's sending his demons to do his dirty work, and they're powerful, possibly more powerful than you. They've not been fading away on his plane for more than two millennia. They've been gaining strength in Aitás."

As the room fell silent, Brand's head swam with an overload of information. Were the pretty blonde goddess and Hard-Ass the Fucking Barbarian really talking about demons? Probably not demons in the Christian sense of the word, which was all Brand—whose parents had never attended church in his lifetime—knew about.

Jesus, what other powers did Lucy possess? And where the *hell* was Cimmeria? He thought Robert E. Howard had made up those stories about Conan. He'd devoured those books as a kid.

What did that make Hard-Ass? Was he human? Or something else? He looked human. Hell, Lucy and Tessa looked human, too, but they claimed to be goddesses.

Questions. Too many damn questions.

And that crack about him not being able to protect Lucy—and Lucy's obvious belief that he couldn't—had hit a little too close to his manhood. He took a fucking beating three nights a week on the ice. His body was rock solid with muscle and able to withstand more physical pain than most of his fellow players.

But if they were talking about actual demons with superpowers… Well, hell, could they be right? Maybe he wouldn't be able to protect Lucy from whatever this demon threat was.

And that would suck. Big time.

Christ, he was getting a headache. Did he even want to try to figure out what the hell they were talking about?

"Brandon, are you okay?"

He turned his head to find Lucy staring at him, concern evident in the tightness of her expression. But he saw something else in her eyes. Pity?

Fuck that. And fuck thinking he didn't want to ask questions. Lucy hadn't sent him away to deal with this herself. She'd invited him to listen in.

"I'm fine. Just a little lost." He ignored Hard-Ass's snort, though it made his hands curl into fists. "Who's Charun?"

"God of Aitás, our Underworld," Lucy answered, her expression loosening a little. "FoGEs are what we," she nodded toward Tessa, "call ourselves. The Forgotten Goddesses of Etruria."

Forgotten goddesses. That's not something that came up in conversation every day, now was it? "How many are there?"

"Well, there were twenty-four at one time, in addition to several minor deities," Lucy continued. "Over the years, we've lost touch with some and others have disappeared completely. We don't know what happened to them. After so many centuries, some of us couldn't find a new purpose to support our existence. It was... an untenable position for some. The world has changed so much over the centuries that some couldn't keep up.

"Tessa used to control the rising and setting of the sun—"

"Until that bitch Aurora took my job," Tessa cut in, her mouth screwed up in an adorable frown. Even angry, the woman lost none of her appeal.

Lucy... Lucy only got more beautiful with each passing second.

"There's no love lost between our pantheon and the Romans', as you might be able to tell." Lucy smiled at Tessa and Brand thought he'd melt into a puddle at her feet. Damn, he had to be off the deep end. "When the Romans assimilated the Etruscans, many of our people adopted the Roman culture and religion. Some of our people remained true to us, but worship had to be conducted in small, secret groups. Though the Romans were surprisingly tolerant of those who practiced other religions, the Roman deities tend to be... jealous."

"Try psychopathic," Tessa muttered.

"And when the Roman Empire fell," Lucy continued, "the Etruscans' ability to control the elements and harness that power made them feared and persecuted by the Christians. The Catholic Church hunted our people and forced them into hiding in the ever-shrinking forests and hidden places of the world.

"For centuries, we remained in Etruria, until many began to scatter across the ocean to the Americas. Most settled along the eastern seaboard, but there are four main cities that house a large number of Etruscans. The largest of those is Reading. This village is a tiny offshoot of those who settled here. Everyone who lives here is *Enu* or *Fata*."

"*Enu*? *Fata*? What are those?"

Lucy didn't bat an eye. "The magical races of the Etruscans. The *Enu* are humans who control power and wield what you call magic. The *Fata*… Well, the *Fata* are the elemental races. The fairies."

Fairies. Right. "So you're telling me Reading, Pennsylvania, is home to an entire race of magical beings from Italy?"

"Yes," Lucy and Tessa answered in unison.

Hard-Ass just shook his head and rolled his eyes, like Brand was a lost cause. And maybe he was because, Jesus, this just got more fucked up.

"And no one knows about this?"

"Well," Lucy said, "obviously we know about it. Not many of the *eteri* do, though."

"And that means regular humans, right?"

Lucy smiled and he felt like he'd just aced a test for his favorite teacher. "That's right."

Okay. Okay, he could deal with this. Yeah, it was a lot to absorb in a short amount of time. But he'd memorized entire playbooks in one night after being traded the same morning. He'd get up to speed.

So does that mean you believe all this?

Brand looked at Hard-Ass, knowing the guy had a plan. A guy like him always had a plan. "So, what are you doing about Charun?"

"You don't need to worry about that, Brand," Lucy said. "You aren't in any danger."

"But you are." Brand didn't even glance her way, just kept his eyes on Hard-Ass. "What happened to Tessa?"

"Charun sent a demon here to capture her and take her back to Aitás." Hard-Ass's voice had dropped another octave. "The demon got her as far as Cimmeria before I caught up. We both almost didn't make it out."

There was a hell of a lot more to that story, but the color had drained from Tessa's face, so Brand decided not to push. He'd get the guy alone later and get the full story.

"So where's Cimmeria?"

"Cimmeria is the border between the planes of existence." Hard-Ass said each word as if they wouldn't rock any sane person's world. "You have to go through Cimmeria to get to Aitás or any of the other planes beyond this one."

Yeah, that was probably another one of those pieces of information Brand didn't want to think about right now, because if he stopped to ask questions, he'd have so many others they'd never move forward.

Brand turned to Lucy. "You need to lie low for a while, disappear. You can come stay with me—"

"He'll find her wherever she goes and *you* can't stop his demons," Hard-Ass said. "I had a rough time and I don't feel pain."

"You're kidding. Like, no pain at all?"

The guy shrugged, like it was no big deal. Huh. Brand had an unusually high tolerance for pain but he still felt it.

"I'm not leaving my home." Lucy's voice had an edge to it that left no doubt as to her sincerity. "And I'm more than capable of taking care of myself. I do appreciate the warning and the concern, but I'm fine. And I'll continue to be fine."

"But Lucy—"

"Tessa. I'll be fine."

The two women stared at each other until Tessa sighed, rising from the chaise. She'd given up. Obviously, she'd known Lucy a lot longer than Brand and knew when to throw in the towel. "Alright, we'll leave, though I hope you'll keep your eyes open." Lucy rose and gave Tessa a hug. "Keep safe, Sister."

"You do the same, Tessa."

As the women said their good-byes, Hard-Ass pinned him with a look he didn't have any trouble interpreting. Lucy was in trouble, no matter what she thought. And Brand was supposed to keep her safe.

"Tess and I will be around if you need us," Hard-Ass said as he tugged his goddess toward him. "Just contact Sal if you want to take me up on my offer. I can have a man here in minutes."

Lucy just shook her head as Brand stiffened at the thought of another man keeping her safe. Jealousy didn't suit him but he'd be damned if she cut him out now.

With a final wave and a sweet grin, Tessa wrapped her arms around Cal's waist as his went around her shoulders. Then the guy spoke a few words Brand didn't understand and they were gone.

And not like walk-out-the-door gone. They were disappear-into-thin-air gone. Brand's mouth literally fell open as he stared at the place the other couple had stood only seconds ago.

Vaguely, he felt Lucy rise and begin to pace but he was still trying to digest this latest development.

Holy shit.

They'd fucking disappeared. Even after everything he'd heard, everything he'd seen, that one took the cake.

Closing his mouth, because he gaped like a fish out of water, he shook his head and caught Lucy staring at him.

"Can you do that, too?" he asked.

She shook her head, "No, I can't. Not any longer."

"But you used to be able to do that?"

"Yes."

She'd lowered herself back onto the chaise and stared up at him with a look he really didn't like.

That look said she'd come to a conclusion about something. And he wasn't going to like whatever decisions she'd made. Damn, how had he come to be able to read her so well in so short a time? "So why can't you now? I mean, you're a goddess, right?"

"Yes, I am. And I can still do parlor tricks…"

She disappeared and he didn't realize until she spoke that she'd reappeared on the chaise behind him. "Like shield myself from your view for a short period of time. But I no longer have the ability to travel great distances. And much of my power is siphoned off to protect my people."

"Your people? You mean the Etruscans?"

She paused and he had the feeling she was going to lay something new on him. But she only nodded.

They fell silent as she got that look again, the one he knew meant she was thinking about him. Hell, he didn't have to be a mind reader to know she was thinking about wiping his memories again.

Fuck that.

Bending, he reached for her, grabbed her by the arms and dropped his mouth on hers. He'd thought to take her by surprise. But she'd been ready for him. She remained still under his hand, her mouth unmoving under his. She made him work for what he wanted. And what he wanted was her surrender.

His mouth moved over hers, sealing their lips together before he teased his tongue along the seam of her mouth. Her taste seeped into his, into his bloodstream, where it ignited a firestorm of desire.

His cock twitched, more than willing to join the battle for her desire. And this was a battle. One he had to win. Because if he didn't… If he didn't win, she'd strip his memories and this time he wouldn't remember a Goddamn thing about their time together.

So he played with her, let his lips work over hers until she finally opened to him. Just a centimeter but he took what she offered and slipped his tongue between her lips, into the warm, moist cavern of her mouth. His tongue slid against hers, coaxing her to play.

She didn't respond right away. He felt her restraint in the tenseness of her muscles, the stillness of her body. He wanted her hands on his body, needed to feel her touch. But she continued to hold back.

Hell, maybe she was done with him. Maybe she'd had her fun, and now that it was morning she'd decided it was time for him to go.

Shit. Maybe he'd worn out his welcome. He pulled back to stare down at her.

"Lucy." Shit, what the hell should he say? He wanted her again. He hadn't wanted another woman like this in years. Maybe ever. "Do you *want* me to leave?"

She didn't say anything right away and a chill swept through him. Her expression gave no clue to what she was thinking; her gaze was inscrutable.

Damn it, he didn't want to leave. He wanted to pin her to the wall, against that mural, and get so deep inside her she'd be able to feel him in her throat. He wanted to fuck her brains out, as crude as that sounded.

But he wanted her to want it just as much. She had last night. She'd been just as hot for him as he had been for her.

Finally she sighed, lowering her gaze as she shook her head. But he had no idea what the hell that meant.

"Come on, babe, just tell me. Do you want me to go? You only have to say the word and I'm out of here."

Lucy shook her head again, though she didn't have a clue what to do.

She knew she should erase his memories and get him home, back to his life. Without her.

But… she couldn't do it. She literally couldn't force herself to whisper the spell that would erase her from his mind.

She wanted him again, like she'd never wanted anyone, god or man. She couldn't look into his eyes but her gaze had dropped no lower than his chest. So broad, so powerful.

She wanted to lean forward and lick those six-pack abs, before she let her mouth follow that sexy-as-hell line of muscle down his stomach to his cock.

The thick outline of it pressed against his zipper, the ridge in his jeans pronounced. Beckoning her, begging for her hands to release him so she could suck him off and feel him explode in her mouth.

Blessed Goddess. She could barely breathe, lust roiling in her gut like a wild animal, stealing her capacity for rational thought.

"Lucy."

Damn it. Every time he said her name, her clit tightened and pulsed as if he'd reached between her legs and stroked her.

She wanted him to do that. Wanted him to take the decision away from her. Every day of her very long life, she'd had to make choices. Life and death. Choices that kept her people safe, kept her *lucani* free from the torment of the *Malandante*, those evil bastards.

That she'd failed several times before only made her more determined not to again. And this man was one huge, raging distraction just waiting to completely destroy her.

Why? She lifted her gaze, determined to tell him he had to leave. But her breath caught at the intensity of emotion written all over his face. His desire, his absolute craving for her made her resolve quiver and fall to pieces at her feet.

And when she opened her mouth to tell him he had to go, she couldn't get the words out.

Because Brandon grabbed her by the shoulders, pulled her up against that gorgeous chest and slammed his mouth down on hers again, kissing her with a need just short of violence.

Her mouth opened under the onslaught, her body bowing under the force. Her hands grasped at his waist, as if she'd fall over if she didn't have something to anchor her.

Oh, Gods, the man could kiss. His lips, firm and hot, moved over hers with purpose, coaxing a response she wasn't sure she wanted to give. And didn't think she could deny.

His tongue forged into her mouth, sliding against hers and making her shiver. She opened farther, letting him in deeper and gave up all pretense of pushing him away.

He groaned and she knew he'd correctly read her actions as surrender.

Her breath caught in her throat as she expected him to take the intensity down a notch, which she so did *not* want.

She wanted—

With a growl, he slanted his mouth so he could get deeper and his hands shot down her back to her waist. No, not her waist. To the front of her robe. He practically ripped the fabric off her body, causing her breath to hitch in her throat.

Gods, yes.

Naked now, her nipples peaked and aching, she tried to pull him closer, to rub her breasts against the soft cotton of his T-shirt and get a little relief.

He wouldn't let her. He held her away from his body, his hands and lips her only contact with him.

Her need grew, clawing at her gut. She moaned a low, desperate sound that caught her off guard.

So embarrassing, and yet Brandon clutched her tighter, and she swore she felt heat blast from his skin, drenching her.

His hands left her abruptly, as did his mouth, but she had no time to protest because he grabbed her off her feet, walked a few steps, then her back hit the wall with a breath-stealing jolt.

She had a second to catch her breath as he lifted her against the wall, the muscles in his arms bulging and his gaze hot enough to peel paint. He practically dared her to tell him to stop.

Tinia's teat, she was drowning in so much lust she didn't think she could speak. And she certainly didn't want him to stop. Instead, she wrapped her legs around his waist and drew his hips into hers.

His thick, hot cock rode up against her clit, the denim of his jeans rough enough to provide good friction as she moved against him.

His gaze dropped to watch her for several breathless moments until he leaned just far enough away that she couldn't reach his mouth.

"Brandon…"

"No way do you get to get off yet." His voice had lowered to a feral growl that made her pussy clench. "Not until you pay for even thinking about taking away my memories again. You're going to be screaming my name before I shove my cock in you."

"I don't scream." She had to force the words out of her mouth, barely able to get enough air to speak.

"You will. Now shut your mouth before I put you on your knees and stuff my cock in it."

Blessed Mother Goddess. She shivered even as her blood flowed like lava through her veins and her muscles tightened in painful need. "Aren't you afraid I'll bite it off?"

His lips curved into a sharp smile. "You like what it can do too much to hurt it, babe. Hell, you're practically begging for it now."

Damn him, he was right. She wanted to whisper the words of the spell to remove his clothing but she was too caught up in the moment to want to change the dynamics now.

So she watched as he lifted her just high enough to get his mouth on her breasts. She'd wondered if he'd slow down, now that he had her under his control. Torment her with slow, teasing licks.

No, he fell on her like a starving animal, attacking her breasts with his mouth and teeth. His lips circled one nipple, sucking it into the heated cavern of his mouth and rasping his tongue over the hardening tip. Her head fell back against the wall, hitting with an audible thump and sending an instant of sharp, shooting pain through her head, quickly replaced by lust.

When he'd made that nipple rosy and so hard it hurt, he switched to the other, giving it the same treatment.

Air became a scarce commodity. Her lungs burned for the lack of it. Still, she'd suffocate before she told him to stop. Not that she thought he would.

He feasted on her, teeth and tongue working her breasts while her hips arched, trying to connect with the erection he kept so selfishly in his jeans.

After what seemed an eternity, he pulled away, his teeth scraping and pulling at her nipple, sending lightning bolts of heat directly to her womb. Damn him, she needed to be filled. She needed more.

She threaded one hand through his short hair, just long enough for her to grip and yank. He didn't fight her hold but he didn't let her just tug his head back either. He must have felt some pain and, if his wicked smile was anything to go by, he liked it.

"Damn you. I want you to fuck me," she said. "Now."

Lowering her an inch at a time until she stood on her feet, he pinned her hips against the wall, her ass smashed against the cool, painted surface.

"I'll fuck you when I'm damn good and ready. Now be a good little goddess and stand still."

He dropped to his knees in a motion so fluid, she thought it had to be magic.

And then she didn't think at all because his mouth had opened on the soft skin of her stomach, just above her mound.

Sweet Mother Goddess, she didn't think she could get any more desperate without making a complete fool of herself.

She wanted to fall in a puddle of lust at his feet but she locked her knees as his mouth slowly kissed and sucked its way to her mound. She kept the curls there trimmed and her lower lips bare.

And now she knew why.

Because the feel of Brandon's tongue swiping over that skin made her have a short, sharp orgasm that left her gasping.

"Hey, baby, I didn't say you could come yet, did I? I think maybe you need a little lesson in control."

"I need no lessons from you, *eteri*."

She tried to force some strength into her words but knew she hadn't succeeded when she felt his mouth curve in a grin, his breath ruffling her hair.

"Is that a challenge, goddess? Because you should know I never back down when someone drops their gloves."

She drew in a breath to answer but it sputtered and died on her lips when he swiped his tongue through her slit.

Burning heat seared her pussy as he licked and nipped at her most sensitive flesh. Thick cream seeped from her sex, so fragrant she could smell it.

Pinned against the wall by his strong hands, she couldn't move her lower body. Her hands tugged at his hair, but he slowed to an even more glacial pace. Her pulse pounded in her clit, which he flicked with the tip of his tongue, wrenching a harsh sigh from her.

When Brandon gripped the inside of her thighs and spread her wider, she could hardly bear the sensation of the cooler air on her heated flesh.

Lifting one leg over his shoulder, he used his fingers to spread her open then fucked his tongue into her channel.

A long sigh shuddered from her as her body gathered in

preparation for another orgasm. But he withdrew just before she could find her release.

"Damn you, Brandon," she groaned, releasing his head so she didn't accidentally hurt him. Instead she slammed her fists against the wall, hearing the plaster crack and not caring in the least.

"You taste fucking amazing. But I know you feel even better when I'm stuffed inside you."

"Then do it. Come inside me, Brandon."

He licked her again before closing his teeth on her clit until she thought she would burst out of her skin with the pleasure.

"When I'm damn good and ready."

His words hummed through the tiny bundle of nerves like an electric shock, firing every pleasure receptor in her body. It took every ounce of her control not to throw him to the floor and pounce on him.

She could do it. She had the strength of a goddess. But she wouldn't. She wanted…

He wrung a groan out of her with his tongue, flattening it and drawing it over her clit, finally allowing her orgasm to break free.

Drawing it out as long as he could, her knees almost gave out as he released her for a second to stand. She felt the bulk of him surround her as he lifted her again with his hands under her thighs.

"Strip me, goddess."

She almost didn't understand his meaning, but at least one part of her brain had to be working. In the next second, he stood naked before her, his cock poised to enter her.

No hesitation, just a slight adjustment and he rammed home, filling her so deep, she didn't think he had a centimeter to spare.

His lips bit her earlobe. "Now I'm gonna make you scream."

She couldn't help herself. She wasn't one to back away from a challenge either. "You can try."

"Oh, baby, don't you know trying is the fun part?"

She expected him to fuck her hard and fast then, tried to prepare herself for a quick release. But he surprised her.

He pulled out at a glacial pace, making sure she felt every ridge, every inch of his hard flesh scraping against hers. Her channel clung, clamping around him like a vise, but he fought the pull and withdrew until only the tip of his cock remained inside. Then he pushed back in at the same speed until the base of his cock hit her clit.

Her body shook, straining. His every movement pushed her closer to completion, but at such a wicked cost. Sweat sheened her body, hers and Brandon's.

Turning her head, she licked his neck, his flavor bursting on her tongue like the finest wine. Her hands, currently kneading his upper back like a cat, slid downward until she reached the clenching globes of his ass. So physically beautiful. A perfect specimen of male.

Hers.

She slipped a finger between his cheeks and felt him groan above her.

"Ah, hell, Lucy. Don't—Aw, *fuck*."

She rimmed the tiny opening of his anus and pushed against it barely enough to matter but he bucked against her like a bull.

Yes.

His speed increased, his hips thrusting faster, then wildly until he seemed out of control.

She didn't care. His cock rubbed against that sweet spot high in her channel, scrambling her brains and making her nerves spark like fireworks.

Biting her tongue, she tightened her legs around his waist and dug her heels into his thighs.

"Brandon."

His head dropped onto her shoulder but he turned into her neck and latched his teeth onto her skin. She'd have a mark there. Another mark. She didn't care. Hell, she wanted it.

"Brandon!"

She screamed. She didn't care. He'd wanted her to and she wanted to please him as he pleased her.

His groan sounded yanked from the depths of his chest as he gave one final heave, breaking her orgasm free and making her clamp around him, milking his answering response until she felt his cum spill down her legs.

Breathing like he'd just done twenty sets of wind sprints, she felt his heart pounding against hers. In perfect sync.

"I win," he said. "But I'm gonna fucking die on the ice today."

Chapter 5

"Will you be at the game tonight?"

Lucy opened her eyes to look at Brandon, lying on his stomach next to her on her bed, his head pillowed on his crossed arms.

After that last bout in the living room, he'd cradled her against his chest and carried her back upstairs. She'd fallen asleep in his arms and woke to find him staring down at her.

She hadn't done that in years, fallen asleep with a man in her bed. It just never happened, mainly because she didn't have sex in this bed. Not since she'd moved here.

She wondered what Brandon would say if she told him where and how she'd been having sex. Would he believe her? She knew he still didn't truly believe she was a goddess.

And really, what normal *eteri* would?

"Can I ask you something, Brandon?"

His eyes narrowed for a brief second before he pushed himself up onto one elbow and rested his head on his hand. "Sure."

"Do you believe in electricity?"

He didn't react immediately, just stared at her with an intensity she recognized from watching him play. She knew he was weighing his answer carefully. Brandon was known on the ice as an enforcer with a wicked right hook, but the man also had a blazing slap shot, quick skates and a mind that was always three steps ahead of the play.

Why he wasn't a star in the NHL was a mystery she'd never understand.

"Yeah, I believe in electricity."

"When I was…" Created? Came into being? Spontaneously appeared? "…young, electricity would have been viewed as magic. And really, what is electricity except harnessed power, yes? Magic is merely another way to harness power."

Nodding, he held her gaze. "I understand the theory behind magic. Hell, I have an aunt back home who makes potions from weeds that'll cure whatever ails you. Last night, you touched my shoulder and now it doesn't hurt. I believe you did that."

"But you don't believe I'm a goddess."

His expression didn't change one bit. "I didn't say that."

Heat began to gather in her belly. A furious, vicious heat that wanted her to snarl and rage at him. But on its heels was a more sober threat. Tears.

And Lusna, the Etruscan Goddess of the Moon, didn't do tears.

"What time do you need to be at the arena for the game?"

He gave an almost imperceptible flinch that let her know he'd correctly interpreted her question.

"You know," he said, his tone calm, almost amused, "I could play stupid and just answer the question. I could play the dumb hockey grunt and ignore the fact that you want me to leave now."

"I didn't say—"

"But I don't play those games. Hell, I don't even play games on the ice. Out there, it's a battle but there's always a winner. If you tell me you're not playing mind games with me, then I'm gonna take you at your word. Now, you tell me you're an Etruscan goddess," he took a deep breath and released it before continuing, "well, then, I guess until someone can prove otherwise, I have no cause to doubt you."

That cold ball of rage died a fast death. Could it truly be that easy?

No, nothing was ever that easy. Men—no matter if they were gods or mortals—would tell a woman whatever she wanted to hear if it advanced his cause. Or got him laid.

She forced a smile that made his gaze narrow on hers. "I'm glad to hear it. And yes, of course I'll be at the game."

It took him a few seconds, but Brandon finally nodded and rolled off the bed and walked across the room to retrieve his clothes from the chair she'd set them on last night.

She didn't say anything, just enjoyed the show as Brandon moved naked across the room. The play of muscles in his thighs and ass was enough to make her mouth water.

At thirty-five, he still had the body of a twenty-year-old. And he got it the natural way. He hadn't been born with it, as had the gods she knew.

No, he earned those muscles on the ice and at the gym. Hard, physical activity that sculpted his body into a work of art.

His scars merely added to the appeal. Even his crooked nose appealed to her in a way nothing ever had. What was it about his man that set her on fire?

And what would she have to do to douse the flames when it came time to get rid of him?

Dressed in his shirt and boxers, Brandon returned to the side of the bed, carrying his jeans. He stopped to stare down at her, heat and a promise in his gaze.

"I knew you weren't there last night, you know." He pulled his jeans up his muscular legs. "Not that it's your fault, but I knew something was wrong. I was off my game all night."

She knew his injury had been her fault. She nodded as he zipped his jeans. "You were and I'm sorry. But I was in the arena, just not in my regular seat."

She didn't think she could live with herself if something else, something worse, happened to him.

Wipe his memories, you idiot. And do it right this time.

The conversation with Tessa and Cal played through her head again. She truly wasn't worried about Charun coming after her. She didn't think he'd have the nerve.

But what if he did? What if Charun sent one of his demons to get her? What happened if Brandon got between her and *tukhulkha* demons? He'd be hurt. He was *eteri*. He didn't have the power to protect against what one of those fiends could throw at him.

She would need all of her powers to protect herself. But she knew if Brandon was in danger, she would protect him at her own expense.

Ugh, when did you become such a sap?

Damn it, she wasn't. If Charun came after her, she didn't want Brandon anywhere near her. Or any of her *lucani*, for that matter. But all she could think about was when she would see Brandon next.

Wipe his memory.

Her chest tightened as she stared up at him. She couldn't do it. And not only because the sun had spilled over the horizon, severely limiting her powers. But she just didn't *want* to.

"Babe, don't even think about it." Fully dressed now, Brandon leaned down and planted a hard kiss on her lips.

She really shouldn't melt every time he touched her. But she couldn't help herself when he kissed her or caressed her—hell, all he had to do was look at her and her entire body surrendered.

She opened to him as his arms wrapped around her and his tongue slipped into her mouth, cutting off any reply she might have thought about making. With no visible effort, he lifted her off the bed and against his body. She let him kiss her, allowed his hand to roam over her naked body, palming her breasts and tweaking the nipples before smoothing down her back to cup her ass and press her mound against that firm ridge in his jeans.

He kissed her until she wrapped her legs around his waist and tilted into him, her sex wet and aching for him again. When she moaned and tilted her head to make him kiss her even deeper, he pulled away and set her back on the bed. Then he looked straight into her eyes.

"If you take my memories, I will turn up here again tonight.

And when I figure out what you did, again, I might just think you don't want me."

He slipped a hand between her legs, stroked her wet lips and tweaked her clit until she shuddered.

"And I know that's not true." He kissed her one last time then headed toward the door. When he got there, he stopped, turned, and flashed her a quick smile.

"Wait for me after the game. I'll tell Chester the guard to expect you."

She shook her head and he was about to argue when she said, "Why don't we just plan to meet here after the game? Is that okay with you?"

He couldn't stop smiling. "Absolutely. I'll see you later. And don't miss warm-up."

—⁓—

"I see you're going to be worthless today. Had a good night?"

Tivr paused as he stocked the beer coolers behind the bar when she entered the bar later that morning.

A hot shower had done nothing for the throbbing ache in her temples. Deities didn't get sick and they certainly never experienced anything as pedestrian as a headache.

Except Lucy was pretty damn sure that's what she had at the moment.

Dressed in her most comfortable black yoga pants and a soft cotton sweatshirt, Lucy wanted nothing more than to head back to bed and sleep for another eight or twelve hours.

But she knew if she didn't at least make an effort to show herself downstairs, her boys would be upstairs and in her face before she could bar the door against them.

Maybe she'd get lucky and only have to deal with Tivr.

He would rag her relentlessly but she knew he wouldn't worry like Caeles.

Caeles was still so young, still a child, even though he'd reached the *eteri* age of adulthood several years ago. The *Fata* aged and developed at a different rate than *eteri*.

"I don't think I need to dignify that with an answer." She sat on the barstool in front of him and forced herself to meet his gaze. "How's the back room looking? I planned to take inventory today but that may have to wait until tomorrow."

Caeles would have offered to take inventory for her, even though she'd never taken him up on it. Tivr knew it was a futile gesture and had given up asking years ago.

Lucy ran the bar. This was her domain. She took care of every detail, from what liquor to stock to what snacks she ordered and how many napkins.

Yes, she was compensating. No, she didn't give a flying rat's ass.

"The back room looks good. You, however, look like shit. You want me to beat the crap out of the guy?"

"You will do no such thing. Ty, don't you dare—"

"Hey, Caeles," Ty called over his shoulder. "Pay up."

Her second son pushed through the doors from the kitchen, where he'd obviously been making her breakfast. He set a steaming plate of eggs, bacon, and home fries on the bar and followed it with a bowl of cantaloupe. Pulling a twenty dollar bill from the front pocket of his flannel shirt, Caeles passed it over to Ty, who pocketed it with the skill of a magician.

She couldn't help herself. She had to know. "Tell me. What did you bet on this time?"

The boys exchanged a glance before they crossed their arms over their chests in an identical motion then turned the weight of their gazes to her.

"You didn't wipe his memories last night, did you?" Ty asked.

Now, when had her children decided she'd lost control of her faculties and decided she needed a keeper?

She had a moment to smile and think how much alike and yet how different her boys were.

With his spiky dark hair and pronounced Mediterranean features, his bare arms covered in black tattooed protective runes, Ty looked like a badass biker who would beat the shit out of you. Worn jeans and a tight black T-shirt emblazoned with the name of some rock band completed the picture.

Caeles, on the other hand, wore tan cargo pants and a long-sleeved plain green T-shirt that matched his eyes. His wheat-colored hair nearly reached his broad shoulders, covering his distinctly pointed ears and curling in a way women would kill for.

Only Ty carried her blood but when they looked at her like that, standing side by side with the exact same expression, she had to wonder.

"I don't see how that's any of your concern," she finally answered Ty's question, giving him a look that should have had him cowering in the corner.

Ty just lifted his eyebrows at her. When she turned that look on Caeles, he had the grace to look abashed.

A flash of him as a baby, abandoned on the porch just outside the door he was facing, came to mind. She'd only found him by chance thirty years ago. He probably would have frozen to death if she hadn't stuck her head outside to investigate a noise.

Wrapped in a blanket, no note pinned to his chest, no name stitched on his blanket. Just a pair of huge green eyes and those ears that marked him as *fauni*, one of the shape-changing Etruscan elemental beings.

Most of the *fauni* had lost their lives during the Purge of 1758 when the *eteri* of Tuscany had turned on their fellow native inhabitants out of fear and ignorance and nearly annihilated the *Fata* population, including the three elemental races, the *fauni*, *silvani*, and *aguane*.

To be a full-blood *fauni*, Caeles had to have a *fauni* father and a *silvani* mother. She never even tried to track down his parents. Hadn't wanted to know why they'd left him for her. She'd taken him as a gift and would have refused to give him up to anyone after she'd taken him in her arms.

"We're worried about you." Caeles finally sighed, his hands held out in front of him in surrender. "You've seemed kind of… off-kilter lately."

She controlled her surprise as best she could. How had she slipped up? How had they known?

"I'm fine, boys, really."

Ty's eyebrows lifted, and a cocky little grin she'd grown to know and worry about curved his lips. "Uh huh. So your hockey player seems like a nice guy. For an *eteri*."

Her back straightened at the sneer she heard in Ty's voice. How dare he? "And when did you become such an elitist?"

Ty's grin widened. Damn it, he'd caught her out.

"I didn't," he said. "You would have asked me the same thing, Mom. I *am* glad to see you interested in someone after all this time. We've been worried."

It was her turn for raised eyebrows. "Isn't that kind of like the pot calling the kettle black?"

He shook his head. "Nope, 'cause we're not talking about me right now. We want to know what it is about this guy that's made you come out of hibernation?"

Hibernation? Interesting choice of words. "Why do you say I was in hibernation?"

Caeles snorted. "Maybe because you haven't shown an interest in a man ever."

"And that's a problem why?"

"It's unhealthy." Ty set his hands on the bar and leaned closer.

No, it wasn't. It was an extremely healthy way to keep her sanity.

"Sweethearts, I don't need a man to make me happy. Hell, I don't even need one to find satisfaction."

As she knew they would, Ty held his hands up in a T-shape as Caeles blushed a bright red.

"Whoa," Ty said. "TMI. But don't think I'm not wise to your tricks. And don't think you're going to avoid the subject. You need affection, not only blind worship."

"I have it. My *lucani* are extremely affectionate and they—"

"Treat you like the goddess you are," Caeles interrupted. "But they don't treat you like a woman. And no matter what else you are, you're a woman first. And you need to be treated like one occasionally. You've been alone too long. You've cut yourself off from all emotion and that's not healthy."

When had her baby become so astute? And so pushy?

She knew they were only trying to help. She knew her sons would never want to hurt her. But they were rubbing her loneliness in her face, and she didn't think she could stand much more of it.

"That's not true. I love you boys so much—"

"We know that, Mom." Ty shook his head and sighed, running one hand through his short hair and making it stick up even farther. "But that's not what we're talking about and you know it. So what is it about Stevenson?"

The honest curiosity in Ty's voice made her bite back her flippant words about the beauty of his body.

Yes, her attraction had started like that. What attraction didn't? But sometime last night, it had changed. She didn't just want to get the man naked and jump his body.

She wanted to talk to him, to hear his voice, to find out what he thought about, what TV shows he liked to watch, what books he liked to read. How perfectly awful was that?

"I don't… I think…" She bit back a sigh and tried again. "There's just something about him. From the first moment I saw him step onto the ice, I knew I needed to meet him. There was… something I responded to instinctively."

The intensity of her reaction to him had actually frightened her a little. So much so, she had gone out of her way *not* to meet him.

"I didn't realize he'd noticed me until a month or so into this season."

She stopped to smile, calling up one of her most precious memories. "The first time he caught my eye on the ice during warm-up, he smiled at me. It was like the moon breaking over the horizon on a clear night. I wanted him like I'd never wanted another man in my life."

Caeles's smile eased some of the anxiety she felt over her reluctance to wipe his memories. "Then allow yourself to have some fun, Mom. You deserve it."

"Just… be careful," Ty said, something she didn't understand lurking in the darkness of his eyes. "Because if he hurts you, I'm takin' him out."

<hr />

As soon as he stepped onto the ice that night, Brand skated down the boards to make sure Lucy was where she was supposed to be.

The tight band that'd wrapped around his chest as he'd driven home that morning loosened when he saw her in her regular seat.

Damn, the woman was a beauty. He wanted to tear down the glass and jump the boards to get to her. He wanted a fucking good-luck-with-the-game kiss and if that made him a sap, well, fuck it, so he was.

He felt pretty damn good. When he showed up at the arena, the team trainer took him into his office to check his shoulder.

"It feels fine and I've got full range of motion." Brand demonstrated for the doubtful trainer.

"Holy shit, Brand." The young guy's voice held a definite note of disbelief. "What virgin did you sacrifice to the devil to get that to heal so friggin' fast?"

Brand had shrugged it off like it was no big deal. "Guess it looked worse than it was."

The trainer continued to shake his head as he told the coach Brand was okay to play.

Now, as he skated by her seat, he acknowledged her smile with a raised stick and a nod. The second time around, he hit up Casey, the young guy who'd been at the bar last night. Casey waved back, his grin wide. Damn, he felt great.

As he stopped to stretch along the boards and bang the glass for the kids in the front row calling his name, he caught sight of the Terrible Twins headed his way, identical shit-eating grins on their identical faces.

As they flanked him, he had to fight to keep a smile off his own face.

"So, dude," Jason started. "She's hot."

"Too hot for you, man," Tommy chimed in. "What she needs is some young studs to do her right."

Brand let the guys talk. He knew if he opened his mouth, it'd only fuel their fire. And every man on the team knew not to rile the twins before a game. They wouldn't shut the fuck up for the rest of the night and someone would end up taking them into the boards. Usually it was the opposite team.

On more than one occasion, one of their own guys had given them a shot. Good thing the kids didn't hold grudges. And had short attention spans. After a few minutes ragging him, they moved off to bother someone else.

Leaving Brand alone to try and wipe the shit-eating grin off his face before the rest of his teammates decided to start in on him.

Luckily, the game turned physical from the first puck drop.

Hard checking from both sides, a few fights, one of which he started because the guy pissed him off by taking a cheap shot at his goalie.

He had two assists and they won the game by a score of five to one, which meant the locker room buzzed with adrenaline and testosterone after the game.

"Hey, Stevie," Lenny yelled across the room, "we're heading for Third and Spruce. You comin'?"

He should. As co-captain, he should celebrate with his team at the local bar.

But he couldn't wait to see Lucy. "Can't tonight. Got a date."

Every man in the locker room turned to stare, which was kind of ridiculous. You'd think he was a monk breaking his vow of chastity, for Christ's sake.

So he hadn't dated anyone this season. It wasn't like it was a big deal. Jesus, you could hear a pin drop in there. Until Jase opened his mouth.

"Dude, don't tell me you actually know that piece of hotness in the seats? Whoa, she looks way too good for you."

He shot the kid the finger as he headed for the showers but he ignored the ribbing from the other guys as his tension melted away under the good-natured and foulmouthed taunts.

He knew they didn't mean anything by it. He'd be doing the same if it were someone else. Hell, it sent him off in an even better mood, if that was possible. By the time he got to Howling Moon, he had a grin that wouldn't quit.

Inside, he headed straight for the bar, nodding to a few familiar faces in the sparse crowd. Only eight people sat scattered around the room in pairs tonight. He didn't see Lucy but he knew she'd be here eventually.

The bartender he'd met two nights ago set a full mug in front of the stool he was beginning to think of as his.

"Hey." Brand stuck his hand over the bar as he slid onto the stool. "I don't think we've been introduced. Brand Stevenson."

The bartender shook and held his gaze. "Ty Aster."

Brand's eyes popped wide. Holy shit. Lucy hadn't mentioned—

"Yeah. She's my mom."

Brand opened his mouth to say something… and couldn't think of a damn thing to say. Ty stared at him for a few seconds, his gaze boring into Brand's, until a hard grin split the guy's face.

"Yeah, I know she didn't tell you, but don't read anything into it. It's not something we draw attention to."

"Why not?"

"Because I could be used to hurt her. Deities are immortal. The *Fata* and *Enu* live for centuries. Jealousy, rivalries, the slightest insults can fester for decades and become deadly grudges. Gods and goddesses are notoriously arrogant and easily pissed off, and they'll use whoever they can to hurt their target."

"So… you're a god?"

"Yep."

"So who—" No, forget that. His mother had raised him better than to ask rude questions. "So what do you do, Ty?"

"I tend bar."

"No, I mean… what does a god do?"

Ty shrugged. "Impregnate a few mortals. Throw some thunderbolts. Change into a wolf and chase a few sheep. Not much, really."

Brand blinked, his mouth opening to say something but he had no clue what to say.

The first part he got. Sex was universal. But what was it about thunderbolts? And… "Did you say change into a wolf?"

One second, Ty stood in front of him. In the next, he wasn't there. Instead, a wolf stared at him from behind the bar. The animal stood on its hind legs, his front paws resting against the edge of the bar.

"Holy shit."

Brand barely heard himself speak through the rush of blood in his ears. He nearly fell off the stool but managed not to embarrass himself that badly.

"Ty, Mom's gonna put a chain around your neck and tie you outside for the night."

Lucy's guitar player joined the wolf behind the bar. Brand spared him a glance, wondering if he'd just materialized out of thin air, then returned his gaze to Ty.

The wolf.

"You're a werewolf."

Holy shit, there were werewolves. Wouldn't that just blow the twins' minds? Just last week, they'd been arguing about who would win a grudge match between Bigfoot and the Wolf Man.

"No, he's an idiot. Hey, I'm Caeles. I'm Lucy's intelligent son. Mom said to tell you she'll be down in a few minutes. Just ignore dogbreath. He'll eventually change back into his even-more-stupid human body."

Brand nearly choked on air when Ty reappeared in front of him and gave Caeles a grin and a gesture involving his chin and his hand.

"*Vaffanculo*, Spock." Ty grabbed a mug and tapped a draft for a man who'd stepped up beside Brand. "Take your guitar and go play with yourself."

Caeles gave Ty a good-natured shove as he moved out from behind the bar, one Ty returned. They looked nothing alike but Brand saw the smiles they exchanged. Brothers. Two sons.

"So, Gretzky, you gonna hang around for a while?"

Ty watched him with a deceptively easy expression but Brand knew a challenge when he heard one.

He nodded. "Yeah, I am. So what can you tell me about Charun?"

Ty's eyebrows lifted toward the ceiling. "Why the hell are you asking about Charun?"

Shit. "She didn't tell you?"

Now Ty's eyes narrowed down to slits. "Tell me what?"

Goddamn, he had a big mouth. Still, he wasn't convinced Lucy had nothing to fear from this Charun guy.

He'd done some Internet research before heading out to the

arena this afternoon. He'd felt like an idiot Googling "Etruscan Goddess Lusna" and "Etruscan God Charun."

But once he'd gotten over the "holy shit, I'm Googling a goddess" feeling, he'd lost himself in it.

Not that there was much information out there. Most of what he found was based on Greek myth. But Lucy wasn't Greek.

And according to most of the sources he'd been able to find online, the Etruscans hadn't left behind a whole hell of a lot of written material. He'd also ordered a few books on the Etruscan culture from Amazon but those wouldn't be here for a few days and—

"Yo, Hockey Stick." Ty smacked him on the arm. "What didn't she tell me?"

Fuck, he'd totally forgotten that Ty had asked him a question. Brand couldn't exactly take the words back now.

"Lucy had visitors last night. Tessa and Cal. They told her Charun is hunting down Etruscan goddesses and consuming them for their powers. He's trying to break out of wherever the hell he is."

"Aitás." Ty's expression darkened. "Charun is in Aitás. Shit, that's not good."

"Lucy doesn't think she's in any danger but I'm not convinced she's safe. Then again, what the hell do I know about Etruscan gods and goddesses?"

Tim's expression lightened a little as he shook his head. "All this must seem pretty strange to you, huh?"

Brand just shook his head. "Yeah, you could say that, considering a few days ago I still thought deities were something you read about in textbooks." Brand caught Ty's gaze. "So what *are* you?"

Ty's mouth tilted up in a smile that must make the girls fall at his feet. "What makes you think I'm any different from you?"

"I mean, what do you do as a god?"

Ty didn't look like he was going to answer at first. Then he sighed. "I'm the Etruscan God of the Moon."

"So your father is…"

"I don't have any idea. Mom's never told me. I only know he's a full god which is why I'm not a demigod."

"That means half god, right?"

"Yeah. You've been doing your homework. You heard of Hercules, right? He's a demigod. Human mom, deity sperm donor."

"And Caeles, is he a demigod?"

"No. Mom adopted him about thirty years ago. He's *fauni*, one of the elemental races of the *Fata*."

Brand shook his head and sighed. "Yeah, ya know, I never went to college. The closest I got to studying mythology was watching *Clash of the Titans* about twenty times when I was six and stuck at home with a broken leg for a few weeks."

Ty laughed, the sound bursting out with an almost magnetic pull. Brand knew if he looked over his shoulder, all of the women in the place would be smiling at the kid. The god.

Aw, fuck it.

"Yeah, I can see your dilemma," Ty said. "Okay, so, the *Fata* are Etruscan fairies, though I suggest you don't use that word unless you want to start a brawl." Ty tapped a beer for a guy who'd walked over from a table. "They're a separate race from humans, older, longer lived and more powerful. The race originated in Europe about a millennium or so before humans showed up. So did all the elemental races. In the beginning, there were three races, the *fauni*, *silvani*, and *aguane*. Over the years, through interbreeding, there are now more than fifteen races of *Fata*."

Brand nodded, as if he understood what the guy was talking about. And maybe he did. Kind of.

"The *Enu* are humans who can work magic, and that's where the Etruscans came from."

Enu. Humans who can work magic. Got it.

Damn, he'd always thought he had an open mind, but this…

Hell, he needed brain surgery to open a hole in the back of his head to be this open-minded.

But the way he felt about Lucy…

He'd never been so damn infatuated so fast in his life. Not even as a teenager when his hormones had been raging.

But it wasn't just infatuation. That would've been easy to ignore. What he felt for Lucy he couldn't ignore.

"So, what makes someone *fauni* as opposed to, uh…"

"*Aguane* and *silvani*. Well, *fauni* have more of an affinity for animals. They can shift into any animal, as opposed to the *lucani* who worship Lucy."

Worship, huh? Well, she was a deity. "*Lucani*. Those are the werewolves, right?"

"Hey, dude, good job on the pronunciation." Casey slid onto the stool next to Brand and held his fist out for a fist bump, which Brand obliged. "Not many people get our name right. How's it going, Brand? Good game tonight."

"Thanks." *I think.* Brand wanted to shake his head to make sure his marbles were still there. "So you're a werewolf."

"We call ourselves *versipelli*. It's Latin for skin shifter."

Ty snorted and Casey gave him the finger. Obviously Casey didn't feel the need to kowtow to Ty.

"I do have a master's in engineering, you know." Casey tried to look offended but couldn't hold back his grin. "Okay, so I was definitely *not* a straight-A student in high school, and I majored in girl chasing during my undergrad days."

Casey's wide grin was infectious and Brand returned it even as his brain started to spin in its track.

Holy shit.

This guy turned into a wolf, too. And Caeles, tuning his guitar on stage, could turn into any animal he wanted. There were creatures—people?—who called themselves fairies.

"Hey, Brandon. Man, are you okay?"

Refocusing on Casey's face, he reached over and placed his hand on the kid's shoulder. "Yeah, I'm fine. Just a little much to take in all at once, ya know? It's gonna take me a little while to get up to speed on everything. But trust me, I'm good at adapting. So, you turn into a wolf under the full moon?"

And there was Casey's thousand-watt grin again. "Actually, I can turn into a wolf anytime I want. The *lucani* usually come into our change when we're teenagers, usually around thirteen or fourteen for boys, sometimes younger for the girls. We can't control it right away, so it's only under a full moon until we're about twenty. By then, we can usually do command performances."

"So if I asked…"

"Yeah, but I haven't filed my nails for a while and Lucy doesn't like when we mark her floors."

Brand felt a laugh bubble up but swallowed it. "I can see where that would be a problem." He looked around the room. "Is everyone else here… *lucani*?"

Casey looked over his shoulder. "Pretty much so. Oh, except for Larth. He's *stregone*."

"And that means…?" Brand asked.

"He's a witch."

Of course he was.

"Hey, Case." Ty set a mug in front of the kid, who didn't look old enough to drink. But he'd said he had a master's degree in engineering. "I think Brand's had all the lessons he can stand for one night."

Casey's grin dimmed again and Brand shook his head. The kid would never be able to play poker. "Nah, I'm good. Just… processing."

"I know it's kind of—"

Casey cut off and turned toward the kitchen door, his expression melting into abject happiness, while Brand felt heat slide up his spine a second before Lucy walked through the door.

Damn, maybe he was developing his own powers where she was concerned.

She wore the same outfit she'd had on at the arena—a deep purple sweater that molded her curves, tight jeans and a pair of black boots with fuck-me heels that would bring the top of her head to his chin.

She let her gaze slide by him the first time around, making sure she acknowledged everyone in the place before she came back to him.

Hell, his smile probably looked as goofy as Casey's and now he had a raging hard-on to go with it.

"Hello, Brand. Good game tonight. You played well."

He swallowed, hoping like hell he didn't embarrass himself when he tried to speak. "Thanks. The team was sharp tonight. The kids are coming along pretty well."

She walked over to the bar and stopped directly in front of him. Their gazes locked. "No injuries tonight, though I thought you were going to take that guy's head off in the second period."

"Yeah, he had a few disrespectful words for my goalie. I made him think twice about using that kind of language around the kid again."

Lucy's husky laugh filled every empty space in the room with shivery anticipation and Brand had to fight back the urge to vault over the bar, throw her over his shoulder, and take her upstairs.

When her laughter died, she continued smiling straight into his eyes. "Since I know how persuasive you can be, I'm surprised he wasn't in any mood to hear you out, considering he took a swing at your head. I'm glad to hear you have no lasting injuries that would impair your... playing."

Damn, he really liked this woman. So much so, he knew right then that he could happily live with her for the rest of his life.

The thought shut him down cold. Was he nuts? What the hell was he expecting to happen here?

Did he truly believe they were going to walk off into the sunset and live happily ever after? With a goddess?

Hell, if he bought into everything she and her barful of worshippers were saying, she was immortal. The best he could hope for was another five good decades.

Shit.

"Brand." Her tone drew his gaze back to hers and he knew she *knew* exactly what he was thinking.

He could see it in her eyes, they were that expressive. "Don't." Then she gestured behind him. "Want to shoot some pool? I'll let you win one or two games."

Her sly grin made his mouth quirk in response. "You can break my balls any time."

─── ∿∿∿ ───

Brand shot straight upright in bed, certain he'd find someone watching them again.

Pale morning light shone down on them through the skylights, lighting the room enough for him to see every corner. He saw no one.

Glancing down, he saw Lucy asleep, naked and curled on her side. Her dark hair curled like a shadow across her shoulders and down her back. Her pale skin looked strangely sallow in the light, almost jaundiced. He reached out to run his hand down her hair, an unreasonable fear gripping his stomach in an icy vise. Damn, she felt hot, like she was running a fever. Was she sick?

"Lucy? Hey, baby, you okay?"

She didn't answer, didn't move.

He actually put his hand in front of her mouth to make sure she was breathing. Maybe this was normal for her. What did he really know about goddesses anyway?

His stomach tightened further as his earlier fears about her immortality and his lack of it rose up like bile.

He found it hard to wrap his mind around the idea that this woman had been alive for more than two millennia. Even worse, the thought that he'd be only a footnote in her life made him want to lay someone out.

Hell, she probably figured this was a fling, a little diversion to pass a few months, maybe a couple of years. Would they even last a decade?

And why the hell was he getting his shorts in a knot anyway? It wasn't like they were going to get married and live happily ever after.

She'd probably laugh in his face if he dared ask. Talk about opposite sides of the tracks. Jesus, thinking about this made his head hurt, almost canceling out the sense of dread now making his stomach roil. What the fuck was going on?

He gave the room another once over, trying to be alert to every—

There. In the far corner. What the *hell* was that?

A shadow had formed, dark and ominous and completely out of place in the increasingly sunny room.

For several seconds, he watched it coalesce as if in slow motion. Almost mesmerized at the out-there sight, he didn't even think to move.

Until he realized anything that looked that bad had to be up to no good. So he got his ass in gear.

Sliding out of bed without waking Lucy wasn't as hard as he thought it'd be. He figured she'd rouse pretty easily. But no, she didn't even move. Christ, just something else to worry about.

Maybe he should wake her? But what if this turned out to be nothing more than his overactive imagination?

And what if it doesn't?

Fuck it. If he looked like an idiot when she woke up, so be it. He slid behind the bathroom door, watching from behind it as the shadow formed into something far different than anything he could have even imagined.

Heart beating a mile a minute, Brand forced himself to calm his breathing so maybe that… that thing wouldn't hear him.

Jesus, what the hell was it? From behind, it had a human form but its blue skin held a faint sheen in the brightening sun and its black hair coiled like snakes down its back. When it turned, Brand could see it had no visible sexual traits—no breasts, no genitals. It had long pointed nails and a mouth full of sharp teeth that it bared in something resembling a smile.

Now fully formed, it sniffed the air then hissed like a snake. The creature immediately honed in on Lucy. Alone. On the bed.

Shit.

"Hey, you butt-ugly asshole." Brand stepped out from behind the door. "What the *fuck* are you?"

He wanted the thing to get the hell away from Lucy and focus on him. He got his wish. The whatever-the-hell-it-was turned and Brand had to force himself not to take a step back.

Holy shit, that was freaky as all hell.

It looked human, mostly. Except for that blue skin and those teeth a shark would be proud of. It had a long straight nose and high cheekbones and a square jaw.

And Brand still didn't know if it was male or female.

Maybe it's neither.

And, whoa. That was a whole other freak-out.

Turning its head, the thing sniffed again, this time in Brand's direction. "Hmm. Maybe that's a question I should be asking you." Its gaze slid down Brand's naked body, making creeped-out goose bumps rise and his testicles want to crawl back inside his body. "What's your name?"

Brand's hands curled into fists at his sides before he forced them to relax. He'd treat the thing like a rabid dog. Show no fear but be ready for anything.

"You don't need to know my name. You just need to leave. I don't think you were invited to this private party."

"So you were having a party with beautiful Lusna. Interesting. Lusna usually sticks close to her *lucani*." The thing drew in another deep breath, its nose actually twitching like a rat. "Now, you're not *lucani* but you're not strictly *eteri* either, are you?"

What the fuck was this thing talking about? "I don't know what the hell—" Wait, maybe engaging the thing in conversation wasn't such a good idea. "You don't need to know what I am. Just know I'll kick your ass if you don't get out of here now."

"Oh, I will be. But not without my prize."

Every muscle in Brand's body tensed, ready to spring into action should that thing go for Lucy. But no, it just stood there, clawed hands on its nonexistent hips, and sniffed again.

Christ, that was creepy. What the hell was it trying to smell anyway? Finally, the thing tilted its head in an oddly female gesture and stared at him with eerie red eyes. Either the thing had been on a bender for the past two years or it was one of those demons Cal and Tessa had been talking about. A real honest-to-G—wait. Honest to God was taking on a whole new meaning lately. And he really didn't have time to think about that.

"Fuck" covered it for now.

"You know, you'd be a lot more threatening if you weren't naked," the blue demon said. "Not that I don't appreciate the show. Very tasty."

And now Brand's testicles wanted to crawl into his chest to hide.

"Dude, you're making me ill." Brand forced the words out from between clenched teeth. "Get the fuck out or I will make you get the fuck out."

The thing laughed, more like it cackled, and it made Brand wince like it'd dragged those nails across a chalkboard.

"Oh, you're very brave, I'll give you that. I can understand what Lusna sees in you. But you're not exactly what you think you are. And that could prove to be problematic."

Okay, maybe Brand was still asleep. Maybe he was dreaming. He'd taken in a lot of information yesterday and they'd had a hell of a lot of sex last night.

Maybe his subconscious was screwing with him, making him see things that weren't there.

Hoping the demon didn't know what he was doing, he let his hands curl into fists and his nails bite into his palms, hard enough to break the skin and draw blood. No, he was awake.

Then he thought about exactly what the thing had said. He opened his mouth to ask what the hell it meant—and the thing jumped at him.

Luckily, he'd been expecting it and was ready. Reaching for its neck, Brand caught it, managing to keep his hands away from the thing's teeth before he tossed it like a venomous snake across the room, away from Lucy.

It hardly weighed anything and it hit the wall with an audible crack. Brand ran for it, intending to beat the shit out of it before it could get back up. He'd nearly reached it when the demon sprang back to its feet, teeth bared.

Christ, that was just nasty. Brand figured he'd probably better not get too close to those, so he rushed it, digging his shoulder into the thing's stomach and driving it back into the wall.

The demon hit hard but got in a good swipe across his back with its claws, making Brand draw away with a hiss of pain. Shit, that stung.

Putting some distance between them, Brand bounced on the balls of his feet and got ready for the thing to make a counter attack. The demon stood, shook its head, then hissed before it ran out the door of the bedroom and disappeared down the hall.

Adrenaline pumped through Brand's veins in an almost painful rush as he tried to catch his breath.

Why the hell had it run? Brand couldn't believe it'd been scared of him. It'd been strong, maybe not as strong as him, but still. It had claws like a tiger and teeth like broken glass. And just what had the damn thing meant when it'd said Brand wasn't exactly what he thought he was? That hadn't made any damn sense at all.

Taking another deep breath, he turned toward the bed—and realized Lucy had slept through the entire thing. Her breathing was slow and steady and her skin looked even more sallow in the brighter light of the sun.

She looked sick.

He ran for the bed, crawling onto the mattress next to her. "Hey, babe. You okay?"

She didn't answer, didn't respond in any way, and now he was beginning to get worried. Hell, he was a lot worried.

"Lucy, hon. Wake up."

She moaned, just a small sound, but enough to make Brand's gut tighten. Bending down, he pressed his hand to her forehead. Burning hot.

"Damn. You're sick. Come on, wake up."

She moaned again, a little louder this time. What the hell was wrong with her? Did goddesses get sick? "Wait right here, I'm gonna go to the bathroom and get—"

"Sun." Her voice, a thready whisper, chilled him even more. "Burns. Didn't close skylights."

Shit, she was allergic to the sun? "How do I close them?"

She tried to lift her hand but couldn't. "Switch… on wall."

He ran for the wall, though it was only a few steps away, and hit the two switches on the wall. The overhead lights flicked on and a faint hum filled the room as blackout shades began to crawl across the skylights.

When he was sure they were working, he ran back to the bed, kneeled next to her and pulled her limp body into his arms. "Damn, Lucy. Are you okay? What can I do?"

Lucy sighed as the shades darkened the room and finally her eyelids fluttered open.

Brand blew out a long breath. "Jesus, Lucy. What the hell—

She turned into him, her body still so hot, and grabbed his head to pull him down for a kiss. He froze for a few seconds, his brain racing but his body stuck in neutral.

What the hell's going on?

Then his body took over and gave into the raging hunger that sent him up in flames. She kissed him like she wanted to devour him. Her mouth fused to his, stealing his breath and his sanity. Her tongue danced along his, enticing him, wiping his mind of anything that wasn't her.

He turned her until her body aligned with his. On her knees now, she pressed against him, her breasts smashed against his chest, her nipples tight little points that dug into his muscles, pinpricks of heat that taunted him.

Her pussy ground against his groin and he reached for her hips, tilting her until his cock fit in the notch between her thighs.

Both naked, he could have sworn he saw sparks fly as their skin meshed, sweat slicking their flesh as the heat sizzled and burned.

Holy hell. She's going to burn me to ash. And I'm going to love it.

———

Burning lust, eating her from the inside out.

Lucy had woken knowing something was wrong. Her skin burned, her pussy ached, and her thoughts jumbled together like a ball of tangled yarn, confused and disjointed. She wanted sex. Needed sex to curb the effects of the sun on her body.

There, that's what had happened. She'd forgotten to close the skylight shades last night. Last night. Brandon. His body pressed against hers, his cock between her thighs, hard. Oh, so hard and hot and long. She wanted to suck it, to bite it, and force him to shaft into her deep and hard.

But she was kissing him right now and she didn't want to release his mouth.

The feel of his tongue against hers made her stomach clench and eased the sun sickness even as it stoked her desire. He tasted her like he couldn't get enough, his lips hard on hers. Forceful and oh, so masculine.

And his groan when she bit down, trapping his tongue in her mouth… Blessed Goddess, it made her pussy weep until her juices flowed down her leg. So good. She wanted him to fuck her. He *would* fuck her.

Lucy pressed even closer, her hands sliding down his biceps to his wrists. With very little force, she drew his hands up to her breasts, leaning back only enough so he could mold her breasts in his palms.

She needed him to pinch her nipples, to squeeze almost to the point of pain. She needed more. He didn't need much encouragement. He cupped her, his fingers tweaking her nipples.

"Harder, Brandon. Harder. I need—"

She moaned as he obeyed, the lick of pain arrowing straight to her clit. Her heart raced and lust pulsed in her blood. She needed more. Harder, faster.

Yet, in the back of her mind, she knew Brandon was only human. His body more frail than her *lucani*. Still, she couldn't rein herself in. Her arms wrapped around his back, her fingers clenching as her nails bit into his flesh.

She heard him hiss in a breath even as she felt his cock thicken further against her stomach.

His hands tightened for several seconds, giving her exactly what she needed until he abruptly released her, tearing his mouth away from hers.

"Jesus, Lucy, I don't want to hurt—"

With a barely coherent cry, she sank one hand into his hair and dragged him closer.

"You can't hurt me. I need you to do me hard and fast. Now."

Through the haze of sickness and her burning desire, she heard him swear under his breath and, for a second, she thought he might pull away. That she'd frightened him with the strength of her desire.

"Open your eyes, Lucy. Come on, baby. Look at me."

No, she didn't want him to see the madness in her eyes. She needed him to fuck her, and if he even suspected… But she couldn't *not* obey the command in his voice.

She opened her eyes and immediately lost herself in the glittering darkness of his. So warm, so mesmerizing. So damn masculine. She leaned forward and let her tongue flick out to graze his jaw and the throbbing muscle at the side. Spicy hot.

"Brandon, please."

She let one hand drift down his back to his ass, where she grabbed a handful and squeezed. The firm muscles clenched and flexed, and when she moved her hands between his legs to scratch her nails along the tight pouch of his balls, she felt his skin go slick with sweat.

"I need you to fuck me. Bend me over and take me. I need it now. Please."

She knew she was begging and she didn't care. All that mattered was that he made her come. Preferably soon. Before the madness took over and she really hurt him.

Blessed Mother Goddess, please don't let me hurt him.

She knew she was close to that edge, where desire became fury. She'd only been in that place once before and she'd sworn never to be there again. She'd been sloppy last night, forgetting to cover the windows. She couldn't be sloppy.

"Lucy—" He groaned as she let her other hand curve around his cock and squeeze. "Oh, *fuck*."

"Now. Hard. Brand—"

He lifted and twisted her, until she was facing away from him.

For a few brief seconds, he held her back against his chest as one hand pinched and kneaded her breast and the other slid between her thighs.

His breath left his lungs in a rush as he felt the slickness of her lower lips and she nearly came when he thrust two fingers into her sex.

"*Yes*. Oh Gods, yes."

The thickness filled her, stretched her. The scrape of rough skin against delicate inner tissue made her eyes close as lightning-hot flashes of sensation shot from her pussy to her womb.

She clenched around him, trying to pull him deeper.

"Fuck, Lucy. You're tight."

"For you. Only for you."

He withdrew in a rush, causing her to sob out a denial and reach for his hand to make him fuck her with his fingers.

Before she could, he caught both of her wrists and pulled them away from her body just as he thrust into her again, harder this time.

Yes.

She arched her back, trying to move her hips but he withdrew his fingers completely.

"No, Brandon. Godsdamnit, fuck me."

"Christ, Lucy, you gotta... Bend over. Now."

She barely understood his words but she knew what he wanted as he pulled her wrists down. She bent until her cheek hit the mattress, her ass at the perfect position. She wiggled her hips, felt his cock brush against her ass cheeks before it settled in the valley between her cheeks.

Her pussy pulsed with need as his heated shaft rubbed against her. The smooth skin of his cock contrasted with the wiry brush of the hair on his thighs and between his legs.

Then it was gone and cool air caressed her ass where only a second ago there'd been heat.

She practically growled at the loss but in the next second, she felt him move into position. The head of his cock pierced her lips and, with a heavy thrust, he sank deep.

Crying out at the luscious fullness, she pressed back, wanting even more. But his hands gripped her hips in a vise so tight, she couldn't move without using excessive force. And truth be told, she liked it too much.

She liked the bite of pain as his fingers dug into her hips, the dragging friction as he pulled out and then heaved back in.

She let herself be taken, let Brandon fuck her hard and fast as she laid there and took it. Her pussy tightened with each thrust, her orgasm gathering with a strength she craved and feared. If it got to be too much, she could hurt Brandon when she came. She'd done it before, though not for centuries.

She tried to rein back some of that passion now.

"Oh, no fucking way." Brandon's voice rasped through her control, breaking the thin strings she'd been holding onto. "I want you to explode. I want you out of control, just like you've made me."

"Can't—"

"Fuck that." He withdrew then slammed into her again, deeper, thicker. Enough to make her lose her mind. "Come, Lucy."

No, she couldn't. She didn't want— He smacked the side of her ass with his open palm, hard enough to make her flinch... and explode.

Her orgasm hit her so hard, her back bowed and her vision went hazy, tinged with red. Her pussy rippled and contracted around his cock, sucking him in, milking his response. He held on for a minute at least, fucking her through the orgasm until he groaned and began hammering into her, his movements jerky and uncoordinated.

She didn't know how she managed to keep her legs from collapsing under her, how she kept her ass in the air. Probably because Brandon held her and wouldn't let her fall.

Hot jets of cum bathed her channel as her body sank into the aftermath. Afterglow, hell. She still burned like a ten-alarm fire but it wasn't painful. No, she was sated. But… she still wanted more. Was afraid she might always.

After a minute or so, Brandon groaned, wrapped his arms around her waist and maneuvered them onto their sides, his cock still thick enough not to slip out.

They lay there, both of them trying to catch their breath. Surprisingly, Brandon seemed to rouse first. He stroked a lazy hand along her hip before he propped himself up on an elbow and pressed a long, hot kiss to her neck.

And she realized the heat she continued to feel was the sun sickness as it burned off. She blew out a sigh of relief. She hadn't lost control. She hadn't torn him to shreds in the throes of madness. No, he'd fucked her into complacency. Wow. Just… wow.

"Lucy, not that I'm complaining, but are you okay? I didn't hurt you, did I?"

She bit back a laugh, knowing he wouldn't understand why she'd done it.

"No, you didn't hurt me and, yes, I'm fine." Now. "I forgot to close the shades last night. I have an intolerance of the sun."

"So it wasn't anything that blue-skinned freak did to you. Jesus, I was so worried—"

Lucy's eyes popped wide as she scrambled around on the bed to face Brandon. "What? What are you talking about?"

Brandon's eyes narrowed as he looked at her. "Damn, you really slept through the whole thing, fight and all? You were out harder than I thought."

She felt all the blood rush to her head and actually thought she might pass out.

"Did it hurt you? Did it *bite* you?"

Vaffanculo, she reached for him, running her hands over his body, searching for even the slightest scratch. The *tukhulkha* demon injected poison through its teeth. One bite...

Blessed Goddess. She searched but couldn't seem to find any bite marks.

She did note his swollen knuckles and the beginning of a bruise on his cheekbone. The damn sickness had caused her to miss those before.

"What happened? How did it get in? Why did it leave? What did it want?"

"Whoa, slow down, babe." He grabbed both of her hands in his and held on. The firm pressure caused some of her anxiety to lessen. But only by a little. "It's gone now. Turned tail and ran, if you can believe that. I'm fine. Everything will be okay. Just tell me what that thing was."

Lucy couldn't stop continuing to check him for injuries. "I can't believe a *tukhulkha* demon got in here without my knowing. I can't believe I forgot to close the shades."

Her hands shook as she ran them over Brandon's face and down to his shoulders until he sat up, gathered her into his arms and held onto her.

"Yeah, we were a little focused on other things last night."

She wanted to laugh but couldn't force the sound through her vocal cords.

"A little focused" was putting it mildly. She'd been so wrapped up in him, she'd forgotten one of her most basic routines.

And this morning, a demon had gotten through her wards to infiltrate her home.

Something that felt a lot like fear slid through her, chilling that afterglow down to nothing.

"Look." Brandon nipped her earlobe. "You rest for a while. I'll throw some things in a bag and you'll come stay with me for a little."

Shock made her mouth drop open as she turned in his arms. How could he even think—

"No. Absolutely not, Brandon. I'm not going anywhere with you. And you can't be anywhere near me. That demon found me here. It got through my wards and my wards are not insignificant. It will find me no matter where I go."

She should've known he wouldn't take that well. His entire body stiffened against her, and that strong jaw clenched.

"Hey, babe." His voice deepened to the point she could almost imagine it was a growl. "You might have slept through it but I went head-to-head with that thing and I'm still here. But that doesn't mean I'm an idiot who wants to hang around to get my ass kicked in round two. And no offense, but you're not exactly well hidden out here. That demon doesn't know who the hell I am. It won't know where to look for you if you come with me."

Could he be right?

She'd had no dreams, like Tessa had had. Charun had had to search for Tessa and only when she got weak was the god able to find her.

And Brandon was right. The location of her home was no secret. All *lucani* knew where to find her, as did the *streghe* and the *Fata*.

But what if the demon came after her wolves or her sons? She couldn't protect them if she wasn't there. She could warn the boys, tell them to lay low. She had no doubt Ty could take care of himself. She'd tell Caeles to hole up with the Downbelow band in the city. And she would stay with Brandon and keep an eye on him.

Before she could open her mouth to agree, he stood, set her on the bed and looked down at her. "Where's your overnight bag and your underwear drawer?"

Chapter 6

LUCY STILL WASN'T SURE this was a good idea, but she had to admit the closer they got to his home, the more safe she felt by his side.

And the more curious she became about the man driving this ancient behemoth of a truck. Brandon called it a classic. She wondered what he'd say if she reminded him that she'd been around when Ford had introduced the first mass-produced car. As a matter of fact, she'd owned one, fresh off the assembly line. Probably best not to bring that up at the moment.

Luckily, the huge black truck appeared to run well, and the inside was spotless and boasted a radio that wasn't even a dream when this car was two decades old.

Apparently they shared a love of satellite radio. But not stations. He'd chosen classic rock. Meaning anything from the '70s and '80s. She tuned hers to the music of the 1940s. Or Sinatra. The man had a golden voice.

What else would she learn about him? She wanted to know everything.

And yes, she knew she shouldn't. She shouldn't be so interested in an *eteri*. Shouldn't want to spend so much time with him. Shouldn't be putting him in this kind of danger. Which just proved she was still in shock after her bout with sun sickness and learning about the demon, or she never would've agreed to come stay at his apartment with him.

Fifteen minutes after packing her bag, Brandon had bundled

her into his truck—the tinted windows affording her relief from the sunlight—then driven her back to the borough of Mount Penn, just outside the city of Reading. He'd parked behind a large older building, not very far from Salvatorus's home. The goat-legged *salbinelli* ran a safe house for Etruscans in the city. If anything happened while she was here, she knew Sal wouldn't be far away.

"The door's just over there." Brandon pointed at the set of two plain steel doors. "I live on the ground floor. The neighbors are pretty quiet. And they're nice too. Mrs. Finegan, my neighbor, is probably at church and the Monteiths upstairs don't get up until around noon on Sundays. They're young. They like to party." He grinned, as if he was remembering one of those parties. "The Salingers left Friday to visit their daughter in Connecticut."

"How long have you lived here?"

"A few weeks after I signed, I found the listing in the paper. Got sick of living in a hotel and, since I knew I probably wasn't going to be called up anytime soon, I figured I'd find a place I liked. Not just something convenient."

With that in mind, she looked at the building again. It'd begun life as a two-family home, probably built sometime in the '40s or '50s. But it'd been carved into four apartments sometime in its past. The building looked exotic, she decided, with its ornate arched windows and stucco facade. She wondered if the building's appearance had been part of its appeal.

"Well, come on then. Let's get you inside while I don't see anyone."

Brandon slid out of the truck then made his way to her side. After he'd made sure her bloodred hooded cape completely covered every inch of her skin, he picked her up and carried her to the door. She thought about protesting. But she liked it too much.

And he had no trouble carrying her and her bag at the same time. Made her want to sigh in abject devotion.

Once he had the door open, he set her down in a hallway that split the building in half and stuck his key in the only door on the left side. Another door on the opposite side sat further down the hall.

Standing there waiting for him to open the door, she felt a slight tug of magic against her own. It wasn't unusual for old buildings to retain traces of a former resident's energy. And since Reading had a larger-than-normal population of magical beings, the fact that there was magic here didn't surprise her.

Still, when Brand swung open the door, the strength of the energy increased.

Waving her through, he followed close behind, carrying her bag. His bulk made her feel protected, cherished. Safe. Even though she knew he shouldn't have been able to beat off that demon. What the hell had happened in her bedroom before she'd awakened?

Whatever it was, she couldn't believe she'd slept through it. Or that she'd been so stupid as to forget to close the shades and had practically torn into Brandon afterward.

Then to let Brandon hustle her out of her home and into his... She was obviously rattled and she didn't rattle easily.

"Sit on the couch, babe. I'll be right back."

Brandon walked down the short hall to the left and through the door at the end, leaving her to look around.

He'd obviously rented the apartment furnished because everything was beige—beige sofa and chair that practically disappeared into the beige walls and beige carpet in the living room to the right of the entry. Oak end table and coffee table added a little color but matched the dinette set behind the small kitchenette to the right of the door.

The personal touches around the room helped save it from being bland. Framed pictures on the side tables, and books. Lots of books. Brandon obviously liked mysteries and thrillers.

A huge television consumed almost one whole wall in front of the TV, and he had an Xbox and a Wii. A library of games and movies any video store would kill for filled the bookshelves on either side of the TV.

And then there were the hockey sticks.

They occupied two corners of the room. There had to be at least twenty of them. Just the sight of them made her smile. She walked over to examine them, noticing they all had tape with a date on the shaft. Milestones, she guessed. There was also a collection of pucks in a basket on the floor, also dated. She'd just begun to take off her cloak when Brand walked back into the room. And set her heart pounding.

What was it about this man?

He was handsome, no doubt about it, but it wasn't just his looks. There was just something about him, something indefinable. And that smile…

"Yeah, I know, it's a guy cave. Sorry. My parents haven't been able to visit lately or it'd be neater. But it's clean. I'm not a complete slob. My mother made sure I knew how to work a vacuum and a dust rag." He put an arm around her and drew her over to the couch before sitting and settling her on his lap. She let him tuck her head under his chin. "So, you want to tell me about this problem you have with the sun?"

She sighed, knowing every piece of information she gave him would make it that much harder to wipe his memories later.

If you even can.

She knew she was coming close to the point of no return with Brandon. At a certain point, not even the most experienced *strega* could completely erase an *eteri* mind because those memories became embedded. Ripping them out meant damaging those parts of the brain.

So what are you going to do?

"I call it sun sickness. As a moon goddess, I harness the power of the moon. The moon reflects the light of the sun, so my power is tied to the sun, but when I'm exposed to the full power of the sun, it's an overload. It leaves me vulnerable."

"And that's what happened this morning?"

"Yes. It had nothing to do with the demon." She pulled away to look up into his serious dark eyes. "I want you to tell me exactly what it said, Brandon. *Tukhulkha* demons aren't known for backing down from their prey."

Brandon sighed. "It said I'm not exactly who—no, it said *what* I think I am. What the hell did it mean?"

Lucy thought about that for a moment, thought about the energy she'd felt when they'd arrived here. "I'm not really sure, but it could mean the demon sees something in you, a hidden trait or the trace of a magical ancestor you didn't know you had."

His eyebrows lifted nearly to his scalp. "You're kidding, right?"

"No, not at all. Many seemingly normal people have traces of the ancient magical races in their blood. Most of them don't have any power at all. Some have an affinity for animals, for nature, but they can't control the elements. That doesn't explain why the demon would run without engaging you, though."

He gave her a wry smile. "So the fact that I love honey and like to climb trees means there's a bear in my past?" He snorted. "Maybe I just plain frightened the thing away."

Shaking her head, she sighed. "I'm sorry, Brandon. As much as I'd like to stroke your ego, I don't think that's what happened."

His smile lit the banked flame of her libido. "Well, I got something else you can stroke."

She burst into laughter at his lecherous look then had to catch her breath when he smiled along with her.

The man made every nerve ending in her body sizzle and pop. That smile... Damn, she'd have to change her panties at the rate she was going. But it wasn't just his looks.

The man had taken on a terrifying blue demon to protect her. After she'd wiped his memories. That wiped away her smile in a second.

"Brandon…"

He nodded, his expression turning serious. "Yeah, I know. We need to figure out what's going on with the— What do you call that thing, anyway?"

"A *tukhulkha* demon. They work for Charun."

"The god of the underworld, right?"

"You've been doing some homework, haven't you?"

"A little, yeah." His gaze held steady. "Is there a chance this Charun guy can do what he says?"

She shivered as a chill ran up her back. "Yes. I think… Yes."

"What would happen to you if he did?"

"I'd cease to exist."

And that frightened her. Hell, it downright terrified her and that made her even more furious.

"Hey, babe. We'll figure something out."

His arms tightened around her, and she fought the urge to sink into him and forget everything. But that wasn't going to happen. She was a goddess of the moon. She didn't do frightened. She was frightening.

"Brandon, I'd like to introduce you to someone later. Someone who might be able to shed a little light on who your ancestors were."

"Yeah, I'd rather not have to call my parents and ask if they're witches or werewolves. So who's your friend?"

Hmm, how could she explain Sal? "Better if you just keep an open mind."

He stared at her for a few seconds before nodding. "I can do that. So, you hungry? I'm not much of a cook but I can whip up something edible."

Sliding off his lap, she stood, tossing her hair over her shoulder and staring down at him. "Why don't you let me take care of the food? Maybe you'd like to rest for a while."

The least she could do was feed him, especially after everything that'd happened. Leaning back into the couch, Brandon let his arm rest across the back of the cushion. He looked relaxed. How did he manage to be so calm all the time? The man had found out only yesterday that magic existed, as did deities. And fairies and elves.

Yet here he sat, smiling up at her as though he didn't have a care in the world. She'd wonder if maybe he'd gotten his head knocked into the boards a few too many times, but that would just be mean. He might not have gone to college but he wasn't stupid. Far from it. He always seemed to be one play ahead.

"Yeah, ya know, rest isn't what I'm thinking about at the moment."

Her lips twitched into a smile at the blatant heat in his gaze. And damn if she didn't feel her sex go slick and hot. How did he do this to her? Maybe he did have some magical powers that she just couldn't sense.

Or maybe she'd finally met the man she'd been waiting for her entire life. The man who made it all worthwhile.

Wouldn't that be the world's greatest cosmic joke? That she'd met the man who she could actually stand to spend eternity with and he'd be gone in another forty or fifty years.

The thought caused her heart to thud painfully in her chest. This was why she didn't allow herself to fall for *eteri*. They lived so few years, in the grand scheme of things.

Better to only use them as a diversion then set them aside before they could hurt you too deeply.

Pasting on a false smile, Lucy turned toward the kitchenette she'd seen when they'd entered the room—and found herself spun around, then lifted off her feet and lowered onto Brandon's lap. She automatically spread her legs so her bent knees fell on either side of his thighs. Her hands fell on his shoulders. She told herself it was to hold him at bay.

But she could already feel her body softening in preparation. So she stiffened her arms.

Instead of being deterred, he leaned closer. "Why do I get the feeling I wouldn't like what you were just thinking about?"

She tossed her hair over her shoulder and gave him her best cool gaze. "I don't know what you mean."

Those beautiful eyes just stared into hers. "Yeah, that's pretty much bullshit. What the hell just happened, Lucy? Whatever it is, it's not good."

There was no way she would discuss this with him. He'd never understand. They never did. She looked him straight in the eyes, ignoring the ache in the pit of her stomach.

"There's nothing wro—"

One hand cupped the back of her head, holding her in place for his mouth to take hers.

But when she expected him to force her to part her lips for his tongue, he tricked her. His lips teased hers, pressing featherlight kisses even as his hand tightened in her hair, almost to the point of pain. The combination left her panting.

Gods, how did he manage it? It must be magic. She had no other explanation for her reaction to him.

And he didn't try to hide his reaction to her. She felt the hard ridge of his cock press against her sex, spread open and covered only by the thin cotton of her yoga pants. Thankfully, she'd worn underwear or she'd be seeping through. As it was, she felt the moisture slip from between her lower lips.

"Take our clothes off, Lucy. I want to fuck you now."

His guttural command caused her stomach to tighten and a hot ball of lust to form in her gut, even as she knew she should be putting him in his place for daring to order her to do anything. She was a goddess. She didn't take orders.

Although she very much worried that she would take any order he gave her. But she didn't have to make it easy for him.

She let her expression harden into the haughty look that had served her well as the goddess in charge of the dark and the denizens of the shadows. That expression had caused war gods to retreat and brought a Titan to his knees.

Brandon simply tightened his hand in her hair and waited for her to respond.

Blessed Mother Goddess, she loved that hint of pain, the edge of dominance that called for her surrender. The surrender she shouldn't give.

Yet who would care anymore that she longed to be dominated by a man? That she longed to give up just some of the control she'd had to hold on to for so long? This man would know. Hell, he already knew.

But will he use it against you, as it had been once before?

That had been a dark time and, with the force of her will, she shoved those thoughts out of her mind. No place for them here.

Here she wanted only to think about pleasure. About Brandon. With barely a thought, their clothes disappeared, reappearing in a pile next to the couch. Brandon didn't even bat an eye this time. He held her gaze and her hair and burned the air around them with the level of sexual desire emanating from him. Which was just about equal to her own.

Now that their clothes were gone, only inches separated their bodies. The heat of his skin seeped into hers, soaking her in his scent. She leaned forward, wanting to run her tongue along his neck, to bite into that square jaw that was showing signs of strain.

So he wasn't as cool as he fronted. Good. How embarrassing it would have been to be the only one going up in flames.

Even though the pain in her scalp intensified, she pulled against his hold until she got her mouth on his neck. Drawing in a deep breath, she licked from his collarbone to just below his ear. Salty taste, musky scent. His own brand of ambrosia.

"You taste wonderful." Another lick before she bit his ear lobe, just a nip, but enough to make him groan, sharp and low.

"You can taste me wherever you want, babe. Just don't stop."

Her mouth curved in a smile as she scraped her teeth down his throat to the hollow. His words were an order but his tone sounded more like a plea.

"Are you giving me an order? I'm not one of your teammates, Brandon. I don't take orders well."

"Baby, you take them so fucking well, I think I might die from how well you take orders. Now fuck me, baby. Take me in, hard and fast."

Every word was a direct strike on her clit. The tiny organ swelled and ached to be touched, her sheath clenched, moist and hot. So ready.

Reaching between them, she wrapped her hand around his cock. So stiff, so silky smooth. She pulled it away from his body, let her hand caress the shaft with a firm, tugging motion. His jaw clenched as she worked him from root to tip, the length growing even more.

The man certainly put some gods to shame. His beautiful cock flushed a dull ruddy color, the tip even darker. She wanted to take him in her mouth and suck on him but she didn't think she could wait. Her body ached with a need that was fast becoming an addiction.

Another forbidden topic. Rolling her hips, she rubbed the lips of her sex over the head of his cock, getting him as wet as she was.

"*Fuck.* Lucy, come on. Take me in."

Ignoring him, she bent farther, his grip on her hair slackening enough that she could reach his nipples. Running her tongue around one stiff peak, she kept stroking his shaft with the other.

Every muscle in his hard body flexed, straining. But he held himself with a rigid control as he let her tease and taunt.

When she could no longer bear the ache between her legs, she gave his nipple one final lick before she straightened, pulled his cock straighter then sank down on the length in one motion. Her sex tight with anticipation, she had to use a little force to get him in, even as wet and ready as she was for him. When she had him fully engulfed, she stilled, absorbing the feel of him. A red-hot brand inside her, thick and throbbing.

Just the feel of him inside eased some of the ache. But it wasn't enough. She started a slow roll of her hips, arching up on her knees to ease him out then rolling again to slide him back in. He held still and she realized she had her hands planted on his shoulders, her nails digging into his flesh, hard enough to make tiny crescents of blood appear.

Gods, she didn't want to hurt him but she couldn't seem to make her hands release him. Her body had taken control from her mind, knowing what it needed and going after it with singular determination.

Her rhythm increased, the friction creating a burgeoning fire-storm of sensation in her gut. She chased that feeling, reached for the building orgasm. She could barely breathe, barely think. She heard Brandon's groan of pleasure echo in the room and it caused her heart to kick into overtime.

Faster, she rose and fell, her head tilting back as he tugged on her hair in time with her motions. She felt his hand cup one breast and lift it, then his mouth covered the nipple and his teeth tugged at the skin. He suckled her hard, her sex tightening with each pull until she couldn't stand it anymore.

Arching just the tiniest bit further, she hit her clit on the base of his cock, freeing her orgasm and letting her fly.

Her cry barely had the strength to be heard over Brandon's harsh grunt as he grabbed her hips and forced her to continue when she would have stopped. He drew out her orgasm and his own. She felt him holding back, shuddering with the effort. No, not fair. She wanted him to fall. She clenched hard on his next inward thrust, squeezing him as if she had her fist around him. And was rewarded by the fiery hot drenching of his seed.

Falling forward, knowing he would catch her, she sank against his chest as he spent himself in her.

For several seconds, all she heard was the thud of Brandon's heart against one ear and his harsh attempts to breathe in the other. After a minute, he ran one hand down her hair, petting her.

The heat from his large body surrounded her, soothed her. She snuggled into him like a child with a teddy bear and closed her eyes.

———

She woke in a bed that wasn't hers to the smell of bacon. And the sound of cursing. Brandon cursing.

Throwing off the covers, she ran for him, terrified that the demon had found them. Though she heard no signs of fighting, she couldn't take any chances—she skidded to a stop in the living room when she realized Brandon wasn't alone.

And he didn't seem to be in any danger. At least, not from a blue demon. However, the two boys now staring wide-eyed and open-mouthed at her should probably fear for their lives because Brandon looked ready to kill them for staring.

Yes, the boys looked young, late teens, possibly early twenties. Maybe they had never seen a naked woman but she found that hard to believe. These two certainly seemed attractive enough. Surely they'd had girlfriends before.

"Shit," Brandon swore under this breath as he turned, cutting off the boys' line of vision.

Until they both leaned to either side, giving the illusion of Brandon having three heads. She bit her lip to cut back a laugh, knowing Brandon wouldn't be amused. He looked panic-stricken actually, as he pulled off his T-shirt and dropped it over her head.

"Shit, Lucy, I'm sorry. I should've warned you but you looked like you were totally out of it. I didn't want to wake you."

She smiled up at him, so relieved he hadn't been in danger and more than a little charmed by the boys' reaction to her.

Twins. She could see that now and finally recognized them from the team's roster. Jason and Thomas Fransechetti.

"I'm sorry for interrupting. I thought—" No, she couldn't say what she'd thought. These boys had no idea what was going on, and she and Brandon had to keep it that way. He knew that, didn't he?

"You're not interrupting anything." He looked her straight in the eyes, and she knew what he was saying without words. He hadn't told the boys what had happened. Hadn't told them about her.

"You're definitely not interrupting." The one with the longer hair waved at her as a goofy smile spread across his handsome face. "Hi, I'm Jason."

"And I'm Tom. And we're really glad to meet you. Damn, Stevie, no wonder you were trying to get rid of us so fast."

Brandon barely moved as Tom slugged him on the shoulder. Drawing in a deep breath, Brandon rolled his eyes toward the ceiling before he turned back to face the twins, making sure he shielded her completely.

She couldn't help it. She had to choke back a laugh. If he only knew how *not* shy she really was. Having sex on an altar in front of hundreds of worshipers tended to erase your inhibitions pretty quickly.

She really didn't understand the pervasive American dichotomy between exhibitionism and prudishness. Instead of standing behind him, she stepped beside Brandon, wondering what he'd do. Lifting his arm, he placed it around her shoulders and drew her close to his side. Good man. He didn't try to force her behind him again, hiding her.

"Dude, aren't you going to introduce us?" Jason asked. "Whoa, bad manners, man."

As Brandon reached out to smack the kid on the side of the head, which only made Jason's smile spread even more, the other twin, Tom, held out his hand, which she took.

"Hello, Tom, I'm Lucy."

Tom's smile, while not as broad as Jason's, was sweeter. And showed off the missing tooth on the right side of his mouth. Jason immediately held out his hand, hip-checking his brother out of the way. She took it as Brandon sighed heavily.

"I didn't mean to interrupt." She glanced up at Brandon. "If you have things to talk about…"

Brandon opened his mouth to speak but Jason beat him to it. "You can stay, if you want. We just… Well, we kinda needed some advice."

"Yeah, I, uh, shit, oh… Damn, sorry, Lucy." Tom gave her an apologetic smile, she assumed for his language, before he turned his attention back to Brandon. "We got a phone call this morning."

"From that douche—uh, that jerk from Sweden." Jason's mouth twisted in a sneer. "He's been yanking Tommy's chain hard about his contract. I mean, we know he can't force Tommy to play over there but he's really fu—uh, pretty damn insistent. He keeps calling and it's annoying as all hell."

Both boys looked at Brandon with the identical expression. They waited for his response like he had the absolute right answer.

"Sounds like you guys have some business to discuss." She smiled at the twins. "I'm going to go get dressed and then I'll make some coffee."

She turned to go but stopped as Brandon turned with her and dropped his head down to meet her lips.

"Sor—"

She put her hands over his lips, cutting off his apology. He had nothing to apologize for. "They need you." She spoke for his ears only. "Do what you need to do. I'll be back in a minute."

He licked her fingers before she withdrew them and she had to work hard to cover the shiver of lust that ran through her. And when he winked at her, she had to smile.

But it faded on her way back to his bedroom. She shouldn't be here. She was going to get him killed. She had to leave.

———

"I'll see you tomorrow at practice. And don't worry about it. I'll make a couple of calls."

Brand stood at the front door, watching the twins throw waves back as they headed for Jason's truck. Of course they weren't waving at him. They were waving at Lucy, standing by his side, her shoulder fitting perfectly under his, her body curved into his side like she'd always been here. He liked that. A lot.

He'd kind of had that feeling once before in his life and he'd been ready to marry that girl. She hadn't wanted to be the wife of a professional hockey player. She'd married the manager of the local grocery store in their home town and had a couple of kids.

Bet she didn't know a damn thing about blue demons and goddesses.

"Brandon?"

"Yeah?"

"Are we going in?"

Shit, they were still standing in the open doorway, in minus-twenty-degree weather. The forecast was for snow later.

"Yeah, yeah." He waited for her to turn and head back into the living room while he closed the door. "Hey, sorry about the interruption. They're good guys, they just need some guidance."

Lucy had curled onto the couch, her legs drawn up, her arm on the back of the cushions. She looked too pretty for his dingy apartment. She also had something on her mind, if that expression was anything to go by.

"No need to be sorry. Those boys look up to you."

"Those boys think I'm a dinosaur."

She shook her head. "You know that's not true. They came to you because they knew you'd be able to help them. They're still so young. You're good with them. I know you've been acting as assistant coach this season. Is that something you want to pursue? Do you want to be a coach?"

Dropping onto the couch next to her, he let his head fall back onto the cushion before he turned to stare at her, trying to understand what she was getting at. Because he knew she was going somewhere with this.

"Sure. Don't all players wanna coach when they get too old to play? We get to stay close to the ice, still be part of a team. I never wanted to do anything except play hockey."

"You'll make a wonderful coach." She reached out to run her fingers through his hair.

He loved the feel of her hands on him. He wanted to close his eyes, maybe spread himself out on the couch and let her run those fingers over the rest of his body.

Her nails scratched at his scalp, slivers of sensation running through his body. If he was a cat, he'd be belly up, purring and begging her to pet him. His eyelids drifted shut as a wave of tiredness swept through him. When did he get so damn tired?

Not that they'd slept much last night but still—

"Hey!" His eyes flew open and he sat up, grabbing her hand off his head. "Don't you even think about putting me to sleep and sneaking out on me."

Her expression showed absolutely no hint of guilt. "Brandon, this isn't going to work. I can't stay here with you. You're at risk every second I'm here. What if the *tukhulkha* demon had shown up when the twins were here? What if it'd hurt them? What if it doesn't run next time?"

Then he'd fight the damn thing until he couldn't fight anymore.

He'd held his own against some of the biggest hitters in any league. No, he'd never gone up against a mythical blue creature before but he'd done okay the first time.

And when they found out what the thing had meant about Brand being different, whatever the hell that meant… Well, maybe that was a little freaky, but if it meant there was a chance of him keeping Lucy, then he'd take it. Because he really wanted to keep her.

"I don't think I can let you go, Lucy. I don't think I *want* to let you go."

She sighed, shaking her head, and Brandon thought he might have to put up more of a fight.

Instead, she said, "Fine. Let me get in touch with Sal and see if he can make a house call."

Sal turned out to be a kid, maybe ten or eleven.

He showed up at Brand's front door dressed in baggy jeans, a black hoodie, and a knit cap pulled down almost to his eyes.

"Hey, man. How's it going?"

Brand stuck out his hand to shake, though he knew his eyes had widened at the sound of the kid's voice. Christ, did he have a two-pack-a-day habit or what? And the accent, pure Bronx. And what was with the kid's eyes? They looked… Hell, they looked old. Darker than his own, almost black. Darker even than the curly hair peeking out from beneath the edge of the hat.

Brand had barely said hi before the kid walked over to Lucy, seated on the couch, and bowed. Literally freaking bowed.

"Lady, how are you? You okay?"

Lucy's expression actually eased a little as she nodded. She was glad to see the boy, almost looked relieved, as if she knew he could fix whatever problem she laid at his feet. "Thank you so much for coming, Sal. I really appreciate it."

"Anything for you, Lady, you know that." The kid hopped up on the cushion next to Lucy and looked back at Brand. "So, what's happenin'? Obviously it's got something to do with the *eteri* here. Caught some of your games, kid. You're a damn good player."

Kid? Had this child just called him kid? "Uh, thanks."

Sal nodded. "No problem. So, you wanna tell me what's going on or do I have to guess?"

"One of Charun's demons came after me last night." Lucy's voice almost sounded strangled, as if it was a struggle for her to get the words out. "It never got close enough to do any damage. Brandon chased it away."

Sal's eyes widened at that and he took another look at Brand, this time staring until Brand started to feel uncomfortable.

There was something about this boy...

"So, you took on a *tukhulkha* demon and you're still here to talk about it. Yeah, that'd make me wonder what the hell was going on with you too."

The kid sniffed, and not just a normal human sniff.

Brand knew, without a doubt, Sal was trying to pick up Brand's scent. Which was just too freaking weird to contemplate.

Of course, Brand was sleeping with a goddess being hunted by a blue demon. Why would— The kid took off his hat and tossed it on the couch next to him.

"I don't smell anything off about you. So—"

"*Holy shit.*"

Brand's mouth dropped open as he realized the kid had horns. Short, stubby, black horns sprouting out of the curly black hair on his head.

"Never seen horns before, kid? You must've led a sheltered life."

"Wha— How—" Brand shook his head, his feet carrying him closer to the couch. He wanted to actually touch them to make sure his mind hadn't just cracked.

Sal laughed and the sound had a definite edge to it. "You think those are crazy, wanna see something really out there?"

"Sal," Lucy released a sigh, "do you really think that's necessary?"

"Hell, after battling a blue demon, how bad could he react?" Sal leaned forward, beckoning to Brand. "Shazam."

In the blink of an eye, the kid was gone and in his place sat a man, if the sideburns and five o'clock shadow were anything to go by.

At least, half of him was a man. The top half. The other half…

Was the lower body of a goat. Covered in rusty brown fur. With little black hooves that dangled a few inches above the hardwood floor.

"Brandon, love, you need to breathe."

Lucy's softly spoken words made absolutely no sense.

He heard them, but his brain couldn't process them because it was busy searching for anything in his brain that even vaguely resembled the thing. A memory popped up out of the depths and through the turbulent sea of his thoughts.

"Pan."

"No, I'm not Pan," the thing said on a sigh. "Had some Latin in high school, didn't you? That little prick is bad for my good name. I'm a *salbinelli*. And you might want to sit down before you fall over."

"Shit. *Holy* shit." Brand forced himself to take a deep breath, because he finally realized he was light-headed. Lucy reached for his hand and tugged him down onto the cushion next to her. He nearly stumbled over his own feet as did.

"Would you like me to get you some water, Brandon? You look a little pale."

Tearing his gaze from Sal, he looked at Lucy, who looked worried. Pale and worried. Shit, he'd frightened his goddess.

Pull it together, asshole, or she's going to think you're a fucking pussy.

Sucking in a deep breath, he went through his pregame mantra in his head.

Skate fast. Head up. Hit hard. Go deep.

After a few of those… okay, more like a hundred of those, he felt steady enough to try to speak coherently. And to try to regain some of the ground he felt he'd lost in Lucy's mind.

She had to be thinking, *Well, if he can't handle a little goat man, he certainly isn't strong enough to handle me.*

Fuck that.

"Sorry." Brand forced himself to focus on the guy's eyes, which still looked pretty freaking old. "My mother taught me better than to stare. It's just…"

Freaky? Terrifying? Trippy?

Sal grinned and waved his hand in the air, dismissing Brand's bad behavior in a second. "No problem. So, Stevenson, what do you think of this new wonderland you've stepped into? Pretty cool, huh?"

"Uh, yeah. Yeah, you could say that."

Sal laughed and slapped one hide-covered knee before he turned back to Lucy. "So, you wanna know what it is about your *eteri* here that made the demon scurry away like the cockroach it is."

Since Brand was still trying to get his brain to form a rational thought, if not full sentences, Lucy told Sal about their visit from Tessa and Cal. Then she turned to Brand. "You'll need to tell Sal about the demon. I don't remember any of it."

Sal's dark eyes widened with surprise. "What the hell happened? Did it hurt you?"

"I'm fine, Sal. It never touched me. I… forgot to shut the skylight shutters last night and had an episode of sun madness. It's passed."

Her tone let Sal know she didn't want him to ask any more questions. Apparently, Sal was one smart… whatever the hell he was.

"Yes, well, that's part of what we need to talk to you about, Sal," Lucy said. "Tell him, Brandon."

So Brand related everything the demon had said, word for word when he could. Sal watched him through narrowed eyes the entire time. By the time he finished talking, Brand felt like the one with goat legs and horns. Sal took another deep breath. Then he shook his head, glossy black curls giving off blue tints from the light. "I'm not getting anything off him, but that doesn't mean he's not. What are you thinking, Lucy? *Berserkir?*"

Lucy nodded. "The heritage would be right, I believe. Your ancestors were Germanic, weren't they, Brandon?"

Yeah, they were, but what did that have to do with any of this? And had Sal said something about a *berserkir?* Brand tried to come up with a reference in his scrambled brain for that word but wasn't having much luck.

So he put that aside and concentrated on Lucy's questions. "Yeah. My great-great-grandfather emigrated in the 1800s from a small town in the German Alps. Family legend claims he had to travel three days to get to the nearest town. A few cousins tried to track it down years ago, tried to trace our family tree and find that village or even a mention of it. Never could."

Sal nodded. "Makes sense. The *berserkir* are notoriously more reclusive than the other *versipelli* families."

Brand's brain went blank except for one question. "*Berserkir* are shapeshifters?"

"Yes, Brandon." Lucy's hand reached out to stroke his arm. "They're bears."

"Well, they used to be," Sal interjected. "The *berserkir* are kind of special in the world of *versipelli*."

Oh yeah, that sounded great. "Special how?" Brand asked.

Sal tilted his head to the side and frowned. "Well, for one thing, they don't become actual bears anymore. They've evolved."

"Bears." Holy shit, were they actually saying his ancestors became bears? "Wait, evolved how?"

"Well, now they take on the characteristics of bears—their strength, their claws," Sal continued. "Their ferocity. They tap into the animal inside without fully becoming the animal. Just one of those quirks of evolution."

Brand looked down at his hands, imagining claws at his fingertips. How fucking weird was that?

He looked back up at Sal. "As far as I know, no one in my family can grow claws."

Sal shrugged. "The traits could be latent in your family. Your great-grandfather may have mated an *eteri*. And your grandfather and your dad. Somewhere along the line, your family lost its mojo."

Bears. Bears were strong. Really fucking strong. "Is there any way to find out for sure?" he asked.

"Yeah, but it ain't pretty and it ain't easy."

Sal's tone indicated it would be worse than he could ever imagine. Something to consider at a later time. Right now…

"Okay, we can deal with that later," Brand said. "Right now, Lucy's safety is more important than whether or not I can grow claws. What are we going to do about Charun? How much danger is she really in? And how do we get her out of it?"

Sal's smile widened before he started to laugh.

Brand's back stiffened and he got pissed off in a hurry. This was no laughing matter, Goddamn it.

Sal must have read his expression because he held up a hand and shook his head as he reined himself in. "Aw, hell, kid, I'm not laughing at you, so chill. It's just… yeah, sorry. Give me a sec."

It took another minute but Sal finally got over his laughing jag.

"Lady, I like him. If you don't mind my saying so, you *could* do worse."

Lucy kept her gaze on Sal. "I like him, too. And I don't want him harmed. Please make him understand that he got off easy this time. He's not equipped to deal with Charun's demons."

"Sounds like he handled himself okay if you ask me." Sal cocked his head Brand's way. "But *tukhulkha* demons are nasty sonsabitches. Their saliva can paralyze, their claws are sharp enough to cut through your chest to get to your heart. Their hair's as strong as wire. They can strangle a grown man with their bare hands and they can open gates between the planes. If they get you into Aitás, you're a goner, because no one leaves Aitás alive."

Well, shit. That sounded ominous as all hell. As his balls tried to crawl back into his body, he swallowed hard. "Okay, I understand the severity of the situation. But that just makes me more worried about Lucy."

"Brand—"

"Lucy." He turned so he could look into her eyes. "Come on. You were completely incapacitated by the sun. What if that thing gets to you during the day? You live by yourself out in the middle of nowhere—"

"Not by myself. One of my *lucani* is always nearby."

"In your home?" *In your bedroom?*

Luckily, he was smart enough not to ask that last question out loud.

But she must have read his thoughts. "Not in my bedroom, Brandon. They don't stay in my home. But the villagers are close enough to come running, if I need them, at a moment's notice."

"Why are you *so* sure you can't be harmed?"

Her gaze slid toward Sal for a brief second. Then she sighed. "Because I have an advantage other deities haven't had since we were worshipped two millennia ago."

"And that is?"

"The *lucani*. When I moved here two centuries ago, I was much like Tessa. I had lost most of my powers. The *lucani* were just beginning to organize themselves into the legion they have today and I made a deal with them. A deal that's been very beneficial to me. They worship me and I give them my protection. By worshiping me, I gain power that I'm able to funnel back to them and enhance their strength."

Brand could tell there was more to this story. "And this is a problem why?"

Lucy sighed. "It's not a problem. It's just… the rituals involve sex."

His back snapped straight and he swore he got whiplash. "Sex. With you."

She nodded. "Myself… and other partners."

Plural.

Brand flashed cold then blazing hot. He opened his mouth to say something, thought better of it, then forced himself to give this some thought.

And not of the "Damn, I'd like to watch" variety. No, he wanted to rip apart the other men she'd taken to her bed. Intellectually, he realized she'd been around a long time. A *really* long time. She'd had other lovers.

Still, he wasn't thinking with his brain at the moment. And that was ridiculous.

Get a grip, idiot. Or at least ask intelligent questions. And not about the sex.

"So this, ah, power boost, what does it do exactly?"

"For one, it allows me to hide my village from the rest of the world. I'm still not sure how you managed to slip through the boundary wards."

She shot a glance at Sal, who shrugged his shoulders. "Maybe your desire for him gave him passage through. I don't know, but it's something to look into."

Brand liked the sound of that, but Lucy's frown made it clear she wasn't buying into it. "What if there's a flaw somewhere, Sal? What if the wards are weakening? We'll need to perform the ritual again—"

"Oh, *no way* in hell."

As soon as the words slipped from his mouth, Brand wanted to take them back.

Shit and double shit, you stupid ass.

She caught and held his gaze, hers turning chillier each second. And her expression made it clear she thought he'd over-stepped his bounds.

Tough shit. She was his. For now. No other man would touch her.

"Brand, I can't let—"

"Use me."

She paused and heat flushed her pale cheeks before she sighed and shook her head. "It has to be someone with *arus* in their blood. If you're not *berserkir*, you won't do me any good."

Well shit. That sucked. "Then let's find out, because I'm really not liking this other men scenario. And you can bitch at me all you want, that's just how I feel."

He thought for sure she'd kick him to the curb. Take her little goat man and his memories and walk through the door.

Instead, her lopsided smile made his pulse race. It began to gallop when she reached out to run her fingers down his cheek. "It's not very appealing to me, either. Right now."

He wondered what she'd do if he told her he wanted to spend the rest of his life with her. He bit his tongue so he wouldn't find out. Swallowing hard, he turned to Sal, his gaze catching on those little black horns, which made him shake his head. "So what do we need to do?"

—◊◊◊—

Lucy watched Brand closely as Sal explained the process.

It wasn't for the faint of heart, but then anything involving running a sharp iron blade through his body wouldn't be.

Brand seemed to take it all in stride. He nodded at the ap-propriate spots, asked intelligent questions and, when Sal was finished, he didn't fall on the ground laughing hysterically or pass out from fear.

He took a breath while he stared at the wall, his jaw set, his mouth a straight line. "So, it'll hurt like hell but I'll be okay by tomorrow?"

She laughed. She couldn't help it.

Brand slid his glance her way and raised his eyebrows. "What? I've got practice."

She threw her arms around his neck and hugged him tight. "You don't need to do this."

His arms wrapped around her with a fierce grip. "Yeah, I do. And not just because I don't want you taking other guys to your bed." She felt his grimace move against her cheek. "Alright, so maybe that's a big part of it, I gotta be truthful. But… if it's true, if I have some of this *berserkir* blood in my veins, it might help explain some things in my background."

She pulled back to look at him but Sal beat her to her question. "Like what?"

Brand's entire body moved with his shrug. "Mainly the aggression. That's how I got started in hockey. It was a way for my parents to run me ragged. I had a lot of energy, and as I got older, that energy turned a little… vicious. I was in a lot of fights as a kid. And since I was bigger and stronger than most of the others, I usually won. My parents spent a few years shuttling me back and forth between doctors and therapists who tried to get me to 'think about' why I wanted to pound the crap out of everyone else."

Sal's laugh was short but sharp, and told Brand all he needed to know about the little goat man's opinion of therapy. Which was exactly the same as Brand's.

"Anyway, the only thing that helped was hockey. I tried basketball and baseball but neither held my attention. Football was okay but there was too much downtime, same with wrestling.

"So, Sal." Brand stroked a hand through Lucy's hair, trying to relieve some of her tension. Knowing it was as much for her as for himself. "If I live through it, I'll be fine, right?"

The goat guy gave a thoughtful nod. "Yeah. I'm pretty sure there shouldn't be any lasting problems. If you live through it."

Pretty sure. Lasting problems. "Then let's do it."

Lucy sucked in a short, sharp breath and her hand wrapped around his bicep. "Brandon, you need to take some more time to think about this. What if something happens? What if—"

"Hey, babe." He pressed his lips against her temple then pulled back, infusing as much confidence as he could into his expression. "I'll be okay. I'm hard to hurt. And I've got you."

—⁓—

Lucy shook her head, feeling in her bones that this was a bad idea, though she couldn't put her finger on why exactly that was.

Brandon looked at her with absolute conviction in his eyes, convinced he was doing the right thing. And that if he had her on his side, he'd come through with flying colors. What if that didn't happen? What if he was injured, damaged? She didn't know if she wanted to live without… What? She didn't want to live without him? She'd known him all of three days.

But she couldn't imagine waking up tomorrow and knowing he wasn't in her bed. Or at least in the next room. And wasn't that the same as living together?

She'd had men throw themselves at her feet, spouting declarations of love and devotion. She'd had gods grovel for the slightest crumb of her affection.

She'd also had one god who'd confused affection with obsession. But she'd survived him. She'd triumphed. She *was* strong.

"Yes. You do. I'll be right here. Everything will be fine."

He looked rock-steady, like he could survive a hurricane. She felt like a boat in rough waters. About to capsize.

His mouth quirked in a lopsided smile before he turned to Sal and nodded. "So what do we need?"

Brand wasn't as steady as he fronted to Lucy.

But he didn't want her to worry and he didn't want her to stop Sal from performing the ritual. And he really didn't want her to use other men to recharge her batteries. Hell, he couldn't even think about it without wanting to rip something apart. Not Lucy. Never Lucy. But he also had to be careful not to let his jealousy get out of hand or he'd take it out on a teammate tomorrow who'd wind up in the hospital.

Sal took a look around the apartment, those dark eyes taking in everything.

"Well," Sal said, "I'm thinking maybe we wanna do this somewhere else."

"Like where?"

"Well, I'd prefer to do it outside, but you'd need to be naked and it's about twenty degrees—"

"Not a problem. The cold doesn't bother me. I grew up in Maine. Northern Maine."

Sal slid a look at Lucy and raised his brows. Lucy bit into her bottom lip and fretted it until it looked like she'd break the skin.

"Alrighty then, polar bear. Outside it is. The *lucani* altar?"

Lucy sighed and her expression cleared, but not before he realized she'd only now given up thinking he wouldn't do this. "Yes, I suppose it should be there. I draw more power there than in the city at Uni's Temple."

"Just wanted to check." Sal looked back at him. "You wanna take a little trip, son?"

"What about the sun? Lucy, it's broad daylight—"

"I'll be fine." She shook her head at his concern. "Sal can

transport us without exposing me to the sun. We'll be able to get what we need at the den to perform the ritual."

"Cat may be around. The girl's getting stronger by the day. You're really going to have to address that soon."

"Yes, I know." Lucy sighed. "But not today. I'll call Kyle, see if he can have the girl meet us there."

"What about Ty?"

She shook her head. "I doubt he'll come if he knows Catene will be there. He's trying his damnedest to make an untenable situation bearable for her."

"Yeah, but you know it's gonna have to come to a head sooner or later."

"Ty is hoping later."

Brand stood quiet, listening to Lucy and Sal talk about people and situations he had no clue about.

He had no idea who Kyle and Catene were, but he recognized Ty's name. Lucy's son.

"Ty can hope all he wants. She's nearly nineteen—"

"And she has a few more years before she needs to know what's going on. Let the child have those years."

It was Sal's turn to shake his head but he took the hint and changed the subject. And gave Brand a look that made his stomach tighten in fear. "So, Brand. This is going to feel a little weird. Just try to breathe."

Sal reached out to touch his chest and in the blink of an eye, his apartment disappeared in a rush of color and sound, almost like he'd stepped into a wind tunnel in the midst of a fireworks display.

Before he had time to really think about what that meant, he found himself in another room. And he didn't mean in another room in his apartment. A room he'd never been in before.

"Brandon?"

He turned to see Lucy, standing by his side, staring up at him with a worried look on her face.

"Hey, babe—"

A wave of dizziness came over him and he nearly pitched over. Lucy grabbed onto him as he reached for something, anything to hold onto. All he found was Lucy.

"Brandon, come here. You need to sit and put your head between your legs."

Bullshit. He wasn't a pussy. He wasn't going to pass out.

"No." He forced himself to take a deep breath, to force back the disorientation. "I'll be okay. Just give me a sec…"

He saw her bite her bottom lip, as if she wanted to argue with him. She didn't. But she didn't take her hand off his arm and that helped to ground him.

After a short time, the feeling passed and he had a chance to look around.

"So where are—holy *shit*."

Sal stepped through what looked like a slit in the wall. No, not the wall. The air. Hell, it looked like he stepped out of an invisible lightning bolt in the middle of the room.

The *salbinelli* seemed to have no problems with his trip. He walked over to Brand, peered up at him for a few seconds before nodding.

"Not bad for a newbie, son. I would've bet you'd be on your ass by the time I got here."

"Thanks for the vote of confidence. And where is here? And how exactly did I get here?"

"Well, here is the *lucani* den, and you traveled by magic."

Magic. Yeah, he'd kinda figured that one out but didn't bother to ask for more of an explanation. His head probably would've exploded. "And a *lucani* den is…"

"Home to a couple hundred werewolves."

Oh, yeah. "Casey."

"Yes, Casey is *lucani*." Lucy looked at him with worry in her eyes. "Brand, are you sure—"

He bent and kissed her, hard and fast. No tongue. Just sealed his mouth over hers and pulled her tight against him. His body reacted to her proximity by pumping blood into his cock and away from his brain, which could use the infusion to actually be able to think.

Damn, he needed to keep that under control, especially since Sal was standing only a couple of feet away and Brand wasn't much of an exhibitionist. A little PDA was okay. A few kisses, holding hands.

But… Lucy melted into him. Her hands flexed against his chest, her hips pressed forward into his and he felt her sigh shudder through her body.

The lust he'd been trying to keep at bay fired up and he wanted to press her back against the wall, strip off their pants and get hot and heavy in seconds. And he wouldn't give a shit if everyone watched.

"Hey, kids. We're about to be descended upon so I'd wrap it up, if I were you."

Brand drew back after another few seconds, opening his eyes to look down into Lucy's. Hers had gone thundercloud gray, turbulent with emotion and desire.

He couldn't help himself. He smiled. The goddess of the moon wanted him. An actual freaking goddess…

Footsteps sounded outside of the room. Lots of them.

With a wry smile, as if she'd read his mind, Lucy reached to stroke her fingers along his jaw and he swore he calmed like a dog being petted.

Damn, he should just offer up his balls to her now. It wasn't like he'd ever find another woman like Lucy.

"Ay, you're starting to drop like flies," Sal muttered under his breath as he turned toward the door. "I don't think I'm gonna live through this."

Brand had no idea what the little goat man was talking about and he didn't get a chance to ask because Sal opened the door.

"Hey, Kyle. Come on in and join the party. We're just getting started."

Sal waved his hand and a hard-ass walked into the room. Brand felt his back stiffen and he had the strongest urge to shove Lucy behind him. He barely stopped himself from reaching for her before she stepped in front of him. As if he needed protection.

And there was definitely something about this guy that screamed danger.

He looked like a hard-core biker. Tats running up both arms and into the short-sleeved T-shirt that barely contained the bulging biceps and broad shoulders and chest.

He had wavy dark hair to his shoulders that didn't look at all feminine and his features were set in stone-cold-killer lines.

Yeah, not a guy he'd want to meet in a dark alley. It'd be a pretty even fight if this guy decided to take offense to Brand's presence. But the guy barely glanced at him. He nodded to Sal as he walked through, then walked up to Lucy and bowed at the waist as if he were at a dinner with the queen.

"Lady of the Silver Light. Welcome."

"Thank you, Kyle." Lucy actually sounded relieved to see the man. "How are you? And Tamra? She's well?"

"We're fine, Lady. Thanks for asking." Kyle let his gaze run over Brand now and he knew the guy was taking his measure before he turned back to Lucy. "What can we do for you? Is there something you need?"

Like maybe tear the guy behind you limb from limb?

Brand didn't think this guy would have any problem with that. He exuded danger like some guys reeked of cheap cologne. Kyle was a predator. Brand had no problem believing that.

"Actually, yes. There is something you can do for me. I'd like Catene to assist Sal and me with a spell."

The guy stilled for a split-second before he nodded. "She's with Margie. I'll call and get her to come over."

Lucy reached for his arm before he could move, her hand resting on his arm without restraining him. "I won't allow anything to harm your daughter, Kyle."

He nodded, but Brand had the sense the guy had to force himself to do it. "I'll just go make the call. Cole's on site. I'm sure he'll be here in a minute. Do you need anything else?"

Lucy's smile looked a little strained. "Not at the moment. Thank you, Kyle."

"Then I'll give Cat a call. Excuse me."

Kyle stepped out of the room, and Brand barely heard his footsteps as he headed away. The guy moved as silently as a ghost. Lucy sighed and she exchanged a look with Sal.

"He suspects."

Sal nodded, his human hands resting on his hide-covered hips. Brand's gaze stuck there for some reason, the sight making him shake his head.

"Yeah, he knows something's up." Sal turned to look at Lucy, pulling a cigar out of his back pocket. "Kyle's not stupid. Neither are Dan and Margie. A girl with three biological parents? Not one you read about. Ever."

Three… "What did you just say?" Brand shook his head as if coming out of a trance. "Did you just say three biological parents?"

Lucy sighed and turned to give him a weary smile. "She's an extraordinary young girl, but it's not something you have to worry about. You have enough on your plate as it is."

But… Holy shit. What the hell else was gonna broadside him today?

Brand caught Sal eyeing him, a gleam in his dark eyes. "What?"

Sal's smile grew about the cigar clamped between his teeth. Brand wasn't a smoker but even he had to admit the damn thing smelled great. Just not like anything he'd ever encountered before.

"Nothing. Just… ever meet a king before?"

A king. His brain worked that one over for a second. Was he serious?

"No, but then I've never been invited to Buckingham Palace for tea."

Sal barked out a short laugh. "No king there, son. But there is here, so you better brush up on your curtsy."

Brand hadn't heard anyone approach. The man just appeared in the doorway, though Brand knew he hadn't arrived by magic.

No, this guy had walked right up to the door. Only he hadn't made a sound.

Lucy straightened beside him and Brand did a double take. Well, holy shit. The woman looked like a goddess.

Regal, haughty. So beautiful it almost hurt him to look at her.

What the holy fuck…?

"Colerus."

"Lady of the Silver Light. Welcome and greetings."

Then the guy actually went down on one knee, as if proposing, grasped the hand she held out for him and kissed it. When he rose again, Brand had to make sure his mouth was closed because he was pretty sure it'd been hanging open for a few seconds.

As the guy stood, Brand took a closer look at him. Colerus was a solid wall, not as overtly muscled as Kyle, but Brand knew the guy would be able to hold his own in a bench-clearer.

Even if he did look too… clean cut. His light brown hair was short enough to be corporate-approved but long enough to show a wave and his sharp hazel eyes missed nothing.

And when he smiled just before he reached to enfold Lucy in a hug… Hell, Brand figured women dropped at his feet all the time.

"Easy, boy." Sal's voice was pitched so low, Brand almost didn't hear it as he contemplated throwing a roundhouse at the guy for daring to touch Lucy. "You'll wind up with a few claw marks if you're not careful."

Colerus finally stepped back and smiled, his expression losing that stiff formality. "It's really nice to see you. It's been a while and I apolo—"

"Cole, no. You have nothing to apologize for. I know how busy you've been. A king's work is never done. And how is Arabella?"

King. This guy was king of the werewolves?

Cole paused for a brief second, as if unsure how to answer. "She's fine, Lady."

Lucy nodded then reached behind her. For Brand. He grabbed her hand and let her pull him up beside her. "Cole, I'd like you to meet Brandon Stevenson. Brandon, this is *Rex* Colerus Luporeale, *legatus* of the *lucani* Legion."

Brand had a feeling that *Rex* word meant something he should be worried about, but Cole shook his hand, his grip firm and their gazes met and held. Cole didn't try to stare him down but Brand definitely felt his curiosity.

"Nice to meet you, Brandon." Cole nodded once more then turned to Sal, his smile spreading as he first shook Sal's hand then did a complicated knuckle-bump thing that Cal figured was their equivalent of a secret handshake.

"Hey, wolf king, how's it going?" Sal took a step back, as if to take in the entire picture. "Looking pretty sharp for a weekend."

"Got a meeting." Cole looked back at Lucy with a slight grimace. "I'm sorry. I can cancel—"

"Oh, no." Lucy shook her head. "No, you don't need to stay. This isn't an official visit. We're only here to use the altar."

"Okay." Cole's eyes narrowed as his curiosity peaked. But the guy didn't ask any questions. Either he didn't give a shit or he knew better than to question a goddess. "Do you need anything then?"

"No, dear. Just some privacy."

"Then I'll leave you to it. I really was just about to get in the car and leave." This time he bent to kiss Lucy's cheek and Brand couldn't bring himself to get upset about it. It was more like the kiss you gave your favorite maiden aunt. Or your patron goddess.

"Stevenson." Cole nodded at him, that curiosity still glowing in his eyes. "Hey, Sal, we still on for poker next week?"

"Only if you want to lose another couple thou." Sal snorted. "Sure, kid. See you then."

And as soon as Cole had disappeared, Sal turned back to Brand. "So, Brandon, what do you think of the *lucani* king?"

King. Ah, the *rex* before Cole's name.

Holy shit. That guy, who could only be in his early twenties, was a king. The werewolf king.

Brand started to shake his head then couldn't stop.

Sal laughed. "Dude, you are providing hours of amusement. And the day's not over. Let's hope you live to provide a little more."

⁓

"So, Catene. Do you think you'll be able to handle this?"

Catene had turned out to be a beautiful copper-haired teenager with bright blue eyes, a smile that lit up an entire room, and two fathers and a mother who adored her. And were worried about her.

Catene didn't seem to be worried, but then she was a teenager. Brand knew from dealing with the young guys on his teams over the years that, at that age, nothing frightened them. They were invincible, immortal.

"Absolutely, Lady Lucy." She flipped that smile toward Brand. "Everything will be fine."

Hell, when she said it, absolute conviction in her voice, Brand knew it would be. Not that he didn't trust Lucy or Sal, but there was something about this girl…

Something her parents sensed or knew. Something that worried them. Or maybe that was just them being parents. Which he still hadn't wrapped his brain around. He'd have to ask Lucy about that whole three-parent deal later.

Then Lucy smiled and all thoughts of anyone else faded. He figured he must look like a fool, grinning at her like he was.

"So," Sal said. "Let's get this show on the road."

"Lady, are you sure you don't want me to assist as well?" Catene's mother, Margie, piped up. "I know I'm not as proficient with this type of spell as Cat, but you may need a healer on hand. I could call Nica…"

"If we need anyone, we'll be sure to get in touch. But thank you, Margie."

Lucy acknowledged Margie's concerns without being patronizing but she'd made herself clear. Only Brand, Lucy, Sal, and Catene would be there for the actual ritual or whatever the hell they were going to do.

Which he hadn't really allowed himself to think about. Probably shouldn't really think about considering the knife Sal held in his hands.

As they'd waited for Catene to arrive, Sal had disappeared for a few minutes before returning with "supplies."

A blanket, a basket filled with who-knew-what—and that blade. Long, lethal-looking. Black handle and dull black blade. Probably best not to think about what he was going to do with that blade. Yeah, they'd explained the process before, but that had been hypothetical. Now that Brandon was staring at that blade…

Not so hypothetical anymore. But he'd do it. For Lucy.

Jesus, had they really only meet three days ago? It felt like he'd known her forever. No, not forever. Lucy would live forever. He'd be gone in a few short decades. Or sooner, if whatever Sal planned to do to him failed.

"Okay, people." Sal's hooves clacked against the floor as he headed for the door. "Let's move out."

They left Kyle and Margie behind at the den's community center, which turned out to be a sprawling log structure in the middle of a community of houses tucked into the woods.

Brand saw a few actual log houses though most were made of stone and none had a second floor. Hard-packed earth served as roads. No asphalt anywhere. No concrete.

It looked almost European, though he'd never been to Europe. He knew they had electricity but he had no idea where it came from because he didn't see any power lines. Probably buried. Of course, it could just be magic.

The sun had just set and there was still enough light in the sky to see to walk as the almost-full moon hung low and just above the trees.

Lucy and Catene led the way, their voices too low for him to hear. They had their arms linked and, though Lucy's lips curved in a smile, he saw stress in her expression.

"Where are we, anyway?" Brand asked Sal, as they walked side by side down a winding path through the trees, away from the houses. The pines provided cover from anyone who might want to pry.

"Rockland Township. The *lucani* own almost half the township though no one but them knows it. Been living here for almost two hundred years, since Cole's grandfather came over from Sicily to take over control of the *lucani* and institute the legion."

"Legion? Like the Roman Legion? Seriously?"

Sal nodded. "Just like that, yeah. No time for a history lesson, but the *lucani* had been a secret legion of the Roman army way back. They were kinda like the Special Forces. They did the dirty work, if you get my meaning.

"They managed to keep it together for centuries after Rome fell, but in 1758 the *Malandante* nearly decimated them and the *Enu* and *Fata* in a purge. That was when most of the Etruscans moved here."

Brand thought for a moment about what that would have meant. No huge cities. Hundreds and hundreds of miles of forests.

"Must have seemed like heaven," he murmured.

Sal nodded. "Too much temptation for some. They ran wild. Not all of them, but a lot. Enough to make it dangerous for them all. They'd splintered into small groups and none of them would've survived if a few hadn't gotten together and petitioned the Sicilian *lucani* king to help them.

"Cole's great-grandfather sent his oldest son over in the early 1900s to bring them into line. And when his father died, he moved the entire operation here to the States. A few families stayed, but the *lucani* legions are based in America now. Right here, actually. With Cole."

"And he controls the werewolf army?"

Sal grunted out a laugh. "Yeah, he does. They have fighters, but mostly the *lucani* run a string of nightclubs across the country. More structure, steady employment and a way to keep the younger males from running feral. It works for them."

Brand just shook his head at the thought of werewolves running nightclubs. It just seemed so damn bizarre.

As bizarre as what the little goat man is about to do to you, right?

Exactly.

"You can still back out, you know?" Sal's voice had dropped to a level Brand shouldn't have been able to hear if he'd been completely human. All his life, he'd just thought he had exceptional hearing and a sense of smell to rival a dog's.

Or a bear's.

Jesus, what if he really was a *berserkir*?

"No, I can't. I have to do this. I… don't want to lose her."

Sal flashed him a wide grin around his still-smoking cigar. "I knew I liked you, kid."

Brand just shook his head and watched the sway of Lucy's denim-covered ass in front of him. So fucking beautiful. That gorgeous dark hair with its strands of pure silver threaded through it. A woman's lush body.

But he loved her strong personality just as much. He loved that she seemed to be completely head-over-heels for him. That she was willing to go through all this for him.

And who wouldn't love a woman who loved hockey as much as she did?

After a few more silent minutes, they stepped into a clearing. Brand swore the temperature rose from almost freezing back in the village to a nearly balmy forty degrees or so here. Weird. But not as weird as the beautifully carved wooden table at the far end of the clearing. And the musical waterfall spilling down the outcropping of rock to the table's right.

Okay, maybe weird wasn't the right world. Magical. Yeah, magical fit. Hell, he'd never been one for fairy tales. Give him a good gritty mystery any day. Still, there was something so freaking peaceful about this place, it felt like one huge tranquilizer.

He stopped at the edge of the clearing, the warmer air heating his skin, the sound of the waterfall soothing his rough edges.

"Brandon?"

Lucy's voice held a tremble he might have missed had he not turned to look at her. Damn it, he hated that he made this strong woman worry. She stared at him with wide eyes, her bottom lip caught between her teeth so she wouldn't say anything, even though he knew she wanted to. She wanted him to say he wasn't going through with this.

Not gonna happen, babe.

He grabbed the fleece sweatshirt he was wearing and pulled it over his head, followed by his T-shirt. The cooler air brushed up against him, making his nipples hard.

The temperature wasn't unbearable. He hadn't been kidding when he'd said he could withstand subzero temperatures. He'd been a Polar Bear swimmer—

He started to laugh, letting his head fall back as the sound ricocheted off the surrounding trees. He knew they were all staring at him like he'd gone made and he just didn't care. The situation was wild, too crazy to be believed, so why not laugh? Damn it, he fucking deserved it.

"So, puckhead," Sal practically growled at him, "you wanna tell the class what's so funny?"

He took a deep breath but couldn't completely stop his laughter. "When I was a kid, I was part of the Polar Bear Club. We used to ring in the New Year with a midnight swim in the lake. It gets pretty damn cold in Maine in the winter, you know."

Then he couldn't help it. He kept laughing. A second later, Sal joined in, his braying howl of amusement setting off Catene. The only one not laughing was Lucy. She just shook her head. He walked over to her and almost had himself under control when he got there.

"You know you're allowed to laugh, right? And it is kinda funny."

He had a brief moment to wonder if his parents had appreciated the irony as well. He'd have to ask them sometime. And that was a phone call he *really* wasn't looking forward to making.

Sighing, Lucy raised her arms and placed them around his neck, drawing him down for a kiss. The second his lips met hers, all thoughts of polar bears fled and he only thought of her. The taste of her lips, the warmth of her body.

He didn't try to make the kiss anything it wasn't, but she almost drowned him with the force of it. Heat and worry and sweet emotion infused her kiss.

When she finally left him up for air, he realized he'd pulled her against him and had a decent hard-on going. Exactly *not* what he needed right now.

"Let's just get through this, okay, babe?"

He heard a strangled cough behind him and turned to see Sal patting Cat on the back as she stared at him with wide eyes.

Brand frowned at the girl. "What?"

She blinked at him, all innocent and sweet and totally faking it, if the amusement in her eyes was any indication. "Nothing. Not a thing. Why do you think anything's wrong?"

Lucy sighed, shaking her head. "Let's get this over with, Brandon. We need to finish before the moon sets. I need all the power I can get."

"Come on over here, big guy." Sal patted that wooden table. "Take off your clothes and lie on your back. And don't worry, dude. You're not my type."

Sal's attempt at lightening the mood put a smile on Brand's face but couldn't lift the sudden weight on his chest as he shed the rest of his clothes and pulled himself up onto the table.

Cat had turned her back while he'd gotten naked and Sal gave him what looked like a velvet table runner to cover his privates. At least he hoped that was what it was for.

He didn't want to be totally naked in front of the teenager. That was asking a little much. He didn't have many reservations about shedding his clothes in company, but he knew as soon as he'd dropped his pants, everybody had been able to tell how freaked he was because his cock and balls had tried to crawl back into his body.

He should've been embarrassed but he figured that was the least of his problems. Sure, he could blame it on the temperature, but they all knew why he'd shriveled. He was starting to get freaked out. And that was unacceptable. He straightened his back and nodded to Sal.

"Alright, son. Lie on your back and put the cloth over your—yeah, that's right."

The wood had been polished until it felt almost like glass against his back. Really cold glass that warmed in seconds. Almost like someone had turned on a heater.

As he shifted around, arms at his sides as he tried to relax, Lucy walked to stand at his head, Sal at his left and Cat on his right.

Cat had removed her heavy fleece jacket and stood next to him in a plain white long-sleeved T-shirt and jeans. She smiled down at him as she rested one hand on his arm while pressing something into his hand.

He lifted his hand and smiled at the four small charms dangling from a ribbon. "What's this?"

"I made you a cimaruta charm," Cat said. "It's for good luck."

He took a closer look at the charms—a tiny dagger, a small flower, a crescent moon and a skeleton key.

"Guess I need all the luck I can get, huh? Thanks, sweetheart. And when this is over, you'll have to explain it all to me," he said.

Cat nodded as she laid both hands on his arms then looked at Lucy before training those blue eyes on Sal.

Cat had a laser-sharp focus that belied her age. Then again, Brand didn't have much contact with teenage werewolves, so maybe they were all this smart.

Above him, Lucy produced the knife he'd seen in Sal's hand not that long ago. She started to chant in a language he didn't understand but sounded an awful lot like the songs she'd been singing the other night. He was guessing ancient Etruscan. Absolutely beautiful.

The sound of her voice eased some of his tension and his shoulders eased down. He took a deep breath, staring up at the knife she held in her palms just above his head. Almost mesmerized by the razor-thin edge.

Cat joined in after a while, her words different, like she was answering or responding to whatever Lucy was saying.

The little goat man was still smoking a cigar, but the scent had changed. It smelled almost like grass. Not marijuana, but the clean, fresh scent of new-mown grass. He was half goat, after all.

Their voices meshed into an almost drugging symphony of sound… and where the hell did he come up with that?

Holy shit, this must be what falling under a spell felt like. Kinda like being high, which he vaguely remembered from his reckless twenties. But without the munchies.

He felt like he was floating, even though he still felt the wood beneath his back.

After at least a minute, their voices stopped. He opened his eyes, hadn't realized he'd closed them. Above him, stars shattered the dark blue velvet sky.

Shit, he must have been out for more than a minute. Or night fell much, much faster out here.

Above him, Lucy passed the knife to Sal, who looked a hell of a lot taller at the moment. Still had his little horns though. For some reason, that grounded him.

Sal caught and held his gaze. "Last chance, man. Say no and—"

"Just do it."

Sal nodded and plunged the dagger straight into his chest.

Chapter 7

LUCY HELD HER BREATH as the blade slid cleanly through Brandon's body until the hilt touched his skin and she knew the point had lodged into the wood beneath him.

Brandon went deadly still. With his eyes closed, he looked like a mounted butterfly.

In her head, she knew he was unharmed. But her heart beat like a trapped bird and her stomach roiled.

And even though she knew they wouldn't answer, she began a silent prayer to the *Involuti*. The founding gods of the Etruscans had deserted their children years ago, but she couldn't help herself. She needed to do something more.

Reaching for Catene's hand, Lucy drew on the girl's pure well of power, calling up the very essence that tied them together, the essence that made Catene the only person who could've provided Lucy with this much energy.

Soon, the day would come. But not yet...

Now, Lucy had to concentrate. Sal needed her strength and the power she channeled through Cat to help him.

With her free hand, she grabbed Sal's and let the power flow through her, completing the connection with Sal.

Immediately she felt Sal begin to pull the power out of her and pour it into Brandon.

Brandon's muscles began to twitch, his body jerking as if Sal had shocked him. The ancient iron blade, blessed by Nortia, the Goddess of Fate, made contact with the solid wood through Brandon's body and allowed Sal to make that connection with Brandon.

Sal used her magic, boosted by Catene's, to seek out what might be hidden.

Dragging her gaze away from Brandon, she watched Sal as he searched Brandon in the most intimate way. Through his blood.

Sal had closed his eyes, using his free hand to grasp the handle of the blade and filter the images passing through the iron and into his head.

Through her connection to Sal, she saw bits and pieces of Brandon's life—family, friends, girlfriends, and hockey. Always hockey. From the first moment his parents put him on skates to his first win in high school to his first professional game.

His love for the sport never wavered, nor did his love for his family and friends. She caught glimpses of his parents, his sisters. He took after his father…

The images cut off as Sal began to focus deeper, looking for ancestral memories carried in the DNA.

Something that would give a clue—

A blast of power blew through Sal with no warning, throwing him away from the altar, away from Brandon.

"No!" Lucy cried out, ripping her hand from Catene's and reaching for the blade. She wrapped her hand around the hilt, ready to yank it out but the blade was stuck, as if some force held it in place.

"Catene!"

The girl had fallen to the ground when Lucy had broken contact, her eyes closed, her face so pale in the moonlight.

"Catene! Oh Gods. Wake up. Sal, I need you. I command you! Get up."

From behind her, Sal groaned. Catene stirred, her eyes fluttering open as she made an attempt to climb to her feet.

"What hap—"

"Catene, run and get Dane. Now."

Catene's eyes widened as she finally stood. "Holy crap. What happened?"

"I'm not sure. I can't remove the blade. We need to get the blade out."

"I'll go get Dane."

Dane. Yes, the *Lucani* doctor. "Go. Get him now. Hurry."

Catene called her wolf in a furious blaze of magic that tugged at Lucy's power. Catene's clothes disintegrated around her as she transformed her body. In seconds, the wolf had replaced the girl and she tore back down the path toward the village.

Damn it. Godsdamnit, this shouldn't be happening.

Fear like she hadn't felt in centuries grabbed her lungs in both hands and squeezed like a vise. Her hands, slippery with sweat, clenched into fists at her sides. She hated feeling so helpless. It made frustration pound through her body. What the hell had happened?

"Whoa, what the he— What am I doing on the— Oh *shit*."

Sal leaped to his hooves, wobbled a bit, then fell against Lucy's hip before he grabbed for the altar to steady himself.

"I don't know what to do, Sal. He's not moving and I can't remove the knife—"

"Hell no, don't take out the blade. Son-of-a-*bitch*." Sal's voice had dropped to a dangerous growl and he hopped back onto the rock he'd been standing on for the ritual. "We broke the fucking spell concealing his powers. Someone—"

"Explanations later, Sal. We have to get the knife out of his chest. I won't lose him. Not like this. Catene went for Dane but I don't think... We need to take out the knife..."

"No. The knife stays. If we pull it out, we may damage him further. Amity." Sal stepped away from the table. "I'll get Amity."

Sal disappeared without another word, leaving Lucy alone in the dark and the cold with Brandon.

He continued to breathe, but just barely.

"Hold on, sweetheart. You have to hold on. I won't lose you. Not now."

She forced herself to speak calmly, as if he could hear her. Inside, she raged at her own arrogance and her failings.

At one time she would've had the power to help him. Even though she was a moon goddess and not a healer, she would've had the strength to hold him here until help arrived.

Now, even though she felt the power of the moon drawing her, calling to her, she couldn't harness enough of it to fix him.

Useless. She was useless and obsolete and—

No, you know what? Fuck that. Heated anger roiled in her gut. Fuck the thought that she was helpless. She was still a goddess. There had to be something she could do. But what?

"Lucy."

Brandon's eyes flickered open as he whispered her name.

"Brandon." She infused her voice with a calm she didn't feel. "Don't move. Please."

"Wha…" He turned his head to look at her, the dullness of his eyes visible even in the dark. "Well, no shit. Sal stuck me."

"Shh." She leaned forward, pressing her lips to his forehead. She refused to let the feel of his cold skin against hers shake her faith that he would survive. "I forbid you to move."

"I like it when you order me around." His mouth curved and she let herself fall into that smile. "Guess we got a problem, huh?"

"You're going to be fine, sweetheart." She refused to think anything else. She said it so it would be true. "Just don't move."

He tried to laugh. "Guess I'm not the man you need me to be, huh?"

"Brandon, you're more of a man than most gods."

He snorted, then winced in pain. "But gods don't die from a little knife wound."

"You're not dying. I won't let you."

"And there's the Lucy I know and love. There now, let me see what's going on."

Lucy nearly collapsed in relief as her sister goddess Amity bustled over to the altar, Sal directly behind her.

"Amity, please…"

"Oh, now, don't sound so worried. It's not as dire as all that, is it?" Amity flashed a bright smile. "Let me see."

Lucy reluctantly drew away from the altar so Amity could see.

Just the sight of her sister goddess's short, rounded little body was almost enough to make Lucy's spirits lift.

As Munthukh, the Etruscan Goddess of Health, Amity knew the secrets of the human body. At the height of their reign, she could cure cancer or heal deadly injuries with the wave of a hand.

But like all of the Forgotten Goddesses, she'd faded. Today, she channeled her remaining powers into her work as a medical aesthetician at the local hospital, helping accident victims deal with crippling disfigurement and cancer victims with the loss of limbs, hair, and breasts.

"Oh dear, that is a problem, isn't it?" Amity patted Brandon on the shoulder, his eyes barely slits at the moment as he watched her. "But don't worry, sweetie, we'll have you fixed up in no time. I'm Amity, by the way. And you are…?"

"Brandon Stevenson. Nice to—"

He broke off, as if unable to draw in enough air to finish, and Lucy's heart seized in her chest.

"And it's very nice to meet you too. I understand you're a hockey player. I very much enjoy hockey…"

Lucy listened to Amity hold a one-way conversation as she stood next to Brandon, her hands on his shoulders.

Amity's voice worked not only on Brandon. Lucy felt a cool serenity pass through her as well. She wanted to scream at Amity. Why would she not shut up and just heal him?

She was about to open her mouth when Sal grabbed her hand and squeezed. Hard. A warning, but why—oh. Amity *was* working.

Lucy looked at Amity's hands, glowing white against Brandon's pale skin. She'd placed her hands on either side of the blade. Still, she couldn't let herself hope. It would hurt too badly...

"No, Lucy." Amity's voice curled around her heart, loosening the dread. "I need you here with me. And so does Brandon. Put your hand over mine. Yes. See, he's getting better already."

Amity's voice had lowered to a croon, as if she were speaking to a frightened child. Though she knew she should be spitting mad at being treated like that, Lucy couldn't help but notice it was working.

Her heart rate began to level off, the weight on her chest eased, and her muscles loosened to the point where she could move without feeling like she would break.

"I think that'll do it. Sal, let's get that knife out now." Amity's voice cut off her thoughts and Lucy drew in a sharp gasp as Sal nodded and drew the blade out cleanly.

No blood. Not on the knife or Brandon's chest. Lucy turned to ask Amity what had happened and was just in time to catch the other goddess before she fell to the ground.

"Amity!"

The other woman drew in a shuddering breath, her body continuing to shake. "I'm sorry, Lucy. I didn't mean to scare you. He'll be fine. Tell Dane..." Her dark eyes closed for a second and Lucy feared Amity had done too much. "Tell Dane to keep him calm and quiet for several hours and then he'll be as good as new."

"Are you okay?"

Amity's smile was brief but visible. "I'll be fine. Just need... a few minutes to rest."

Then her eyes closed and her body went limp.

Lucy felt tears well as the voices drew nearer, and bright beams of light slashed through the forest. Flashlights.

So much harsher than her beloved moonlight.

"Lady, let me have Amity."

Tinia's teat, this was all her fault. She should've told Brandon no. Should've put a stop to this before she nearly killed him and possibly injured Amity irreparably.

"Lucy, come on," Sal said. "Dane and Cat will be here in seconds and you don't want them to see you on the ground like this. Get up."

No, it wouldn't do to have her wolves see her like this, would it? Defeated. Even if it were true.

All her fault.

"Now, Luce, if you wanna blame anyone, blame me." Sal had taken Amity from her arms and held the other goddess against his sturdy body. "But do it later because they're here."

Turning, she saw Catene fly up the path, dressed in sweats and running sneakers. The *lucani* doctor, Dane, followed right behind her, as did three or four others. She lost count because Dane began to ask questions.

The next few minutes swirled into a haze of demands and shouted orders as Dane examined Brandon and prepared him to be moved back to the den.

Someone had had the foresight to bring a stretcher and Lucy watched carefully as four *lucani* transferred him to it.

"Mom." Ty suddenly stood beside her, his hand on her elbow. She didn't know if he'd been there the entire time or if he'd just shown up. How could she not have known?

"Mom, let's go. Dane said Brandon's going to be fine but he wants to get him out of the cold air."

She stared up at Ty's beloved face. "Is Catene okay?"

A brief flash of fear in his eyes made her tense but it disappeared almost immediately. "Yeah, she's fine. But she's worried about you. And so am I. Don't make me carry you back."

No, that wouldn't do, would it? She had to be strong. Especially for what she knew she had to do when Brandon woke.

She straightened her back and forced every last shred of emotion into a tiny little box in her chest. "Then let's go."

Chapter 8

BRAND CAME AWAKE SLOWLY, fighting through sludgy black unconsciousness.

He had the sense that his entire body should be one painful ache.

Which it wasn't. Actually, he felt pretty damn good. And that probably meant only one thing. Whatever Sal had tried, it hadn't worked.

All successful ventures required a little pain, right? He could only assume he'd failed. He tried to open his eyes but they felt like they had weights on them.

"He's waking."

"Should we get Lucy?"

A pause. "No. Not yet. Let me make sure he's really okay before we get her hopes up."

Get her hopes up? What the hell?

He fought against the darkness that wanted to consume him again and felt the warmth of a hand stroking his forehead. Not Lucy. He knew Lucy's touch.

"Shh, Brandon. You need to remain calm. Stop struggling against the spell. We want you to stay still. We need to make sure everything's working properly before we let you get up and move around."

He wanted to fight against that voice, a female voice that sounded young. But it wasn't Cat and it definitely wasn't Lucy.

"'z she 'kay?"

Shit, that sounded like gibberish, even to his thick brain, but apparently whoever was listening to him could understand.

"Yes, Lucy's fine. You've been out cold for several hours. She finally laid down to get some rest. You wouldn't want us to wake her, would you?"

"No, huh uh."

He swore he could hear the woman smile. "Of course not. Now just go back to sleep."

No, he needed to make a phone call, needed to call… who? Shit, he had obligations—

Brandon opened his eyes and stared for several minutes at wood beams in a ceiling he didn't recognize. Good workmanship. Nice joints…

He must have fallen back to sleep because bright sunlight peeked around the edges of the shade on the one window to the left of the bed. Turning his head, he looked for a clock, though his internal clock told him he was late for practice.

"*Shit.*"

He sat up in bed then froze, waiting for the pain to start. Headache, muscle aches, nausea.

Nothing.

He looked down. Naked chest. Lifted the thin sheet covering him from the waist down. Naked everywhere. And erect. Holy hell, he had an erection that wouldn't quit. So of course, he wanted to know where Lucy was.

"Well, good morning. We were beginning to worry."

A pretty blonde walked into the room, stethoscope around her neck, wearing light blue scrubs and a nurse's smile. He shoved the sheet down into his lap, hopefully covering his damn unruly cock.

The woman pretended not to notice what he was doing as she reached for his wrist and he held it out automatically for her to take his pulse. He opened his mouth but she beat him to it.

"Before you ask," she slipped her stethoscope from around her neck and stuck it against his chest, "Lucy's in the next room. She's still sleeping. Whatever you guys did last night, you did it up good. You're nearly healed though, and Amity and Dane said you'll be fine after you're rested."

"I've got a game Thursday." The response was automatic. And true.

The nurse smiled. "Yeah, well, I don't think you'll be playing. The doctor will be in to talk to you soon. Just lie back and relax. I'll make sure Lucy knows you're awake. I'm Tam, by the way."

"Brandon."

Her smile widened. "Yes, I know who you are. Hell, everyone in the den knows who you are."

With her hand on his shoulder pressing him back into the bed, he lay back, wondering if that was good or bad. He meant to ask until he felt Tam's fingers exploring the faint scar on his chest.

"Damn. That almost looks like I didn't have a knife shoved through my heart."

Tam's eyes narrowed down into slits. "Do you remember what happened? I'm not trying to pry. In fact, I'm not asking for details. I'm only asking if you can recall what happened or do you feel like there're pieces missing from your memory?"

What the hell did he remember from last night? He remembered the altar and he remembered a big-ass knife. He remembered Sal lifting that knife and—

He sucked in a deep breath and looked down at his chest. "I remember Sal shoving a knife through my chest. After that, I'm blank."

"Then I guess you can rest easy because that's exactly what happened."

He took a deep breath… and swore he caught Lucy's scent. Damn, his sense of smell had always been better than anyone else he knew, which made the locker room after a game a hellhole for him, but it'd never been that good.

Maybe Lucy was coming toward him.

"Brandon? Are you okay?"

As a matter of fact, the more he concentrated, the more he realized there was a different level of scent.

And his eyesight… Everything looked clearer. And brighter.

He blinked. "Uh, yeah. I'm fine."

"And nothing hurts?"

He gave that one some thought. "No…"

"Then I'd say you were pretty luck—"

"I think you'd better get out of here."

Tam's eyebrows shot up to her hairline. "Brandon, what—"

He'd been truthful when he said nothing hurt. What he felt wasn't painful. But he knew exactly what he was feeling even though he hadn't felt it in years.

"Go. Leave. I don't want to hurt you."

"What's wro—"

"Get out!"

The words came out as a roar and Tam made for the door. Backwards. Never taking her eyes off of him. Probably a smart move on her part because if she'd looked away, he may have leaped for her. As she shut the door to the room, the lock clicking into place made the rage boiling in his gut intensify.

Where the hell it came from, he had no idea. He only knew what it was because he remembered the feeling from when he'd been a kid.

That frightening sense of losing control combined with the heat of fury.

Something had happened last night, something that threatened to turn him into a ravening beast. Control. He needed to find some before he tore this room apart. But the rage bubbled and burned.

Go ahead. Tear it up. They did this to you. They made you like this.

No, they hadn't made him like this. This was him and yet, somehow, he'd managed to keep it contained. Now, this feeling had a way out and it wanted to take it.

He tried to contain it, tried to shove it back in that little metaphysical box he'd always known was there but could ignore before. Now he couldn't find the right combination to lock the box.

He shoved himself off the bed and landed on the floor, planting his feet on the cold wood planks and trying to let that coolness seep into him. Didn't work. He wanted to rip something apart with his hands. Wanted to—he caught her scent again and he knew what he wanted. He wanted her. She was his and he had to have her.

He lunged for the door and yanked but it stood against him. Muscles straining as he pulled the handle, he fought to open it but it wouldn't.

That roar… that sound that wasn't his and yet had come from his body.

Jesus, that was freaky. What—

He banged on the door and watched his claws rake deep furrows into the wood.

His claws…

What the *fuck*.

He held his hands out in front of him, staring at the claws that'd sprung from his nails. Fucking *claws*. Long, lethal-looking. Sharp as hell and bone white.

"Brandon."

Her voice through the door. His woman's voice. He wanted to sink those claws into her—

"Brandon, are you okay?"

Fuck, no. "No, I'm not safe. Stay out, Lucy."

"What's going on? Tell me."

What the hell did he say? *Hey, I got these pretty, new, deadly weapons attached to my hands. Come in and let's play.*

God, she smelled amazing. He wanted to push his nose into her neck and draw in her scent. He wanted to put his mouth on her neck and lick her skin. And then tear into her.

"You've got to stay away from me, Lucy. Just stay out there."

"Brandon. I'm going to open the door. Step away, okay?"

"*No*. You can't—I don't want to hurt you."

"You won't. I know you won't. Brandon, I'm going to open the door."

It hit him then. The sound of her voice acted like a stream of ice directed at that fury in his blood. He latched onto that feeling, struggled to contain the heat and the anger.

The door cracked open, just a few inches. Enough to let him get a bigger taste of her smell.

Then Lucy began to slip through the crack and he knew, in that split second, that he wasn't going to be able to stop himself.

He grabbed her by the wrist and yanked her all the way into the room. She gasped and the sound hit him like a sucker punch deep in his libido. The growl that erupted from his throat scared the shit out of him. He sounded like an animal. Hell, he felt like an animal. One that couldn't control his urges.

Instinct demanded he push her against the door and flatten his body against hers. He didn't want her to be able to get away.

Leaning down, he shoved his face in her neck, drawing in her scent. He smelled no fear, though how he knew that, he didn't have a clue. But, holy God, he knew he smelled her arousal. Spicy hot and so fucking—

He grabbed her shoulders and held her immobile. She didn't try to move, as if she knew he wouldn't let her. She merely stared up at him with those beautiful pale gray eyes and breathed.

He felt her breath brush against his skin, making every hair on his body stand on end, and his cock pulsed and thickened as blood pumped it into an erection.

"Lucy."

He shook as he tried not to do what his body was urging him to do. Which was shred her jeans with his claws, lift her against the wall, and fuck her brains out. Just thinking about it made him burn.

"Brandon. Go ahead. Just do it."

He shook his head. She didn't mean it. She couldn't mean it. Struggling against the need to bite her, he settled for a lick instead. His tongue slicked its way up her neck to her chin.

As her taste exploded on his tongue, he knew it wouldn't be enough. And when she drew in a deep breath that sounded more like a gasp, he knew he'd just lost the fight.

His hands shot to her hips as his mouth opened over the soft skin on her neck. He tried to remember not to hurt her with his claws… Jesus, he had freakin' claws.

But he got lost in her taste and her smell. His entire body had focused on her, and he couldn't stop.

He sucked on the skin of her neck as she tilted her head to the side to give him more access.

With his heart racing and his blood pounding in his veins, he bit her, hard. Not enough to break the skin. Just enough to leave a mark. To make sure everyone knew she was his.

She cried out but he heard desire in her voice, not alarm or pain. As her arms circled his shoulders, she pressed closer, her hips angling forward, seeking out his erection.

Naked. He wanted her naked. He reached for the button on her jeans, barely noticing that his claws were gone. Maybe they'd never been there. Maybe he'd only imagined them. At the moment, he couldn't have cared less. He wanted her. Needed her.

He shoved her jeans down to her knees as she kicked off her shoes. She'd been wearing red sneakers and they hit the ground with a soft thud, allowing her jeans to slide to the floor. The tiny pair of black bikini underwear gave way with barely a breath of sound, leaving her naked. Christ, he could smell how much she wanted him, see the evidence on her pussy lips, wet and slick.

He dropped to his knees, lifted her left leg over his shoulder, and covered her clit with his mouth. No build up, no foreplay. Just full-out attack.

Her head made an audible thud against the wall as it fell back, her hands reaching for his head. Her fingers grabbed at the short strands of his hair, tried to find purchase but couldn't.

So she cupped the back of his head and tried to force him even closer.

Wet and hot, she tasted so damn good he would've been content to eat her out all night. He sucked on her clit ruthlessly, never stopping for breath until he felt her body shudder on the edge of orgasm. Then he shifted his focus to lick at the seam of her sex, lapping at her flowing juices before working his tongue into the tight confines of her sheath.

Her short cry of frustration made him growl in satisfaction. She'd come on his command. He fucked her with his tongue until he'd worked her up again then drew back to bathe her stomach with his kisses. Her moisture covered his face and he felt like a glutton, but he couldn't stop.

His cock fucking throbbed, aching and hard. Each of her ragged breaths drew him closer to that edge where he came completely undone and rutted on her like an animal.

No, he needed to hold onto some semblance of control. But her smooth skin and her breathless cries made it impossible.

Letting her leg slide off his shoulder, he stood. Grabbing her hips, he lifted, her back sliding up the wall until he had her exactly where he wanted her.

The perfect height to—

She leaned her hips forward, the wet lips of her sex brushing against the sensitive head of his cock. Electric sensation shivered and danced along the shaft, making him grit his teeth against the need to shove into her until she begged him for mercy.

He wanted her to scream his name, needed to hear her voice as he took her. But first...

The head of his cock breached her, just enough to lodge in place as her pussy clenched. Tight. So fucking tight.

Yes, she was wet, but she was just as aroused as he was and her pussy would be tight as a fist.

Goddamn, that's what he wanted. Wanted to feel her squeezing him, caressing him. Now. He thrust hard, sank deep even as her body practically fought against the invasion. But when he breached her, she sucked him in as if she wouldn't let go.

That animal he sensed inside himself reared up and took over then. His hips began to pump, working his cock in and out in a piston-fast motion that cranked his blood pressure and sent his libido into overdrive.

His mouth latched onto hers, stealing her breath and sucking it into his lungs. When he began to see stars in front of his eyes, he broke apart to suck in air, his hips continuing to pound against hers. He stared into her face, watching her expression slacken even further into ecstasy.

He stroked harder, faster, felt his body tense as she tried to move with him. The bare skin of her neck called to him and he put his mouth over the tight tendon and bit. Hard. He couldn't help himself.

Christ, he wanted to taste blood and that was just fucked up. Still, he couldn't stop. He barely managed to stop his teeth from breaking the skin.

Tearing his mouth away, he let his head fall back even as he pushed his body harder against hers.

His cock felt swollen and ten times more sensitive than it'd ever felt before. Each time he retreated, he growled and shoved back in that much faster.

Her hands, which had been clenching tight to his shoulders, began to flex, as if she were fighting him. It made his beast rear back on its hind legs and roar.

And made him go at her that much harder.

Total domination. She had to give in. He had to have her complete submission or he'd fuck her until she gave it to him.

But he felt her pressing back against him. She wouldn't give him what he wanted. She twisted, as if trying to get away. Her head shook back and forth. She wanted to deny him his prize. Her orgasm.

He pulled out, fighting her hands as she tried to keep him against her. But she couldn't match his strength.

Setting her on her feet, he turned her to face the wall, lifting her arms and pinning her wrists above her head with one hand. She moaned, and wriggled her ass against his groin, drawing a harsh growl from him.

"Fuck me, damn you." Her voice sounded hoarse and rough with need. "You know you want to. Just do it."

It was exactly what he wanted but he refused to let her control any of this. So instead, he fit his cock into the seam of her ass and pressed hard, making sure she understood exactly what he was promising. She shuddered and moaned then went pliant beneath him, one cheek pressed to the wall.

"I'll do it when I'm Goddamn good and ready. I'm going to fuck you until you can't stand."

Leaning in, he pressed his nose behind her ear to breathe her in, then licked a path from just below her ear to the tip of her jaw. Then he nipped her jaw and strung a series of kisses down her throat as he ground against her.

Her eyes fluttered shut as she drew in a huge breath, her lips parting to release it.

"Then do it already."

Goddamn her, she was taunting him, pushing him. She pushed

back against him, her hips rotating, rubbing his cock with those smooth ass cheeks.

One hand on her wrists, his other reached around the front of her to slip between her legs.

Her sweet, slick essence coated his fingers and he speared them into her pussy without warning, just to feel her writhe. She clamped down on him with a moan, making her sheath that much tighter. He had to use more force to penetrate her now.

His cock throbbed and he realized he'd been rubbing himself against her, almost to the point of getting off.

Pre-cum seeped from the tip, just as her essence flowed down her legs. Pulling his hand away required concentration but he did it, grabbing his cock and angling it down.

He had to bend his knees to get at the right angle but he got distracted by the feel of her wet lips sliding against his heated cock. Christ, he could get off just like this.

His hips naturally took over the rhythm, rubbing against her heated skin, feeling her body quake with each pass.

"Brandon. Blessed Goddess, fuck me."

"When I'm damn good and ready."

"I know you're ready now. I can feel it—"

With just a flex of his knees, he pierced her and sank as deep as he could go in this position.

Lucy released her breath in a harsh exhalation that sounded almost pained to him. Still, he couldn't stop.

He moved closer, knocked her feet with his own so her legs spread even more. It gave him a few more inches of depth. And made her moan out his name.

With one arm around her waist and the other still holding her wrists pinned above her head, he let his hips pound against her ass.

The position made her so fucking tight, he could barely stand it. Somehow he managed to hold off his orgasm, to push into her and push into her until she hung limp in his hand. Her body merely a receptacle for his, she finally gave him what he needed and let him have her.

When she came, she didn't tense at all. Instead her body went liquid around him, fiery hot and clenching. Grasping his cock and squeezing until he couldn't hold back.

With a low growl, he pushed as deep as he could go and held tight. He exploded, his seed pumping deep.

The orgasm went on for minutes until he honestly thought something was wrong. But Christ, he didn't want to pull out. And he swore he was still hard.

The hand at her waist slid across her stomach and arrowed straight down to her clit. He flicked the little nub and felt her twitch around him.

He'd just come but he was still hard and getting harder. He could go again. Right now. So he did.

Chapter 9

WHEN HE WOKE, IT had gone dark again.

So dark, he couldn't at first tell whether he was blindfolded or it was just that pitch black.

He reached for his eyes... No blindfold.

"Shh, Brandon, just lie still a while longer."

Ah, he knew that voice. He loved that voice. That voice made him hard and ready. Even now, when his blood felt like frozen slush in his veins, he felt his cock begin to fill.

"Lucy."

"Yes. Everything's fine, sweetheart. Just lie still."

Sure, he could do that. Frankly, he didn't know if he could do much of anything else.

Jesus, everything fucking hurt. What the hell had happened? The last thing he remembered was falling asleep after nailing Lucy up against the wall like a madman. And that sure as hell hadn't hurt.

"Are you okay?" Damn, his voice sounded scratchy, raw. Deeper somehow.

"I'm fine, Brandon. You need to lie still."

"Why? Did something happen?"

Finally, his eyes were starting to adjust to the dark, enough for him to see shapes.

"Nothing happened. You... just need to rest some more."

He turned his head toward her voice and saw her sitting next to him on the bed. He couldn't see her expression but he knew by the tone of her voice that something was up.

Her hand settled on his chest, a comforting weight that sank heat into him. He felt that warmth trying to seep through his body, trying to dispel the cold.

Her head lowered and she began to chant. Though he couldn't understand a word she said, he knew it was the same language she'd been singing in the other night.

He wanted to reach for her, tried to lift his arms but they were too damn heavy. He opened his mouth to speak but he couldn't get his vocal cords to work.

Now what the hell was wrong with his voice? Panic wanted to eat away at him but Lucy's voice soothed him. He wanted to close his eyes again.

But he had questions about... Hell, what questions did he have?

Something to do with what had happened earlier today. Something about a knife.

The little goat man, Sal, had stuck a knife through his chest. He glanced down at his chest.

Huh. No knife hilt sticking out. And since his heart was beating, he figured the fact that the knife was gone was a good thing. He glanced around. No Sal. No Cat either. The teen girl with the beautiful hair had helped Sal stick a knife in his chest.

Okay, maybe his brain needed a few more hours of sleep to be able to function properly because right now, he definitely felt fucked in the head.

He closed his eyes, concentrating on calming that strange, almost detached panic. And banishing the cold. Why had Sal stuck a knife in his chest?

Berserkir.

Okay, that he remembered. They'd been trying to find out if he had *berserkir* blood.

"Lucy." He swallowed a few times, trying to moisten his mouth. "Did it work?"

Lucy lifted the hand she'd been resting on his shoulder to his mouth and continued to chant.

Okay, he could take a hint. Besides, he didn't really feeling up to moving.

And he loved listening to her voice. She sang like an angel... Wait, was that mixing metaphors, considering she was an Etruscan goddess?

Okay, that sounded a little more like him, even if it was only in his head.

After a few minutes, he actually started to feel more like himself.

His blood unfroze, his brain began to put things back into the right order. His memories of earlier today lined up and he knew it was only a matter of time before he had the answer to his last question.

He relaxed, letting her voice wash over him until finally she went silent and drew her hands away.

"Brandon, open your eyes now. How do you feel?"

She sounded tentative, worried. He opened his eyes to see her expression reflect the same feeling. Shit, maybe he didn't want to know what'd happened.

So instead of thinking about that, he concentrated on her question. He hauled his upper body off the bed then swung his legs off the side of the bed and planted his feet on the floor. He sat there, waiting to feel light-headed or nauseous.

Nothing. He felt fine.

Well, actually... He felt better than fine. He felt energized.

And strong as hell.

Like he'd pumped a few hundred pounds and popped some steroids to go with it.

"I feel okay. Actually, I feel pretty strong. It worked, didn't it? Whatever you and Sal did, it worked."

He couldn't hide his grin but she bit at her bottom lip, worrying the soft flesh as she nodded. "Yes, but there were... complications."

Okay, that didn't sound good. He looked down at himself, trying to figure out if he was missing any body parts or—claws. He remembered claws.

Holy shit.

"Can you turn on a light?"

He needed to be able to see more clearly. He had to—

A lamp on the bedside table clicked, and light flooded the room. Blinking a few times to get his eyes used to the light, he lifted his hands to check out his fingers. Then breathed a sigh of relief.

No sharp white claws where his nails should be.

"No, you didn't imagine them," Lucy said. "You'll get accustomed to how they work in a few days."

His gaze flashed back to hers. "So I really am a... *berserkir.*"

"Yes. I'm sorry, Brandon."

"Sorry? Shit, why are you sorry?"

He was a frickin' bear without the heavy fur coat. He was strong enough to protect her now—

"Because we broke the spell. If I'd known... If we'd realized sooner what was going on, maybe we could have prevented the spell from breaking, maybe—"

"Wait. What spell?"

Lucy grimaced, worrying her bottom lip with her teeth. "Well, we're not one hundred percent sure but we believe your parents had a spell cast that bound your *berserkir* powers. They probably had it done when you were a child. I assume they wanted you to lead a human life and never know you were different."

Shit, that meant his parents... "So my parents are *berserkir.*"

She nodded. "At least one, but I'm guessing both because the binding spell was so strong."

His parents were *berserkir.* Memories from his childhood started to play through his mind. The scratches on his parents' headboard shot to the forefront. What kid wanted to think about his parents having sex, much less rough sex? Yeah, he'd seen the scratches but he'd pretty much forced them out of his mind.

What the hell else had he overlooked as a kid?

"Holy shit," he breathed, "the entire town I grew up in. They're all in on it."

His town wasn't big but it was isolated as all hell. No hotels, no bed and breakfasts. If you had family coming to visit, they stayed with you in your home or they didn't stay overnight. But that happened rarely.

No one ever sold their house if they moved away. They either kept it or sold it to one of the other families.

Hell, the town was so isolated, he and all the other kids had been bussed almost forty minutes both ways to attend the district's high school. The younger kids were taught in a four-room building until they hit seventh grade.

Almost every single child who'd grown up there had left for bigger cities and never looked back. It was practically ingrained into them from birth that they would leave, get jobs "away." Meaning anywhere except where they'd grown up.

"Probably." Lucy's voice drew him back to the present. "I've seen it happen before. Your parents wanted a different life for you than they had. Don't all parents want better for their children?"

"Yeah, but to hide what I am? What if I have kids? Fuck, what about my sisters' kids?"

"The binding is a blood ritual. Your sisters' children probably had the spell passed to them through the blood. And your sisters probably mated men who are not *versipelli*. Their children would have only a fifty percent chance of being able to shift anyway. That spell was so strong, you nearly died when Sal accidently broke the binding."

Brandon just sat there, shaking his head. The lengths to which his parents had gone to allow him to live the life he had now, it amazed him.

He remembered being a teenager and practically crawling the walls to be able to get away from his no-stoplight town. Hockey had been his savior. For others, it'd been college.

"Guess their plan worked. Shit, I couldn't wait to leave."

He was still shaking his head when he realized what Lucy had said. He turned to look at her and she met his gaze straight on.

"Wait, what do you mean, broke the binding?"

"Exactly what I said. When Sal… pierced you with the blade, he disrupted the spell. You can now access your *berserkir* powers. Since I don't know much about *berserkir*, I think you might want to call or go visit your parents."

"I've got games."

She dropped her gaze for several seconds before taking a deep breath and lifting her head, as if it was so hard to do.

"I don't think you're going to be able to play, Brandon. At least not for a few weeks. You're going to need time to adjust—"

He blinked at her, stunned. "Weeks? I can't be out weeks."

Jesus, just the thought of missing Thursday's game gave him a case of the shakes.

Lucy's expression had turned stony. "You'll have to tell your coach you've had a family emergency—"

"No, no way—"

"—and you had to leave immediately. Tell them your father's had a heart attack, tell them your mother's come down with a deadly disease. You can't get on the ice until you know how this is going to affect you."

"What do you mean, affect me?"

But he already knew. He could feel the change deep inside. Almost like a coal smoldering in his gut. Earlier, when he'd fucked her against the wall…

"You'll need to test yourself, see what your limits are," Lucy said. "How hard you can throw a punch. You already had a killer slap shot. Now, you might literally be able to take someone's head off with it. If you get into a fight with someone, you won't be able to control your claws. Not yet. It's going to take time for you to master everything that being a *berserkir* means."

He froze as another thought occurred to him. "Am I going to change into a bear? A real fucking bear with fur and fangs and…"

Holy fucking shit. His brain had gotten stuck on that image and now it wouldn't release him. Could he handle that? Or would he freak out and have to be put in a cell for freaked-out werebears?

He felt a laugh bubble in his chest, but in his head he knew it sounded kind of scary so he tried to suppress it.

"No, you won't." She reached for him then, put her hand on his arm, and suddenly he could think clearly again. He put his hand over hers so she couldn't get away and take his sanity with him. "Do you remember what Sal said earlier? About how the *berserkir* had evolved? You won't become a bear but you will take on some of their traits. The claws, the fangs, the strength. You will learn to control them, but until then you'll need to lie low. Sal's promised to help. And I'll do whatever you need me to do."

Was that guilt he heard in her voice? "Lucy, why do I get the feeling you're not too thrilled about this? I did this for you—"

"But I gave you no choice!"

He frowned. "What? What the hell are you talking about? I told Sal—"

"I should have known something would go wrong." Releasing him, she got up to pace. The second her hand left his, he felt that spark, that flare of heat and… aggression. Yeah, that was the word he was looking for. Aggression.

He gripped the side of the mattress, forcing himself to stay on the bed, not to run her to the ground or grab her arm and throw her down on the bed every time she passed by him.

"Sal *broke* the binding. We can't replace it, can't fix it. We can't put you back to the way you were." She stopped to take a deep breath. "Your life will never be the same, and this is all my fault."

He shook his head, trying to see it from her angle, but there was a little part of his brain that kept telling him she was right. This was her fault. He'd never play hockey again. He'd be a freak and an outcast.

All her fault.

With a growl, he grabbed her arms, yanking her to him then flipping her onto the mattress beneath him and covering her with his body.

And she let him. She didn't fight him, didn't yell at him or tell him to get off. Which meant he was in way more trouble than he'd thought.

He opened his mouth to tell her, again, that this wasn't her fault… and decided to show her instead.

Bending down to her, he kissed her. He let himself revel in the heat and the taste of her. Her scent tangled around his fast-growing lust and he pried open her unresponsive lips and plundered her mouth.

She let him kiss her, let him take what he wanted. And it pissed him off even more.

He didn't want her docile. Fucking her into submission was different than having her just give in.

Swinging his leg over her, he planted his knees on either side of her hips and held himself above her, trapping her beneath him.

He almost thought she wouldn't meet his gaze, but she did, and now he really could see the guilt in those stormy gray eyes.

Stealing another kiss, he drew back so he could see her entire face.

"You still don't get it, do you?" he said. "You still don't understand that this is what I wanted. I *want* to be strong. I *want* to be what you need."

She shook her head. "But I never wanted to have the choice

taken away from you. I—We almost lost you during the ritual. You almost died when the spell broke. You didn't…"

She bit her lips and drew in a shaky breath. Out of the corner of his eye, he saw her hands clench into fists. "I cannot live my life like this. I can't."

Frustration made his voice sharper than he wanted. "And how have you been living your life all these years? Have you let anyone get close to you? Ever? You act like nothing affects you. But when I touch you, you burn, baby. Don't you wonder why that is? Huh?"

Lucy didn't have to wonder. She knew. She loved him. She'd been half in love with him before she'd ever met him. Ridiculous but true.

And now that she'd had him, she knew why she'd never allowed herself to fall in love. Because the loss would be too great for her to bear. She'd become so damn weak in the past few centuries. Yes, she'd been protecting her *lucani* as best she could. The only way she knew how.

But then this man had skated onto the ice and she'd lost her heart. Just another weakness she couldn't afford. And one she didn't want to give up.

Staring into his beautiful eyes, she lifted one hand to trace the slightly crooked nose then let her finger brush across those talented lips.

"I don't need to wonder." She pressed against his lips and he sucked her finger into his mouth. The wet warmth of his tongue made shivers dance up her spine. "I know exactly why."

She loved the feel of his mouth on her skin. Wanted more than anything to be able to forget her responsibilities, to toss caution to the wind and simply love him.

Hated that in three short days, he'd become more important to her than protecting her people.

She couldn't do it. She couldn't give him what he wanted and remain strong enough to keep her *lucani* safe. But neither could she give him up, not after what he'd sacrificed for her.

She lifted her head to press her lips against his, felt his hesitation just before he gave in and kissed her back.

Blessed Goddess, she was selfish. Winding her arms around his neck, she brought him closer.

He held back for a few seconds, as if to proclaim his dominance, and that was okay. She could allow him some power, particularly here. In bed.

She needed to show him that he wasn't merely her plaything. That he held an equal amount of power in this aspect of their relationship.

He kissed her until she could barely breathe, then he moved, getting off the bed to stand by the side. Startled, she just stared at him.

"I've got to call the coach, tell him… Hell, I'll tell him I have a family emergency and need to head home for a few days. We don't have a game until Thursday. We've got time to figure this out. Okay?"

Sitting up, she nodded, willing her brain to stillness instead of rushing through thoughts at breakneck speed. He was right in this. No decisions needed to be made at this moment.

―――

Lucy left Brandon alone in the bedroom to make his phone calls while she headed out to find some hot chocolate.

She knew Sal had made some, she could smell it, and right now, she would sell her firstborn son for a mug. Ty would understand. He let her get away with murder.

Following a short hall, she found herself back in the common area of Cole's home in the den. He had another property several miles away where he actually lived but this served as his headquarters.

Comfortable furniture, an open floor plan in the main living areas and enough decorative touches to make it feel welcoming to anyone raised in the Etruscan ways. Or who'd lived through the heyday of the Etruscans. Like her. Her *lucani* were nothing if not loyal.

She'd expected to find only Sal in the kitchen at the back of the house. She paused halfway through the entrance when she realized it wasn't Sal.

"Ty? What are you doing here?"

He looked at her with eyes the color of his father's, a blue so dark it looked almost black, the exact shade of the sky at full dark with no moon and the sun nowhere close to rising.

They looked so much like his father's that she'd tried to disguise them when he'd been a baby so no one would ever suspect whose child he was. So he wouldn't be a target.

"Should be obvious." He shrugged, broad shoulders moving under the black cotton T-shirt emblazoned with the name of another band. Her son had a thing for music. Something he'd gotten from her. Thank the Blessed Mother Goddess, he'd gotten most of his traits from her. "I'm checking on you."

"I'm fine."

He snorted and stood to pour her a huge mug of chocolate from the pot on the stove. "Yeah, right. That's why you look like you've gone a few rounds with that *tukhulkha* demon."

Setting the mug on the table, he waited until she took a seat before he slumped back into his chair across from her. "You fell for him, didn't you?"

Thick, fragrant steam billowed up from the mug and she drew it into her lungs, feeling the magical stress-relieving powers of the chocolate seep into her bones. "Did you come to interrogate me, my love?"

He snorted. "Yeah, like that's gonna happen. No, I'm just here to make sure you're okay."

"And I'm fine. Have you checked on Catene?"

Low blow, yes, but she didn't need her son picking at her now, asking her questions she couldn't answer.

"Wow, you're definitely running scared if you threw that at me already."

And she should've known he'd see right through her. Obviously, it wasn't all that hard right now.

"Mom—"

"Ty, please." She held up one hand. "I could do without the examination, at least for now. Especially with Brandon so close."

His sharp gaze held hers. "No worries there. He won't hear us unless I want him to. Cone of Silence spell. Works like a charm."

Ty had always had quite the fascination with comic-book superheroes since their debut in the early twentieth century. And he'd never been a slouch in spell casting. Which was probably why he and Catene—

"Mom. Don't push him away now. You need him."

She lifted the mug to her lips and took a healthy swallow, willing herself not to tremble. "I'll get him killed. He nearly died during the ritual."

And how much worse would it be if he died trying to protect her? If she couldn't keep him safe?

"But he didn't. Hell, the guy was strong enough to pull through having a knife plunged into his chest. Don't you think—"

"He's not strong enough to stand against a *tukhulkha* demon. He shouldn't have to be. But neither do I have the strength to send him away and I might as well just sign his death sentence."

"Whoa, Mom, going for the Oscar today? Chill."

Her lips lifted in a slight smile. "And how old are you, sweetheart?"

"Younger than you and don't you forget it. Seriously, Mama, what happened?"

"He's a *berserkir* and we accidentally released the binding spell holding back his powers when we did the ritual last night. He wants to be enough for me but I took the choice away from him. Now he has powers that may make it impossible for him to ever play hockey again and he could get himself killed defending me from a *tukhulkha* demon sent by Charun."

She waited, expecting another smart-ass response, but Ty looked to be deep in thought.

So she sat back to sip her chocolate. Ty presented such a carefree attitude to the rest of the world, most people forgot her son had a steel trap for a mind.

"He told me about the demon attack the other night and I looked up Tessa and her Cimmerian. They filled in the rest of the blanks. You know Charun will be coming for you because you actually have some power left. He's upping the stakes."

"But I am stronger and I have the *lucani*." And now she had Brandon, even if she shouldn't. "Charun's demons will think twice about coming for me again."

Ty shook his head. "So they'll just go after Nortia or Amity or one of the others."

Frustration began to boil in her veins. "And what do you suggest we do? We can't take the battle to him. Charun's too strong in Aitás. We'd be handing ourselves over to him on a platter. No, we merely need to protect ourselves until he gives up this stupid idea."

"So basically you're going to hide?"

Yes, it sounded cowardly. But she had to think of her sons, her *lucani*. And Brandon. People depended on her.

"And isn't that what we've all been doing for the past two millennia? Why should this be any different?"

"You know why, Mama." Ty leaned forward, his gaze intense and piercing. "You know the time's coming. Cat's birth—" He stopped to take a breath, forcing himself to unclench his fists on the table. "Everything's changing and we need to get up to speed."

She stilled, then realized she couldn't ignore what he'd said. Ty never talked about Cat lately unless he had a damn good reason. "I thought you didn't want Cat to be burdened yet?"

His expression screwed up with total frustration and she saw so much of herself in him at the moment, she wanted to be someone else, someone who could make it all better for him. Her sister goddess Tessa had a maternal instinct a mile wide yet she had never been blessed with children.

Lucy was a hunter goddess, fierce, strong and icy cool. During her prominence, she'd ruled the night and its denizens with a steel grip and swift retribution.

She'd created the *lucani* on a whim when the king of a small city had come to her and begged her to give him protection from those who would try to take his land. She'd given him the ability to shift into a wolf, him and his entire city.

She'd taken on a powerful god who'd wanted to bend her to his will and she'd walked away with her sanity and her son.

Now, she melted at the feet of one man and was seriously considering an irrevocable act that would forever change the life of a nineteen-year-old girl. And free Lucy from her continued obsolescence.

"I'm sick of waiting." His voice sounded like a low growl and he shoved away from the table to pace the floor. "I hate knowing what's meant to be and I hate having no choice in the matter. I hate that her choice is nonexistent. And I love her so much it fucking scares me."

Running a hand through his already messy hair, he looked wild, and for the most part he was. He'd taken to running in his pelt much more now than he ever had before.

All because he feared the changes they'd both known were coming. And which they'd been ignoring.

Charun's pursuit was forcing her hand and she didn't like feeling she was being backed into a corner. She tended to come out fighting when that happened and that never ended well for anyone.

She had much more to lose now. Or… maybe she just cared more about what she had to lose.

Either way, she needed to come up with answers. Soon. For all their sakes.

"Ty, sweetheart, you're going to wear a path in Cole's floor. The decision doesn't have to be made this minute. We have time."

A lie. She knew it and so did Ty.

He shook his head. "No, we don't."

"Hey, Mom. How's it going?"

"Brandon, honey, how are you?"

Yeah, how the hell did he answer that one?

"I'm fine."

Andrea Stevenson paused and Brandon had a second to wonder if she could actually read minds in addition to growing claws. "What happened? Were you injured?"

"No, it's nothing like that. I'm fine. I've just… I got a question for you and I need you to answer me straight up."

Another pause and Brandon saw his mom so clearly in his mind's eye. She was flexing her hands, straightening and curling her fingers like…

Shit. Curling his own fingers around the charm Cat had given him before the ritual, he shook his head. How many times had he seen his mom do that and joked that she reminded him of a freaking bear, clawing the trees.

"Brandon, you're worrying me. What's wrong?"

Just spit it out. "Are we *berserkir*?"

He heard his mother gasp and then the clatter as the phone hit the floor. Next he heard her yelling for his dad. Screaming would probably be more like it.

And crying.

Shit, he'd made his mom cry. Damn it, he should just bounce his head against the wall a few times himself because when his dad caught up to him...

He heard Robert Stevenson's voice in the background, his deep, steady tone trying to calm his mother, trying to get her to say something other than "He knows."

Yeah, really could've handled that better.

It took at least a minute before he heard someone pick up the phone. Then his dad sighed as he brought the phone up to his mouth.

"Hello, Son."

Oh, hell. His dad sounded just as bad as his mom, practically on the verge of tears.

"Damn it, Dad. I'm sorry, I shouldn't have just dropped that on Mom. I thought about coming home but we've got games and... Shit. *Shit.*"

"Brandon, are you okay? Did something happen? Did... Did you hurt someone or did... How did you find out?"

"It's kind of a long story and we probably shouldn't get into it on the phone. Look, I'm fine, honestly. And I didn't hurt anyone. I met someone and, well, I met someone who let your secret slip. Our secret, apparently. I just needed you to know that I know. And that I need to take a few days off from the team and I'm gonna use you and Mom as my excuse. I don't think the coach'll actually call to check up on me but if he does, I need you to cover for me. I'm gonna tell him you were injured and I need a few days for emergency leave."

"Brandon, how... what..."

"Dad, really, it's okay. I even get it." Kind of. At least, he understood the need to want your kids to have a normal life. Later there'd be time for questions and answers. "I just need to know you'll do this for me."

A pause as his dad took a deep breath. "Of course we will. And you're sure you're okay?"

"Yeah." He might not be later, but he didn't need to get them riled up now. They'd want to come down here and help and he didn't think he could deal with that right now. "We'll talk, Dad. Just not now. I gotta go. Just tell Mom I love her, okay? And I love you too."

"Brandon—" His dad sighed. "We'll be waiting for your call."

"I promise. As soon as I can. Love you both."

He hung up so he couldn't hear his mother crying. Then he called his coach and lied through his teeth.

Chapter 10

LUCY COULDN'T STOP WATCHING the hall, waiting for Brandon to emerge from making his phone calls.

She was so focused on waiting for him, she missed Catene slipping into the room.

"Lady Lucy, can I come in?"

Lucy turned to see the girl standing in the doorway to the kitchen, literally wringing her hands. Catene's blue eyes held shadows and she worried her bottom lip with her teeth.

"Of course. Come here and sit with me."

Catene practically ran across room to get to her but checked herself before she hit the couch where Lucy sat. As if she were afraid of Lucy.

Gods be damned, she'd never wanted to make the girl afraid of her. But she had kept her at arm's length because of her own selfish fears.

Reaching for the girl's hand, she drew Catene down onto the sofa and wrapped her arm around her shoulders.

At nearly nineteen, Catene stood a few inches taller than Lucy but was just as lushly built. And so damn beautiful, from the copper hair to those sapphire blue eyes. She looked nothing at all like Lucy... but then, maybe that was the point.

Catene looked almost startled at the show of affection from Lucy but she covered it fast by staring down at her hands, now twisted together in her lap.

"What's wrong, Catene?"

"Is Brandon going to be okay?"

"He's already healed and Dane doesn't expect there to be any lingering health problems."

The issue of his being *berserkir*, well, that was something else entirely.

"Was it... Was it my fault, Lady? Did I screw something up? Did I mess up the spell somehow? Did I—"

"Catene, sweetheart, no." Lucy pulled the girl closer, feeling the fear eating at her from the inside when Catene laid her head on Lucy's shoulder. "It was nothing you did. If it was anyone's fault, it was mine. I didn't take the time to consider all the consequences. I didn't look closely enough at the situation because I wanted *him*. And I let that blind me to everything else."

"But how could you have known what his parents did to him as a child?"

Lucy's lips twisted in a wry smile. "That's the problem with being a goddess. You think you should know everything."

"How is anyone supposed to know everything?"

Lucy just shook her head. "You're not. But no one tells you that."

Catene paused, as if thinking that over. Then she took a deep breath.

"Lady, I don't think I'm the person everyone needs me to be."

Lucy froze. Did the girl actually know? She knew Ty hadn't told her. Lucy wouldn't put it past Nortia to say something to Catene about what her future held. But her sister goddess would've told Lucy. Probably. Maybe.

"Catene, what are you talking about?"

"I know how much power I have." The girl's voice shook, just as her entire body did. "And I know I'm supposed to use it to help my community. But, Lady, I couldn't help Brandon. I didn't know what to do... I couldn't think and—"

"Catene, shh. Listen to me." Lucy ran a hand down the girl's bright hair, hugging her closer. "You didn't panic. You kept it to-gether and that's all anyone could have asked for. Sometimes there is no right way to handle a situation..Sometimes you do the best you can with what you've got."

And this girl was doing one hell of a good job, considering she didn't have all the pieces of her own puzzle.

"Mom."

Lucy squashed a smile at the hint of anxiety in Ty's voice. Only one person was able to put that note in his tone.

Catene stiffened beside her but didn't turn to look at Ty. And as much as Lucy wanted to ease this awkwardness for her son and this very strong young woman, it wasn't her place. They'd have to work it out for themselves.

Just as she and Brandon needed to find their way. Together. She was responsible for him now.

"Ty, is something wrong?"

"No, nothing's wrong. Just checking in with you."

And the fact that Catene sat here beside her meant nothing to him. Right.

"I'm fine, Ty, but I'm sure Catene could use some sleep. Why don't you walk her home?"

Of course, sometimes people could use just a little bit of a shove in the right direction. Catene stiffened next to her but her breath caught in her throat and she started to bite that lip again. Across the room, Ty looked like a rabbit caught in the headlights of an oncoming car. He had been the one to say they didn't have that much time.

Well, my son, consider this my first step toward doing something about this messed-up situation.

Then Ty blinked, and his face cleared back to his default expression—bored indifference. She would have smacked him across the back of his head if he'd been closer. Now who was hiding? Instead, she stood, pulling Catene to her feet as well. The girl could barely stand, she was that tired. Apparently she hadn't slept at all yet and it was almost Wednesday morning. "I want you to get some sleep, sweetheart. Ty will take you back to Kyle's or to your mom's, whichever you want. And Ty, I want you to stay and make sure she's okay. Do you understand?"

That order wasn't merely her interfering with their lives. She was worried about the girl, worried about what might happen if Charun realized who Catene was. What she was.

Ty's mouth flattened into a straight line but he nodded. Good. He understood. Not that she thought he'd leave Catene, but sometimes men needed to be reminded of certain things.

Lucy didn't think he was aware of the deep breath he took before he came forward, hand outstretched for Catene's.

After a split-second hesitation, the girl reached for him with her back straight. She tossed her hair over her shoulder as her chin tilted back and Ty's gaze followed the flow of copper.

The naked longing on his face nearly cracked Lucy's heart, but he hid the look between one blink and the next, took Catene's hand and tugged her toward him.

As Catene blinked up at him, he brought his free hand up and brushed it along those bright waves. Then he shocked the hell out of both of them by dropping a kiss on her forehead.

"Let's go, Catene. I'm pretty sure Kyle's crawling the walls by now, waiting for you."

They disappeared out the front door after grabbing coats from a rack on the wall. And Lucy stood there, just staring at the door until she heard Brandon clear his throat behind her.

"Everything okay?"

She turned to find him leaning against the wall to her left. The man looked steady as a rock, his dark gaze glued to hers, broad shoulders strong enough to take everything she'd thrown at him the past few days.

Simple jeans and a white T-shirt shouldn't be so damn appealing, but on him they looked edible. Especially with those bare feet.

"I should be asking you that. How did your parents react?"

Sighing, he rubbed a hand over his short dark hair. "About as well as you think. Shock, tears, a whole hell of a lot of what-the-fuck."

She took a few tentative steps toward him, then decided the time for being tentative had passed.

She still had Charun's demon on her ass. Brandon may have lost the career he loved because of her. And after so many millennia, she was tired of putting aside what she wanted for what she needed to do.

Her steps quickened until she fairly flew across the floor to him. Wrapping her arms around his waist, she tilted her head back as she felt one hand cup her nape while the other pressed against her back and drew her even closer.

He didn't kiss her right away, though. He stared down into her eyes, searching for something. And when his gaze narrowed and he lowered his mouth to cover hers, she figured he'd found whatever it was he needed to see.

His lips moved over hers like liquid heat, coaxing a response she held back only so he'd keep kissing her like this. Like he loved her.

The hand on her back began a slow slide upward, under her hair, wrapping his fingers in the strands and tugging her head back even farther. His tongue breached her lips, making her moan into his mouth even as his hips arched into her so she could feel his thick erection straining against the zipper fly.

Her hands flexed into his back, making him groan into her mouth. She wanted him again. Right here. On the floor, on the table, she didn't care where. She only knew she needed to be naked now. Their clothes fell to the floor next to them; lucky she hadn't just disintegrated them.

Brandon didn't even pause for a split second. He merely tilted his head to get a better, deeper angle on her mouth and let his hand slide down her back to cup her ass.

The next thing she knew, he'd lifted her with one hand on her ass, the other still plastered to her neck to hold her mouth on his.

He started to walk and she barely had time to realize it before he set her on the dining table. At least, she figured it was the dining table from the smooth, cool wood beneath her. Without a word, he put his hand on her shoulder, pressing her down until her back hit the table.

"I'd go down on you and eat you like breakfast but I can't wait."

She wanted to tell him she didn't care what he did, just so long as he made her come, but she couldn't form the words. Her brain had fallen into neutral while her body dropped full-gear into lust.

She could smell her own arousal, practically taste it. She wanted to taste Brandon but she wanted him to make love to her even more than she wanted to kiss him.

He apparently felt the same. Grabbing her legs, he slid his hands down until he had her ankles, which he then lifted to his left shoulder.

It put her at the perfect angle—

He thrust into her, his thick cock feeling even fuller because of the way he had her legs pressed together, and forced a moan from her throat. Sinking deep until his thighs pressed against her ass, he held there, staring down at her, one arm wrapped around her legs.

That gaze made her so hot, so needy. She needed him. More. Always. His free hand reached for her breasts, palming one and massaging it until the nipple was so sensitive, the ache spread through her entire body. Her clit throbbed, tucked between her thighs, untouched. Her sex pulsed around his swollen shaft, as if enticing him to move.

Instead he just stood there, watching her, switching his hand to her other breast and playing with that nipple until she could barely breathe, and each tiny ripple of her sex around his cock threatened to throw her into orgasm.

Which was exactly what she wanted. She wanted to come, but first she wanted him to shaft hard and deep and fill her with his seed.

Lifting her hips, she tightened those muscles that were already clenched around him and watched his eyes narrow even further. The muscles in his arms trembled and she felt that quiver pass through the rest of him. Even in his cock, which seemed to swell even more.

"You know I love you, right?"

It took her a second to realize what he'd said in that soft, soft voice, but she heard the meaning loud and clear.

Tears welled but she blinked them back. Instead, she nodded. "Yes, I know. And I love you, too."

She wasn't about to lie or hold back anything now. Not when every second brought her closer to a vow so true, it would change not only her existence but the lives of her son and the *lucani*, as well. She owed him that. And he would own her from now until their time was done. His expression hardened into pure sexual bliss and finally, *finally* he began to move.

Slowly at first. Not what she'd been expecting. She'd expected him to ravish her like he'd done in the other room. But this was more a claiming.

He withdrew as if savoring every friction-filled second, his eyes closing even farther but never completely. He never broke their connection and she fell into a state of heightened bliss, where every thrust pushed her closer to the brink of meltdown and every retreat made her moan in abject delight.

It made no sense, nothing made sense. Only Brandon's control of her pleasure made perfect sense.

Sweat began to slick his body as he worked her, his cock sliding smoothly, eased by her free-flowing juices. The wet sounds rang out in the room, as did the sound of his thighs smacking her ass.

He groaned and spoke her name, lighting off a series of sparks low in her gut. The first sharp orgasm struck her and she cried out, her hands reaching above her head for the side of the table, to anchor her, ground her. Her eyes tried to close but she forced them to stay open, to watch his face as he pounded into her now, fierce and hot. His gaze burned, the connection between them palpable.

And when he came, she watched him throw his head back and his hips forward, lodging his cock deep inside. His chest rose and fell and she felt each panting movement against the back of her thighs. Which just made her shiver and shake.

And when he laid openmouthed kisses along the backs of her calves, the heat that had started to dissipate after her orgasm gave a little flare.

But just as she thought he might want another round, he gave a little laugh and pulled away just far enough to help her sit up.

"So now what?"

His question wasn't unexpected. The man certainly was direct. But she conveniently sidestepped the question she knew he was asking. The one about what the future held for them.

"Now I think we need to speak with my sister goddesses and try to determine what, if anything, we can do about Charun."

They got dressed, though Lucy had to admit she wished he'd just stay naked.

Brandon had a beautiful body, so wonderfully male. Even the scars added to his appeal. She wanted to run her tongue over each and every one of them, to bite the strong muscles in his arms that flexed as he pulled up his jeans and the abs that rippled when he pulled his shirt down over his head.

He caught her staring and his mouth curved in a wicked grin

but just as he opened his mouth to say something, Sal burst through the front door.

"Lucy! You've got to come quick."

Fear coated his words, digging into her with sharp talons. Brandon turned as she scrambled to finish buttoning her jeans.

"What's wrong? Sal, what is it?"

The *salbinelli* skidded to a stop in front of her, his hooves scratching the wood floor in his haste.

"Attack at the village. *Tukhulkha* demon. Several injuries. Cole's already sent a team including Kyle and the *sicari*."

An ice shaft plunged directly into her heart. She might have fallen over if not for Brandon, who wrapped an arm around her waist and plastered himself to her back. She appreciated the solidity of him because her body went boneless with fear.

"I can send you and Brandon directly to the bar." Sal had already begun to draw power. She felt it gathering in the air around them. "You'll be there before the cavalry but maybe your *berserkir* will be enough to scare it off again."

"Then send us." The firm command in Brandon's voice made her heart begin to beat again.

She nodded when Sal looked at her and he wasted no time transporting them. They arrived in the middle of a fierce battle. The fury of sound stunned Lucy for a few brief seconds as she took in the scene.

Three wolves lay on the floor of the bar, unmoving. Caeles slumped, bleeding and unconscious, barely keeping at bay the *tukhulkha* demon that'd attacked them the other night, while another demon wrestled with two other wolves.

Brandon made a move toward the two wolves and their demon but she grabbed his arm before he could get ahead of her and wade into the fight.

"Caeles. Brandon, you need to get Caeles and the injured wolves out of the fighting."

Brandon's gaze arrowed in on her son, lying motionless on the floor. Then he looked at the others who were still fighting. Nodding, he crouched down and headed for her son.

She knew the demons had sensed her presence the moment she appeared and they hissed in unison when she headed straight for the closest.

That one's lips pulled back in a snarl that showed off its impressive sharp teeth. The venom those teeth could pump into a victim would paralyze anyone, including a deity. She had no doubt it would work on her, which was why she wouldn't get bit.

"Brian, James, go help Lidia and Trev. Casey, come here to me."

Her wolves paused for a brief second before Brian and James took off across the room to aid the others. Casey backed up until he stood by her side. The demon facing her smiled, flipping the dagger in his hand over and over. Mocking her.

"I see you brought your new pet with you. Sorry about the others," the demon motioned at the floor, "but they did attack us first."

"Only after you invaded my territory." She gave him her haughtiest glare. "You should leave now, before one or both of you meet an untimely end."

The demon laughed. "Oh, you know I don't care about my colleague over there. We don't exactly form lasting bonds the way you sun planers do. Those of us who live in the twilight planes know we can only count on ourselves. That one is just a… convenient distraction."

A distraction, Lucy knew, that would fight until it either died or accomplished its mission.

"What I don't understand," the demon continued, "is why you don't just come with us? Why would you want to see your pets injured?"

Out of the corner of her eye, she saw Brandon reach Caeles. She figured Brandon would pull her son behind the bar to protect him. At least, that's what she hoped he'd do. Then stay there, out of the way so she wouldn't have to worry about him.

"They're not my pets and I don't want them to be injured. But when you attack, they defend. You should know that."

"Yes, they came to the boy's defense quickly. And the boy put up a hell of a fight. He really did. You trained him well. Too bad it won't matter."

"You won't take him or any others today." Lucy made sure she kept eye contact with the demon, keeping its focus squarely on her. "And I will never go with you. You're outnumbered. You need to leave before we kill you."

"Outnumbered?" The demon turned its head to the side and showed off those teeth in another grin. "Now that's an interesting concept, isn't it? I guess it all depends on your point of view, doesn't it?"

Lucy didn't like the sound of that. She didn't like the demon's cocky attitude or its too-comfortable stance. With a thought, she conjured her bow into her hands. Made of oak from the forests of ancient Etruria, the plain crescent bow looked exceedingly normal. But its string was made of braided hair from her own head, its accuracy unmatched and its strength legendary.

As a moon goddess, she'd had a bow in her hands since before she could remember. It was an extension of her arm, of her very senses.

If she released the cocked arrow, she had no doubt she would drive it through the demon's black heart, giving her time to cut its head from its neck and kill it.

"Ah, the fabled Titan Killer, the bow that felled Astraeus. How unimpressive it looks, but then I guess you shouldn't be deceived by looks."

Shock blew through Lucy at the demon's matter-of-fact statement. How could it know what she'd gone to such lengths to hide? For so many years, she'd lived with the truth of what she'd done. That she'd murdered her son's father.

No one was supposed to know. No one *could* know, otherwise she would have been hunted down and dismembered by now.

The Titans may hate each other but they were like a pack of feral dogs when it came to protecting their own. If they'd even suspected what had happened with Astraeus, nothing could have saved her.

And if they knew Ty was his son… They would have killed him. The Titans allowed none of their children to live. Their offspring tended to kill them if they didn't kill them first.

Most people thought those Greek myths were just stories.

Stupid.

So how had this demon known what no one else could? And did it even matter now?

No.

The safety of her *lucani*, her sons, and Brandon were all that mattered right now. She took the shot. And watched the demon's eyes widen as it realized she had it dead to rights. In the split second it took for the arrow to reach it, the demon tried to dodge out of the way.

It was only somewhat successful. The arrow scraped a furrow along the side of the demon's head as it sprang forward, trying to get to her.

Or was it?

Instead of leaping for her, it bounded toward the bar.

Toward Brandon and Caeles.

Lucy spun to follow and caught sight of the demon just before it disappeared behind the bar.

She cried out a warning to Brandon but a second later, the demon came flying back over the bar as Brandon flung it with an animalistic snarl nearly across the room.

Blessed Mother Goddess. She hadn't truly understood what Sal had meant when he'd tried to explain how the *berserkir* had evolved beyond their animal. Brandon hadn't transformed into a bear but he'd taken on the spirit of it.

Dagger-sharp claws sprouted from his fingers, and he had

dangerous-looking fangs. His body had seemed to expand and grow at least several inches. As she stood, frozen in place, he leaped over the bar, flinging himself after the demon as if he meant to tear it to pieces.

She stood there, rooted to the floor. The fighting continued all around her, the sound of it jarring and confusing. She'd nocked another arrow but couldn't shoot a demon without hitting one of her wolves or Brandon.

Brandon landed on the demon but the demon had been ready for him, rolling onto its back so it caught him with its hands and feet and pushed him back.

Brandon stumbled, knocking into the wolves who were battling the other demon and scattering them, giving the demon an opening to attack.

One of the wolves howled in pain as that demon swiped its claws across his haunch. She had to do something. Anything.

She lifted her bow but Brandon recovered and leaped back at his demon, cutting off her shot. She changed her aim but the wolves had swarmed the other demon. She couldn't get off a shot without possibly hitting a wolf.

Then she saw it. A third demon had Caeles slung over its back and had almost made it through the door to the kitchen.

"No!"

Fear pumped through her veins as she realized her inadvertent cry had warned the demon she was onto it.

It took off through the kitchen, with her in frenzied pursuit. Her only thought was to retrieve her son. She knew it was foolish. Knew it was the only thing she could do. Everyone else was engaged. It's what they'd planned all along. How could she have been so stupid?

She ran full out, but the demon outpaced her, even with Caeles bouncing on its shoulder. It headed into the forest and she lost sight of them, her breath catching in her throat painfully.

Rage bubbled and burned as the light of the sun mocked her,

sapping her strength and causing her to stumble. She fell farther behind, even as she heard the howl of a wolf behind her.

She pushed back to her feet, forcing herself to continue, to follow. She couldn't lose Caeles. A black wolf caught up to her, those topaz eyes clearly marking him Kyle, Cole's lead *sicari*. The king's assassin.

"It has Caeles." She could barely speak the words through the fear tightening her throat and the lack of breath. "Kyle, you've got to—"

Kyle raced ahead without waiting for her to finish, a streak of black among the brown tree trunks. She tried to keep up but couldn't. The damn sun's rays were overpowering her and sapping her strength. Stumbling over a tree root, she hit the trunk then fell to her knees.

More wolves were behind her but they weren't going to make it in time to help Kyle.

The ground shuddered beneath her as the demon opened a portal between the planes. She didn't have to see it happen to know that's what had happened. She felt the power it used, felt the rush of sensation and the utter terror of knowing her son had been taken. Tears streamed down her face, though she hadn't realized she was crying. Behind her, more footsteps sounded.

"Lucy!"

She turned and found herself engulfed in Brandon's embrace. Her face pressed against his chest, his arms holding her together.

"Your wolves took down one." He spoke directly into her ear. "The other got away."

She bit back a sob. "They took Caeles. They took my son."

"Shit!" His voice rumbled deep in his chest, and he followed it with a growl that should have made her nervous but didn't. She looked up to find Brandon still sporting fangs and felt the prick of his claws through her clothes.

She also smelled blood and her stomach roiled. "Tinia's teat, are you injured? Brandon, let me see."

Panic made her pull back so she could let her hands check his body from shoulders to waist. His T-shirt had several tears and so did his jeans but every cut seemed superficial.

As her hands ran over him, she felt him revert back to his natural form, almost as if the magic was leaking out of him now that the threat was gone and the adrenaline had faded.

"Lucy, calm down. I'm fine. Just a few scrapes."

A large black wolf bounded back to their side. It yipped at them, then made a beeline back to Lucy's home.

"Come on, baby." Brandon tugged on her hand when she didn't know quite what to do. "Let's get back. We need a plan."

Chapter 11

"I DON'T BELIEVE THEY'RE going to harm him, Lady. They want you. They're going to use Caeles as leverage or bait."

Leaning against the bar, Brandon watched Kyle with the same careful stare he'd give a rabid pit bull. The man looked calm enough, but Brandon swore he could feel the waves of deadly intent coming off the guy.

Earlier, Brand had asked Sal what *sicari* meant.

Assassin.

Yeah, Brand had absolutely no problem believing Kyle was an assassin. This guy could kill you with one hand tied behind his back before you ever realized he was in the same room. Probably with that same look on his face.

"We need to come up with a plan—"

"There will be no plan." Lucy slashed a hand through the air in front of her. "When the demon makes contact, I will tell it I'll make the trade."

Brand wasn't the only one who had a loud objection to that. Kyle and Sal began to argue as well. Lucy didn't appear to be listening to any of it. She only continued to stare through the front window of the bar. Around her feet, five *lucani* lay sprawled in their wolf bodies, panting and exhausted. To her left, Kyle's mate, Tam, tended to the three worst cases along with the *lucani* doctor, Dane.

The conscious wolves whined and pawed at the floor, apparently adding their two cents to Lucy's crazy plan.

"Lucy." Brand grabbed her hand but she wouldn't look at him. "Lucy, Goddamn it, *look* at me."

Everyone else went silent, tensing as if waiting for an explosion. And from the look on Lucy's face, maybe they were going to get one. Her anger was starting to bleed through the carefully composed mask of her face. He had a feeling that if she released her hold on that anger, she could bring down the building.

He had no trouble seeing her as a goddess in that moment. Regal and fearsome. But she was still the woman he loved.

"You can't give yourself up. I won't let you."

Someone actually gasped. He assumed it was Tam. It sounded female. He probably should've taken that as a warning but there was no way he would let her commit suicide. And from what she'd told him, that's what would happen.

Charun would consume her and she would cease to exist. Sounded like suicide to him.

"You do not tell me what I can and cannot do."

Wow, her voice sounded much more lethal when she spoke normally than it would have if she'd shouted. And her gaze, hell, she could cut glass with it. He didn't care. He refused to back down. She wouldn't hurt him. He just couldn't make himself believe she would. "I can if what you're planning is suicide. I refuse to lose you. Not now."

"My life has been over for centuries."

Shit. *Shit.* This went deeper than just Caeles's kidnapping. His chest ached as if someone had stuck a knife through it recently. Hey, whaddaya know, someone actually had. This hurt worse. Damn it, she couldn't do this to him. Not now.

"And mine only really started the night I met you."

He hadn't meant to just blurt that out, not in front of an entire room full of people. Even if he did mean every word of it. He should've waited until he got her alone, waited until she wasn't so worried about Caeles, when she wasn't so stressed.

Shit, he really was an idiot—

She reached up to cup his cheek in one hand as she stared into his eyes, searching… For what, he didn't have a clue.

Then she sighed and shook her head as she drew back her hand. "I can't be what you want, Brandon." Then she turned away, dismissing him between one heartbeat and the next. "Sal, Kyle, we need to talk. Outside. Now, plea—"

"Bullshit."

Brand picked her up in his arms and headed for the stairs to the second floor. He expected her to scream and yell. To beat on him with her fists while she called him names. Instead, she went deadly still and silent.

He took the stairs two at a time, vaguely realizing that he barely felt her weight. What he did feel was her stone-cold fury. And he knew it was about to break all over him. Yeah, he'd probably broken about five hundred rules of goddess etiquette, especially considering he'd just defied her then snatched her up and stormed out of a room filled with her worshippers. He didn't care. He couldn't lose her. Not now.

When he reached the living room, he set her on the couch then stood in front of her, waiting.

"Lucy."

She lifted her gaze from the hole she'd been burning in the wall to his left and he nearly took a step back. Jesus, she looked ready to kill. As if she didn't know or care who he was. Only that he stood against her.

"You can't give yourself over to the demon. It's suicide."

She didn't answer this time. Only stared at him with that burning gaze.

And fear began to ice his blood. Not fear that she'd hurt him, although she looked like she could tear him limb from limb. No, he feared he wouldn't be able to reach her and he'd lose her to the grief he saw in her eyes. That she'd actually go forward with her plan and he'd never see her again.

Christ, he'd just met her. He'd had four fucking days with her and he wanted at least another hundred years, if not an eternity. He knew they didn't have forever. Knew she would still be here when he was long gone, but... Fuck, it hurt that she wouldn't fight, at least just a little bit, to be here with him.

"There has to be another way, Lucy. Or did you not mean what you said? Don't you love me?"

She didn't answer, and he felt that vise on his chest crank a little tighter. Alright, he'd try another angle.

"Do you think this is what Caeles would want you to do?"

Apparently he'd said the magic word because he saw the first crack in her composure as her eyes narrowed.

"You don't have any idea what Caeles would want me to do."

"No, but I know I wouldn't want my mother to give up her life without at least a little bit of a fight."

She took a moment, as if to collect her thoughts. And when she finally spoke, her tone was precise and refined. "When I took Caeles into my heart, into my home, I promised that I would never abandon him. I won't leave him to be tormented and abused by a *tukhulkha* demon. Or to spend an eternity tormented in Aitás by Charun. My days are numbered. The countdown started nineteen years ago. I was just too arrogant and foolish to realize what that meant."

Brand shook his head. "What happened nineteen years ago? Tell me what you're talking about, Lucy. Please."

She shook her head, though he didn't think she was telling him no because she continued. "I didn't realize at first, and then when I finally saw what was right in front of my face, I still refused to believe."

"Believe what?"

Her eyes closed and he finally saw some of molten anger slip away. But it was leaving an aching vulnerability in its wake. And that cut him to the bone.

"That I was truly obsolete."

"Lucy—"

"Nineteen years ago, my replacement was born."

He blinked, unsure she'd said what he thought she said. "Did you say replacement?"

She continued on as if she hadn't heard him. "My *lucani* are strong enough without me and the *Enu* and *Fata* no longer need a goddess to control the course of the moon. But nature has its own plan and when one tree dies and falls to the ground in the forest, another springs forth."

He tried to sift through the meaning behind her words, tried to understand what she was saying, but he was still missing pieces. He did know one thing, though. "Your people love you."

"They worship me out of habit." She spat the last word like a curse. "I do not want to be a habit."

"They respect you. They look to you for guidance—"

"I am useless!" The fury was back and it was directed inward. "I've been kidding myself for decades, for centuries. It's time to stop. And it's time to do what I should have done when the girl was born."

"Lucy, come on. Just talk to me. Explain to me what you're talking about so I understand. Don't shut me out now. Not now."

With a shuddering breath, she finally looked at him, really looked at him. "The girl, Catene. When she was born, I knew, but I didn't want to believe. Now, I can't ignore the signs any longer. It's time to transfer my remaining powers to her so she can lead the *lucani* through the next age. She's always been meant for Ty. It's time to make her place official.

"And when we transfer my power, I'll be useless to Charun. But the demon won't know that, of course, and it will trade me for Caeles. Caeles will be freed."

"And you'll be gone."

She shrugged as if her fate didn't matter. Christ, he swore he felt her slipping away from him with every second.

"Does Cat get a say in any of this?"

"Catene knows. Even if she's never said anything, she knows there's something special about her. And even if she doesn't know exactly what it is, she knows her future is with Ty. Even if he refuses to acknowledge it."

"So you're just gonna push this on her, whether she wants it or not?"

He saw the trace of anguish that flashed through Lucy's eyes before she blinked it away. "She understands duty, Brandon. She loves her people. She'll make a damn fine goddess. And I will save my son."

He understood where she was coming from. Christ, it all made perfect fucking sense now. Except the part where he lost her forever. That part made no fucking sense at all.

"There's gotta be another way, Lucy." He reached for her shoulders, felt the warm heat of her body seep into his and wanted to shake her until she understood. He couldn't lose her. "I need you to fight because I don't want to live without you."

Her gaze softened as she stared into his eyes, changing from hard silver to a liquid gray that drew him closer, drew his lips down to her to kiss her with an increasing desperation.

Her hands cupped his jaw as he slanted his mouth to get a better angle, to let him slip his tongue deeper into her mouth and suck in her essence. She let him take what he wanted, let him ravage her mouth, which just made him even more desperate. He swore he felt her slipping through his fingers already.

"Lucy, please—"

She laid her finger over his lips, shutting off his pleas. "Sal is coming up the stairs. I need to speak to Catene. Kyle will fight me on this and I can't blame him. But even he understands destiny. And this is Catene's destiny, which I've denied her for too long."

"Fine, do whatever you need to do with Cat. I'm not saying don't do it. But please, Lucy. Don't just toss your life away like it no longer means anything."

"If I can secure Caeles's safe release, that will not be throwing away my life."

Frustration had him grinding his back teeth together. "Fine, I get that. I understand. But what if we can find another way? What if we can find a way that doesn't involve certain death for you?"

Her lips tilted in a semblance of a smile. "I'm willing to entertain ideas. But I won't allow Caeles to be harmed."

Brandon felt like he'd been given a reprieve from a death sentence. "Great, that's great. Then let's talk to Sal and figure this out."

"Yes. Then I have a long-overdue conversation to hold."

"When do you want to perform the ritual?"

Lucy blinked, unsure if she'd heard Catene correctly. Then she took a hard look at the girl.

Her clear, bright gaze stared back, a little fear but no outright terror in her expression, nor confusion over what was to happen. Lucy looked down at the girl's hands, found them steady and still on her thighs.

Kyle had delivered Catene ten minutes ago, his expression so dark, Lucy had felt Brandon stiffen beside her. She knew Kyle wouldn't hurt her but he could be persuaded to take out his frustration on the nearest punching bag. Right now, she knew Brandon would be happy to oblige. They could kill each other if they weren't careful. Kyle's wolf was so close to the surface and Brandon's *berserkir* was so new to him.

Just another worry to add to the growing list. Which included Cat's confounding reaction.

"Catene, are you sure you understand what I'm saying? If we do this, you become the repository of my power for the Etruscan people. You will take over the mantle of the moon goddess and all the responsibilities inherent."

"Will I be a goddess?"

"Yes, for all intents and purposes. At least, that's what I believe. I don't know what will happen. This has never been done before."

"Then how do you know this is what's meant to be?"

Cat's question held no aggression or fear, just plain and simple curiosity.

Lucy just shook her head. "I've known since the moment of your birth. I can't explain it any better than that. Just as I think you've always known you were meant to be more than a *lucani* with *strega* powers."

Cat's gaze slid to her father, Kyle, who'd shoved himself in a dark corner and seemed to be holding himself there through sheer force of will, before recapturing Lucy's.

"Yes." Her voice dropped to just above a whisper. "I've known for a few years. I just didn't completely understand."

And she'd had no one to talk to about it. Lucy had avoided the subject completely and Ty had distanced himself as she'd grown from adorable child to enticing teenager.

The girl hadn't wanted to upset her parents by telling them what she'd suspected. How do you tell the parents you adore that you'd been born to become the new Goddess of the Moon? That the powers she controlled would only get stronger, as she faced an uncertain future as a goddess in a world where deities were myths and her own people might not really need her anymore?

Lucy leaned forward and grabbed Cat's hand. "I'm sorry. It was not my intention to spring this on you so abruptly. I honestly thought we'd have more time to work our way through this, to let everyone come to grips with what this meant. I never expected Charun to threaten my son or force my hand. But I can't allow Caeles to pay for my mistakes. And… there may be a way to hide the fact that you've taken my powers. At least for a little while. Long enough to keep you safe from Charun until you know better how to protect yourself."

"Will I have to go away?"

The first hint of distress entered the girl's voice and it tore at Lucy's heart.

"I don't know. It may come down to that, yes." Catene's gaze dropped but Lucy squeezed the girl's hand until she looked back. "But if my idea works, no one beyond the people we choose to tell will know what's happened. Besides, most of our people no longer hold to the old ways. They don't worship because they know their deities' powers are fading even as their individual power begins to grow."

Another fact of life Lucy had been ignoring. "Change is coming, Catene. I don't know how or what will happen when it does, but I know you feel it too."

Cat shot another quick glance toward Kyle's corner before she nodded. "Yes. It's almost like the pull I feel during the full moon. I can almost touch it, it's so tangible. But it always slips through my fingers."

"Yes." Lucy smiled, amazed at the girl once again and knowing she shouldn't be. "That's exactly how it feels. You are meant to help guide our people forward. They need strong leaders. You and Ty will give them that."

Cat's gaze dropped and she started to worry her top lip between her teeth. "What if he refuses? What if he… rejects me?"

That was all the girl said, but Lucy heard the rest of her question as clearly as if she'd spoken.

What if he rejects me like he's been doing for the past year?

Lucy smiled, shaking her head. "Ty's known since the moment

of your birth what you mean to him. He's been by your side since that time. But he's still only a man, sweetheart. And you were a beautiful young girl, who only recently became a woman. Cut him some slack for giving you a little breathing room. And for not wanting your fathers to behead him."

Cat's laugh was short but natural. And it lifted a little bit of the fog Lucy had seen starting to cloud the girl's expression. When Catene lifted her gaze once more to Lucy's, it was with determination.

"Then let's do this."

Carpenter Barbie, the Etruscan Goddess edition, waited for them in the dimly lit hallway of a building in center-city Reading, holding a hammer and two very large, old-looking iron nails.

"Nortia," Lucy held out her arms to the other woman, who threw hers around Lucy's waist and squeezed tight before stepping away again. "Thanks for coming on such short notice."

The blonde cocked an eyebrow and a hip in her skin-tight jeans and form-fitting black sweater.

"You didn't exactly give me a choice, babe. Besides, you and I both know you need me for this. Only I can cut fate's strings. For now, anyway." Nortia shook her head as her lips curved in a grimace. "I mean, I saw the signs begin five centuries ago. I knew this was coming. I guess I just tried to put it out of my mind. Are you really sure it's come to this?"

Lucy nodded, arms crossing over her chest as if protecting herself. "Yes. I'm sure."

With her hands rubbing her arms, Lucy looked cold. Without another thought, Brandon stepped up and wrapped his arms around her body, pulling her back against him. He thought she'd resist, want to stand on her own. Instead, she let herself sink into him. And that actually made his worry kick into overdrive. Goddamn it, he couldn't lose her, not now. It wasn't fucking fair.

"Brandon, a little tight, dear."

He immediately loosened his arms. Shit, now he'd almost hurt her.

Lucy rubbed her hands on his arms, as if to comfort him. "Nortia, I'd like you meet Brandon Stevenson. Brandon, this is my sister goddess Nortia."

He took the delicate-looking hand the little blonde bombshell held out to him and met her direct green stare straight on.

"So you're the hockey player everyone's been talking about." Nortia looked him up and down as she released his hand. "Nice to meet you. I'm Fate, so don't fuck with me or my sisters or you'll find out why they say Fate's worse than death."

He didn't exactly know how to respond to that as Lucy began to laugh. "I believe the saying is 'a fate worse than death,' Norty."

The blonde flipped her hair over one shoulder and gave a shrug. "They also say 'Fate's a bitch' and those who've gotten on my bad side know that's for damn sure."

"Unfortunately, her bark is as bad as her bite." Lucy smiled up at Brand, though her lips held a faint quiver. "She's the Goddess of Fate, if you haven't already figured that out."

"I was kinda going in that direction, yeah. Lucy…"

She reached up and pulled him down with one hand on his jaw. Their lips met in a kiss that could have very easily combusted but didn't. They both knew it wasn't the time or the place. Her smile made him take a deep breath.

"I'll collect on the rest of that later," he said, before pressing one more hard kiss to her lips.

"I'll make sure you do."

He stared into her eyes for a few more seconds, willing her to see how determined he was. Then he forced himself to release her.

They were back at an altar but this one was in center city Reading. In an honest-to-God marble temple that looked like it'd been transported out of ancient Italy.

Mosaics covered the floor, marble columns reached to the ceiling, and an altar of marble ten times as ornate as the one in the woods sat large as life in front of the room.

This altar looked like it'd seen more than a few sacrifices in its time.

Christ, he felt like he'd been transported back at least a couple of thousand years. Cat and Lucy had exchanged their jeans and shirts for freaking togas, although they didn't call them that.

Only Nortia and Sal would be allowed in the temple during the ceremony. Cat's parents had wanted to be there but Cat had shook her head and told them no.

Kyle had argued in a low, furious voice. Kyle's mate, Tam, had turned away with tears in her eyes, while Margorie, Cat's mother, had tried hard to hold back her own tears while her mate, Dan, just shook his head and stared at the ceiling. Nothing changed Cat's mind. She just said no, hugged each member of her family, then turned and walked into the temple.

Lucy had already gone in, and Brand had started to pace like an expectant father. The hallway provided enough room for him to do so without rubbing up against anyone else.

He heard faint noises from the kitchens of The Cellar, the restaurant that occupied the front of the building. Christ, he'd actually eaten here a couple of times with the coach and his wife and he'd never suspected. Hell, who would suspect that a temple to an Etruscan goddess would be here anyway?

Sal was the last to enter the room, hooves clicking against the marble floor. He didn't look at anyone as he drew the heavy wood doors closed with an audible thud.

Brand slumped back against the nearest wall and prepared for an excruciating wait.

—∽∽∽—

"Catene, I have to ask again." Nortia stared the girl straight in the eyes, her gaze piercing. "Are you absolutely sure you want to do this? Knowing that your life will never be the same?"

Lucy realized she held her breath as Catene stayed silent. This entire plan hinged on the girl's willingness to assume her role. If she didn't, well, Lucy would still be trading herself for Caeles and Charun would be one goddess closer to escaping Aitás.

"I *am* prepared, Ladies. I just… there's so much I don't know." Catene turned to Lucy, her eyes shimmering with unshed tears. "Lady Lucy, I'm going to need your help. I don't want to do this alone."

Lucy grabbed the girl's hand, her heart breaking at the fear she now saw in the girl's eyes. "You won't be alone, Catene. You'll have your parents. You'll have Sal and Nortia and Amity and the rest of the pantheon by your side. And Ty will be here for you. You know that. He won't let you down."

"What if I'm not strong enough, Lady?" The girl had her *cimaruta* charm, much like the one she'd given Brandon, clutched in her own hand. "What if I can't be what they need me to be?"

Lucy smiled, knowing that in this, at least, Catene had nothing to worry about. "For the past millennium, I've been mostly useless to our people. I've been able to use what little power I have left to strengthen the wards on the *lucani* den and my own little village. I've also been able to boost Cole's powers, but Catene… I just don't have the power you do. Our people need someone young, someone fresh. They need you. Everything you do will be different because you're a different person. I can't tell you how things will go. Not even Nortia will be able to tell you that. A goddess's fate isn't set like a mortal's is. And even mortals can change their own fate if they're strong enough."

"Or they beg enough," Nortia added.

Lucy gave her sister goddess a slight smile, knowing Nortia's defense mechanism against emotional turmoil was sarcasm.

"You will find your way just as we did. And it will be the right way because it will be yours. Do you understand?"

After a few silent seconds, Catene nodded. "Yes. I understand. Okay." Catene grabbed Lucy's hand and squeezed tight. "I'm ready."

Lucy felt her lungs release the breath she'd been holding in. "Okay. Nortia?"

"Well, since we're all winging this," Nortia twirled the hammer in her hand like a baton, "we better get started. Lucy, Catene, on the altar. Sal, get your chant on. And let's all pray to the Great Mother Goddess that we don't fuck this up."

Lucy didn't know how much later it was when she opened her eyes.

She only knew she felt empty. As if someone had taken a giant ice cream scoop and used it to clean out her body.

"Lucy, don't move." Nortia's voice seeped through the ringing in her ears. "The transfer's almost complete."

Forcing her eyes to focus, Lucy stared at the ceiling above her.

She felt the warmth of Catene's body next to her as they lay side by side on the altar but she couldn't tell if the girl was awake or unconscious.

Probably the latter.

Lucy had lost consciousness for a short period of time after Nortia had given her the hammer and she'd pounded one of the nails into the wall of the temple right by the door.

Every December, in her role as the Goddess of Fate, Nortia cut the strands of fate of the past year, basically wiping the slate clean for the next year, by hammering one of her nails into the doorway of this temple.

When Lucy had pounded her nail into the wall, she'd cut her own fate's strings.

She was pretty sure that's when she'd passed out, so she wasn't sure what had happened to Catene when she'd removed the same nail and repeated the ritual, making Catene the repository of Lucy's power.

It shouldn't have been painful. But that emptiness *hurt*.

She refused to cry, though. Instead, she thought of Brandon. His warm dark eyes. His easy smile and the intense look he got when he was making love to her. Yes, thinking about Brandon making love to her was much better than thinking about anything else.

"Lucy, how are you holding up?" Nortia's hand gripped hers.

"I'm fine." Physically. "How's Catene?"

Nortia didn't answer right away and Lucy turned to focus on Cat's face.

Her breath caught in her throat. Blessed Mother Goddess, the girl looked so pale. Beautiful, but so still... like Snow White in the glass casket. All they needed were a few dwarves to make the scene complete. Of course, they had Sal, but he certainly wouldn't want to be compared to Sleepy and Grumpy, although Grumpy did occasionally fit him...

Lucy closed her eyes and allowed herself to drift off again, dreaming of her own Prince Charming waiting to kiss her back to life.

Brand heard the faint sound from inside the temple at the same time Kyle and Dan stood abruptly.

Apparently *berserkir* heard just as well as *lucani*.

Margie and Tam, who'd taken his place pacing the hallway for the past five minutes, stopped and ran back to their mates just as the door opened and Sal stuck his head through.

"Everybody made it through." Sal put out his hand to stop Kyle from barging past him. "You're gonna need to give Cat a few minutes. She doesn't want you to see her yet."

"Is she okay?" Margie's voice held tears and she had to take a deep breath before she continued. "Is everything…"

She couldn't continue and Dan tightened his arms around her.

Sal reached for Margie's hand. "She's gonna be fine." Then he turned to Brand. "You need to come in."

The air left his lungs in a rush, as if someone had hit him.

Something had happened to Lucy. He knew it. He could barely smell Lucy. How was that possible? Pushing off the wall, he slid past Sal. The *salbinelli* wouldn't have been able to stop him. He had to get to her and nothing was going to stand in his way.

But when he saw here, so still and pale on the altar, his heart fell into his stomach and he nearly stumbled. He barely noticed Cat, standing at the side of the altar as Nortia helped steady her.

Reaching for Lucy's nearest hand, he laced their fingers together. "I know she looks bad but we can't find anything wrong with her." Sal let his hand fall on Lucy's shoulder. "We just haven't been able to wake her."

That worried Sal. Brand could hear it in the guy's voice. He tried not to let that freak him out more than he already was. Which was pretty damn freaked out. He didn't say anything, just watched Lucy for any sign that she was waking.

Damn, she was cold. He shrugged out of his coat and lifted her so he could wrap her in it, then held her in his arms. "Can I take her back to my place?"

"I think she should go to the *boschetta*," Catene spoke in a low, careful tone, as if she was relearning the language. "Nica and Mom can keep an eye on her and I'll be there—"

"No. I need to be home for the demon to find me."

He looked down to see Lucy staring up at him, her gray eyes so dull, it made his heart hurt. "Jesus, Lucy, you're in no condition—"

"I need to go home. I'll be fine after a few hours' sleep. That's all I need. You and a bed, Brandon. Please."

He wanted to give her anything she wanted but she looked so weak. Fear made his stomach cramp and he looked at Sal for guidance.

Sal just shook his head. "Lucy, you should let the *streghe* look after you—"

"No. I need rest. And the *streghe* can do nothing for me that a few hours of rest will not accomplish. I'll have Cole send a few *sicari* to patrol. Sal, I'll be fine."

Would she be? Damn it, he'd make sure she was. Sal apparently realized he wasn't going to get anywhere with her so, with a sigh, he capitulated.

"But you need to take it easy. I don't know how much I need to stress that."

She smiled, but it looked weak. "And I plan to, Sal. Please, just send us home."

Minutes later, Brandon carried Lucy from her living room, where Sal had transported them, to her bedroom, where he set her on the bed. He released a tired sigh as she started to rise.

"Lucy, you need to lie down."

"And I will. But first I want a shower."

She looked so damn fragile, he didn't want her to be standing, not even for a shower. "How about a bath?"

Her smile made the gray of her eyes brighten for a brief second. "Only if you agree to wash my hair."

"Sweetheart, don't you know yet? I'll do anything for you?"

He had water running into the huge claw-foot tub in seconds and went back for her. She'd already shrugged off his coat and was working on her toga when he returned.

"Here, let me."

He reached for the gold brooch holding the whole thing together at her shoulder. It looked like a miniature shield, but with a brilliant ruby at its center. Ancient and heavy, the piece felt warm in his hand. But her skin was so cold.

"Come on, babe. Let's get you into the water."

After carrying her into the bathroom, he stood her on her feet for the five seconds it took to get the toga to fall to the ground. Then he set her as carefully as he could in the tub. She leaned her head against the rim and sighed, her eyes closing as her expression slackened with bliss.

"This was the best idea." Her speech sounded weak but not slurred. "But it'd be better if you were in here with me."

Which was exactly where he wanted to be, though he planned to keep his shorts on. His heart rate still hadn't returned to normal and he didn't think he'd be able to get an erection even with a helping hand. But why take chances?

Stripped down to his boxers, he eased in behind her, the heat from the water soaking into his skin, loosening tight muscles, then put his arms around her as gently as he could.

"I'm not going to break, Brandon." She lifted her arms to rest them on top of his.

He heaved a sigh of relief and let his arms tighten around her the tiniest bit more.

"So everything went according to plan?"

She paused and he had the awful sensation the other shoe was about to drop.

"I suppose so," she finally said. "Catene and I are still breathing, I no longer feel those powers that I associated with being a goddess, and Catene's power has increased exponentially. I assume that means everything went according to plan."

Pressing his lips to her ear, he kissed the lobe. "I'm sorry you had to give up that part of yourself, Lucy. And I'll say this again and again until you understand exactly what I mean. I don't want you to commit suicide to save Caeles. Let's come up with a plan where everyone gets out alive."

"Wouldn't that be nice?"

Her voice had lowered and deepened, as if she were falling asleep, which probably wouldn't be a bad thing. After what she'd been through, she'd need to rest, especially if they were going to take on a demon and get back her son.

For the next few minutes, Brand let her rest against his chest and just breathe. The hot water surrounded them in a haze of jasmine-scented steam. He'd smell like her when they got out but he was okay with that. More than okay.

Hell, he didn't care if he smelled like a shampooed French poodle as long as she was around to notice. And speaking of shampoo… Grabbing the glass cup on the table next to the tub, he used it to soak her hair then picked up the tube of shampoo from the same table.

He worked the thick liquid into the long strands of her dark hair, massaging her scalp as he did. Her moan of sheer, sensual enjoyment had his skin tightening all over.

Forcing back his ever-present desire for her, he rinsed the shampoo from her hair then turned to pick a bath gel.

There were four kinds and he picked the one that reminded him of her. Moonlit Night. A little musky, a little floral, all woman. Perfect.

Instead of putting the gel on the sponge, he poured it into his hands. Starting at her shoulders, he smoothed the gel onto her skin. Silky bubbles formed, the scent combining with the bubble bath to create a heady perfume.

He washed every inch of skin he could reach without moving her, rubbing her still-tight shoulders and arms.

Stroking up her stomach, he cupped her breasts in his hands. He worked the pebbled nipples into stiff peaks with his thumbs and forefingers, watching her chest begin to rise and fall at a much faster pace as her head pressed back into his chest.

"Shh, sweetheart. Just relax."

Releasing her breasts, he used the cup to rinse her body then shifted her forward so he could reach her legs. He rubbed at her tight calf muscles, kneaded her thighs and hips until he brushed the small triangle of hair on her mound.

Breathing in sharply, she tilted her hips up, pressing his finger-tips into her flesh.

"Brandon." Her voice tried to loosen the strings of his tight control, but he refused to let it. He didn't want to tax her strength but he knew she gained power from orgasms. So he'd keep his dick in his pants. So to speak.

He knew she needed to rest, so he wouldn't draw this out. He'd learned enough about this woman in the four intense days they'd shared that he knew how to bring her off as quickly as possible. Letting his fingers slide between her thighs, he went straight for her clit. The little bundle of nerves was swollen and she flinched when he flicked it.

"Brandon." Her voice sounded like a moan.

"I know what you need, babe. Let me give it to you."

Her head turned on his shoulder, and he felt her lips graze along his throat, making his blood thicken.

Alright, he could do this without embarrassing himself by coming all over her back.

But if she moved her ass one more time—no. Pushing those thoughts aside, he used his fingers to caress her clit, starting with a slow, steady motion. The bubbles in the water created a silky glide as he rubbed her clit then slid down farther to play with her swollen lips.

Her hips shifted and pressed forward. She wanted more and he gave it to her. He increased the speed of his fingers, flicking her clit then sliding back down to play at her slit.

Lucy tensed, a moan passing through her lips on a breath of air as she inched closer to climax. He increased his speed but not too much, just enough to send her over the edge.

She shook, a full-body shudder that lasted almost a minute and left her boneless against him. His arms wrapped around her again, holding her tight against his body until the water had cooled considerably. Then he took her to bed.

⎯⎯

Lucy came awake with a start at the mental prod.

It's time. Meet me in the forest near the head of the small stream.

The *tukhulkha* demon holding her son.

Behind her, she felt the steady rise and fall of Brandon's chest. He slept now but she knew he'd awaken at the slightest movement from her. She didn't want him involved in her mess. Which was such a joke at the moment. He was most likely stronger than she was now. She needed him. She wanted him in her life and it was time she started acting as if she trusted him with her life. Something she'd never done with another man.

Rolling onto her back, she turned her head to look at Brandon. So beautiful, all those muscular lines chiseled and well defined, even in sleep.

She leaned forward to press a kiss against his lips and pulled back to watch his eyelids open to reveal dark, dark eyes.

"It's time."

She watched awareness fill his gaze as his lips quirked into a hard smile. "I'm ready."

Pushing away the doubt that wanted to paralyze her, she nodded then rolled to the side to sit. She felt remarkably refreshed. Apparently some things would remain the same.

The bed shimmied as Brandon got up and began dressing. She followed suit, choosing comfortable jeans and a bright pink T-shirt. The burst of color lifted her spirits and she knew she looked good in it. Which shouldn't mean a damn thing at this time but she needed every little bit of help she could get. Finally, she pulled on a pair of red hiking books and walked downstairs in silence with Brandon's arm around her shoulder.

Surprise, followed quickly by despair, hit her when she realized she hadn't felt the four *lucani* who waited in the bar for her. Some things *had* changed.

Kyle and his three fellow *sicari*—Duke, Nic, and Kaine—sat at the bar. They stopped talking and stood when she and Brandon walked in. The men bowed, and Kaine curtsied though Kyle knew damn well she no longer deserved the honor.

"Lady Lucy—"

"You no longer need to call me that, Kyle. You know—"

"I know you are still Lusna and will always be Lady Lucy." Kyle's gaze burned steady. "That won't ever change."

She had to swallow several times before she could manage all of two words. "Thank you."

To which Kyle nodded and continued. "Now, we need to put a plan together to get Caeles back without sacrificing you. And I think I've got an idea for that."

Kyle transferred his gaze to Brandon. "How would you like to play stupid human?"

"Won't work." Brandon shook his head. "That demon knew there was something different about me. It knew I was *berserkir* before anyone else did."

Kyle just nodded. "That's what we're counting on. You'll be the distraction. It'll expect you but you'll smell different than you did before. We're hoping that'll give us enough time to get Caeles and kill the damn thing. We need to send a message to Charun that no matter how many demons he sends to capture our goddesses, they'll fail because we're stronger."

"And what am I supposed to do?" Lucy asked.

"You need to stay out of that thing's way, Lady. We don't know if it'll be able to sense your… changes. We're going on the assumption that it won't or, if it does, it won't be able to figure out what's different until it's too late."

Kyle fell silent, watching her, waiting for her decision. Just as if she were still the *lucani*'s favored goddess. She couldn't let them down.

"Sounds like a plan. I'll let the demon know I'm coming."

Kyle and his *sicari* melted into the forest in two seconds flat.

Brandon couldn't hear, see, or smell them. Damn, they were good.

His job was to be more conspicuous. To attempt to be invisible, knowing he wasn't that good. But it might just be enough to throw the demon off. Might being the operative word.

Lucy had walked into the forest ten seconds after the *sicari* and Brandon followed seconds after her. He didn't have to see her to keep up. His sense of smell and his hearing had increased since his *berserkir* had been released. Even his eyesight had gotten sharper.

He found it relatively easy to keep up with her and even managed to keep his bumbling to a minimum.

That acrid scent he remembered from before reached his nose after about five minutes. The demon was out there. And close. Had it tracked Lucy from the house without any of them knowing? Probably. Fuck. Brandon took off at a lope, forgetting about trying to be silent. He needed to get to Lucy now. Because somehow the demon had managed to outmaneuver them.

"You didn't really think it would be that easy, did you. Lusna? Did you really think you'd just traipse into the forest with your *berserkir* and take your son back without paying the price?"

Lucy wasn't surprised when she encountered the demon only halfway to where it'd told her to meet.

She'd known this wouldn't be as simple as walking into the forest. She'd known the demon would find a way to catch her off guard. To catch everyone off guard.

"I fully expected to pay the price." She stopped several feet from it. "Where's my son?"

"On the other side of the gate, keeping company with a friend of mine. Bet you didn't know you had a gate between the planes in your own backyard." The demon patted a blue hand on the trunk of an ancient oak that stood tall and strong in the midst of younger pines, oaks, and maples.

Lucy shrugged, happy to be able to disappoint. "Of course I knew. My fault was allowing myself to believe you didn't."

"Then, Lady Lucy, allow me to gloat just a little at getting something past you."

"Don't take too long." She forced herself to casually cross her arms over her chest. "My *berserkir* will be here soon enough and he will not happy."

"Did you really not expect me to come with backup? Your *berserkir* may be strong but he can be slowed. And by the time he catches up, you'll be gone. Same for your *lucani*, who are only now realizing they've been outmaneuvered. If they get here before we leave, Caeles will be thrown into Aitás."

Lucy knew the demon would do it. She'd gone into this knowing their plan probably wouldn't work. She'd been willing to give it a try but she wasn't willing to let Caeles pay the price for her mistakes.

"If we go right away, I'll release Caeles when you pass through the gate into Aitás."

"You will release him back onto this plane."

The demon smiled. "Such a stickler for details. But of course he'll be returned to this plane. He's not the prize we want."

After a slow breath, she waved a hand in front of her. "Then I suggest we get this over with. Because Brandon is stronger than you think."

—∽—

The demon hit him broadside as Brandon raced after Lucy.

He'd realized there were two demons only seconds before this one had leaped on him and taken him to the ground. Brandon didn't even have to think about growing claws or fangs. They just suddenly appeared in a burst of white-hot pain that lasted only seconds.

As he and the demon went to the ground, Brandon used his claws to rip at its arms as they struggled.

The thing was wiry strong, but no match for Brandon in a rage.

And he was mighty pissed off. Apparently *berserkir* blood came with anger-management issues way worse than anything he'd previously been capable of.

So he used the anger. He let the rage fuel his power and when the demon rolled away only to come at him seconds later, Brandon let it get close. Let it think it'd gotten the drop on him.

He took a bone-rattling blow to the head but managed to dodge the thing's teeth as he used his claws to swipe at the creature's back.

The demon staggered back but Brandon sank his claws into its sides.

Furious screeches rang out as the demon tried to get away but only managed to work Brandon's claws deeper. The scent of blood hung in the air, mixing with the acrid, ashy scent of the demon.

The demon snapped at Brandon's neck, and instinct made him pull back, ripping his claws out in the process. Poison. Had to stay away from those teeth.

Brandon brought his hands up into a defensive position but the demon didn't make a move toward him.

And when it fell over in front of him, he realized why. He'd killed it with his bare hands. Bare claws.

Shit. Brandon's stomach flipped. He'd seen his share of blood on the ice, spilled enough of his own, but this…

He'd killed this creature. It didn't matter that the thing would've done the same to him. He'd never done more than break some guy's nose on the ice.

Jesus, he was gonna be sick. He drew in a deep breath. And another. No, he wouldn't. He couldn't. He didn't have time. He knew this wasn't the demon Lucy had been dealing with. This one's features were rounder and it wasn't as tall. The other one was probably dragging her away while he stood here hyperventilating.

Fuck that.

Fear made his feet fly, no longer worrying about how much noise he made. He breathed in as he set off, honing in on her scent. He was close. So fucking close. Not bothering with the trail, he barreled through the undergrowth and the shrubs.

He had to be close. He hadn't been that far behind. There! He saw a flash of color ahead through the trees. A flash that disappeared into a tree. Not behind a tree. Through it.

Without thought, he leaped for that black pit in the thick trunk of an obviously ancient tree. For a second, he thought for sure someone had played a trick on him. That they'd painted what looked like an opening on the bark so he'd jump for it and knock himself out. Like the coyote from the old cartoons, always after the roadrunner. Always fucking things up.

Not this time. Brandon sailed into the darkness, then fell. And fell.

—⁓—

Lucy heard someone approaching, just as the demon opened the portal. She hoped the damn blue bitch closed the portal fast because she knew whoever was coming would follow her.

No such luck.

A heavy body hit her hard and she went down, taking the demon that'd been holding onto her arm with her.

Mist enclosed everything in a gray shroud. Where they'd landed, there was no sun. Blessed Goddess, had the demon taken her straight to Aitás?

"Lucy! Run!"

"Brandon? Brandon, oh gods, get out of here!"

But she knew he couldn't. What little light there'd been from the portal was gone. The gate had closed.

The mist made it so hard to see. She was moving but not under her own steam. Someone was pulling her. She reached out for whoever it was and felt thick, strong forearms.

"Brandon!"

"Quiet, Lucy." He whispered into her ear and relief poured through her body. "Don't fight me. Stay–"

He groaned and fell away as the demon attacked him, knocking Lucy to the side and into what felt like a tree.

She had a brief moment to gasp in relief. Now she knew they weren't in Aitás. There were no trees in Aitás. That meant there was hope.

Blessed Goddess, she no longer had her powers, but that didn't mean she was useless. And she'd just decided she was sick of playing the helpless victim. Her eyes were used to seeing in the dark. She blinked a few times to accustom her vision and she quickly took in the scene.

At least the demon had meant to keep its part of the deal. Caeles lay bound and seemingly unconscious on the ground yards away from where Brandon and the demon now struggled with each other.

Not wanting to draw any attention, she kept low to the ground and scurried toward Caeles. She was trusting Brandon to keep the thing busy while she got to her son.

When she was sure Caeles was okay, they could join Brandon and try to get the hell out of wherever here happened to be.

Behind her, she heard fighting, flesh landing on flesh. Punishingly hard blows that elicited grunts of pain from both fighters.

She reached Caeles and started working on the rope binding his wrists and ankles. He roused just as she tossed away the ropes.

"Caeles, don't move," she whispered in his ear. "Don't draw their attention."

She knew he heard her because he stilled. His head turned slowly so he could watch the fight.

Brandon was holding his own, but Lucy could see his strength starting to flag. Her stomach gave a sickening twist as he took a blow to the face that snapped his head back.

She needed to do something before he was seriously injured. Looking down at Caeles, she saw his eyes narrowed in contemplation.

"Brandon needs a distraction, something to—"

Caeles shifted so fast she barely had the chance to understand what he was doing before he leaped to Brandon's defense.

He'd shifted into a bear... a huge black bear with fearsome teeth and dangerous claws.

The demon didn't respond quickly enough and Caeles caught both the demon and Brandon and they went to the ground in a tangle of arms and legs.

In the misty darkness, she watched as Brandon and Caeles wrestled the demon. Brandon had spared a quick glance at Caeles, his eyes widening before he'd had to return his entire attention to the blue demon.

The demon began to thrash wildly, fists and feet flying, connecting with flesh in audible thuds. It caught Brandon in the side with a vicious kick, sending him flying in the opposite direction, away from her. When Brandon didn't get up right away, she ran for him, keeping a wary eye on Caeles and the demon as she did.

Fear for two of the men she loved most in the world made her light-headed. Caeles seemed to be holding his own but he'd need help to win. And they had to win.

She knew they were close to Aitás. It was the only reason the demon would have brought them here. The longer they stayed, the more danger they were in of another demon coming to help.

By the time she reached Brandon, he was already shaking his head and getting back to his feet. He nodded once to her before he threw himself back into the fight.

Lucy gasped as she saw blood seeping from the back of his head. Too much blood. Godsdamn. Her hands curled into fists so tight, she swore she felt the bones crack. She could stand here no longer. She had to hit something, had to smash that demon's face—

"Hello, Lusna."

Lucy froze. She recognized the voice, though she hadn't heard it in almost two thousand years. Shit. This had all become so much worse. Lucy forced herself to take a slow breath as she turned, schooling her expression into a polite greeting. "Culsu. It's been a while."

"Yes, it has. You seem… different, Sister."

Rail-thin with negligible curves and curly, pale gray hair that reached her hips, Culsu, Lady of the Blue Gate, stepped forward. Her pale skin appeared to glow in the misty gloom, as did her silver eyes, the slimness of her body reflected in the sharp angles of her face.

Goddess Culsu had an ethereal beauty just this side of eerie. Her voice sounded sweet as spun sugar, but her ruthless personality was enough to strike fear into the heart of any sane creature.

As guardian of the gate to Aitás, Culsu made the decision as to where the newly dead ended their journey. Would they be sent to the black pits or merely into holding for the next reincarnation?

"*Tukhulkha, cesasin,*" Culsu ordered the demon to halt. "Call off your men as well, Lusna."

The demon had already stepped back when she called out to Caeles and Brandon to stop.

Caeles caught Brandon back with a large paw on his shoulder when Brandon would have rushed to her side. She met his wide-eyed gaze with a calm nod then turned back to the Underworld Goddess with a forced calm. The blood running down his neck made her heart beat like a trapped bird in her chest.

"Culsu." Lucy deliberately continued in ancient Etruscan, knowing Culsu didn't have a firm command of English. What goddess who spent her life in the Underworld would? "Why have you sent your demons to attack me?"

The goddess's slim, pale eyebrows curved into half moons. "I haven't. Why would I?"

Culsu looked sincere and she had no reason to lie right now. "Then you didn't know Charun was using the *tukhulkha* to kidnap goddesses back to Aitás?"

Culsu blinked, the only outward sign of her surprise. "No. Why would he?"

"Because he wants to leave Aitás."

True bewilderment showed in her frown. "Why would he wish to do that?"

"Why don't you ask him?"

Culsu paused. "I will the next time I see him."

"And when will that be? Have you seen him lately? Have you talked to him?"

Another pause, this time longer. "No. I haven't seen him for centuries, but that's not uncommon."

"Then be careful, Sister. He's seeking goddesses to consume for their power. He's already taken Mlukukh. He tried to take Thesan. He sent this demon to take me."

"And what would he do with your powers?"

"Leave Aitás."

Culsu frowned, her eyes narrowing to slits. "But that would upset the balance."

"I don't believe he cares. Watch your back, Culsu. We don't know what he's capable of."

"And so I will. But now I think you must leave. Your man is about to expire."

With a cry, Lucy spun, just in time to see Brandon's eyes roll back into his head as he went boneless. Shifting back into his human form, Caeles caught Brandon before he hit the ground.

"Shit. Mom, there's a lot of blood."

Caeles's fear barely registered through her own. She only knew it was bad. They had to get him back to home. Back to doctors who could heal him. Back to Amity.

"Culsu, please. You must send us back."

The goddess shook her head. "I can't open that gate. My only power lies with the one into Aitás. The demon must take you through any other. Or you could open it yourself." She paused and studied Lucy closely. "But you can't, can you? Your powers are already gone. Why?"

Lucy barely heard the other goddess. She could feel Brandon slipping away from her with every second. His eyes were closed and his chest barely rose and fell.

Culsu would not allow the demon to take her into Aitás but her life wouldn't be worth living if Brandon died.

"Lusna, what happened to your powers?"

She turned on the other goddess then, allowing all her anger and fear to show. "I gave them up for him. I don't expect you to understand, but you must get us out of here so I can find someone to fix him. I love him, Culsu."

The other woman merely stared at her before looking at the demon. "Take them back. She's of no use to Charun as she is now. And tell him I want to talk to him."

The blue demon sneered. "I'll release her and her toys because you're right. She's worth nothing any longer. Just an empty shell. We'll be seeing her back here soon enough."

The demon walked to a huge tree, laid his hand on the trunk, and muttered a spell that brushed against Lucy's remaining *arus* like a cold breeze.

Goose bumps rose on her skin as the tree disappeared and sunlight poured through. Without another word, she motioned for Caeles to bring Brandon and she pushed them into the light.

She turned back to Culsu, just before stepping through the gate. "Watch your back, Culsu. He'll turn on you too, if you're not careful."

The other goddess shrugged, such a graceful movement. "It wouldn't be the first time."

Chapter 12

BRANDON OPENED HIS EYES and found himself staring at the wall of his bedroom.

He immediately reached out to see if Lucy was in the bed with him and sighed when he realized she wasn't. Where was she? Had she left him?

Sitting up, he immediately put a hand to his head, which throbbed like he'd had it bounced off the boards and the ice before taking an elbow to the face and dropping gloves with Ryan Flinn.

Of course, the NHL's biggest bruisers were nothing compared to blue demons. He probably should be grateful his head was still attached. A headache was a small price to pay for still being alive.

But if Lucy wasn't here, would it matter that he was still breathing? He didn't want to live without her. She'd told him she loved him. Where was his goddess now? Had she brought him back to his apartment so she could disappear?

His heart fucking hurt at the thought. He took a deep breath in preparation for swinging his legs off the side of the bed and caught her scent. She was still here. He nearly went light-headed with relief. Or maybe that was his body telling him he needed to take it easy.

Fuck that. Lucy was here somewhere and he needed to find her. To wrap his arms around her and feel her breathing against him. He wouldn't believe she was still here unless he actually saw her, touched her.

He sat up as carefully as he could, realizing he'd been injured pretty badly from the feel of things. Managing to get himself into an upright position after a few minutes, he planted his feet on the floor as he sat on the edge of the bed, then remained there for another couple of minutes until the room stopped spinning.

He lifted his hand to his head but pulled it away with a hiss after he barely touched the back where the throbbing was the worst. That *really* fucking hurt. But that was the only place that did, so he'd count himself lucky.

He was still here, awake and mostly alert, so that had to mean he was out of the woods. Right?

Ignoring the little voice in his head that told him to lie back down, he listened instead to the ache in his gut that needed Lucy to ease it. Pulling on sweats, he followed his nose straight to her.

She was on his couch, looking as if she'd sat down for a second but fell asleep without meaning to. Exhaustion showed in the dark circles under her eyes and the paleness of her skin.

But she was breathing. And here. And he'd never seen a more beautiful sight.

Easing onto the cushion next to her, he gathered her into his arms and moved her onto his lap. He didn't want to wake her but he needed to hold her against him.

He thought for a second he'd gotten away without waking her, but when she drew in a short, sharp breath, he knew she'd woken.

She moved slowly, letting her head fall back so she could lift her wide gaze up to his. "Brandon."

"Hey, babe."

"How do you feel?"

"Like I got beat to hell and back by a blue demon."

Her lips curved slightly but her eyes darkened as she placed her hand on his shoulder, so gently he barely felt the weight. "That's because you did. Amity assured me you'd be okay but you've been asleep for so long, I wasn't sure…"

She shook her head as if she couldn't finish and her eyes welled with tears.

"Hey, babe, I'm fine now, right? Yeah, I've got a hell of a headache, but it's nothing a few"—*or an entire bottle of*—"aspirin won't cure."

Panic flared in her eyes. "Should I call Amity back? Maybe there's something she missed, something she could do to—"

"Lucy." He put his fingers over her lips, cutting her off. "I'll be fine. Hell, I've hurt worse than this after a few games. As long as you tell me you're not going anywhere, everything will be fine."

She didn't answer right away and a pit opened in the center of his stomach. Shit, maybe she still intended to leave, just walk out and he'd never see her again.

"I'm not good for you, Brandon. Since we've met, you've nearly lost your life three times in as many days."

"Lucy—"

"No, just hear me out." She shook her head, eyes so full of tears, it made his heart hurt. "I'd come to believe I'd never find a mate. And then I met you."

Now, that sounded better. "And you knew I was perfect for you."

And there was the smile he'd been waiting to see. "I knew you were trouble. And that if I let myself love you, I'd never want to give you up."

Now, didn't that just make the ache in his head ease while creating a new one lower in his body. "But you knew I was the one, didn't you?"

Her smile faded as her eyes cleared and brightened. "I did."

"Just like I knew you were the one for me." He leaned closer, careful not to move too fast though the pain was nearly gone. "So where do we go from here?"

She answered right away. "You already know I'm willing to go to hell and back for you. I've given up immortality because I don't want to live without you. I want to be wherever you are for however long we have together."

His smile nearly hurt, it was that big. "Ah, babe. Right answer, because that's exactly where I want you. Everything else, we'll figure out. My career, your world… which side of the bed you want to sleep on every night."

"But—"

He kissed her. Slow, soft. Not a lot of pressure. Just enough to show her he meant business. And to cut off whatever else she might be thinking.

He kissed her until her lips softened under his, and her arms wound around his shoulders. She shifted on his lap until she'd positioned her legs on either side of his and pressed her luscious body against him.

Since he wore nothing more than sweats and she wore only one of his T-shirts, he was relieved when his cock started to rise. At least everything still worked. And worked really well, apparently.

His hands fell to her smooth thighs, stroking along silky skin. He shouldn't even be thinking about how good she would feel naked and rubbing against him. Her breasts against his chest, her nipples poking into his skin. Like they were now, only bare skin to bare skin.

"Brandon." She leaned forward, her lips brushing against the curve of his ear. "You're not in any shape for anything other than sleeping."

"Honey, I'm up for anything you can throw at me. Including yourself."

Her hips sank just a little closer, then close enough to rub her bare sex against his fast-hardening cock, covered only by a thin layer of cotton.

Sensation shot through his body, making him draw in a sharp breath as his hands slid up her thighs, pushing under her shirt then around to palm her perfect ass.

Lucy froze, her gaze shooting back to his. "Brandon."

He loved to hear his name on her lips. He leaned forward for another kiss, more forceful this time as he played his tongue along the seam of her lips. She let him in with a little sigh, her eyes closing. The taste of her eased the pain in his head until it was barely noticeable. Probably because most of the blood had gathered lower in his body.

Releasing her lips, he kissed his way to her ear. He needed to be sure she heard him clearly. "I need to be inside you, Lucy. I need to know you're here and you're mine."

With sure hands, he reached for his sweatpants and lifted his ass just enough to work them down and free his cock. With one hand, he held it away from his body. With the other, he grabbed her hip and pulled her down onto his erection.

Her eyes flew open as she sank onto him, her wet heat encasing him. As she took him completely inside, she cupped his face in her hands and stared directly into his eyes as he began to thrust.

"I won't go anywhere without you, Brandon. I love you too much to lose you."

"And I love you, Lucy. I'll worship you for the rest of my life."

Author's Note

My husband is a huge hockey fan and, throughout the more than twenty years we've been married, his obsession has infected me.

We're lucky to have our own ECHL team, the Reading Royals, in our town and have had tickets since game one. From October through April (and sometimes beyond), we can spend as many as three nights a week cheering on our team.

The roster is always changing because of call-ups. The ECHL is a farm league. Our guys want to move up to the AHL and finally, hopefully, to the NHL. Many of them don't. Some get their shot and grab hold with both hands. James Reimer is a former Royal. So are Jonathan Quick, Rich Peverly, Barry Brust, George Parros, and Ryan Flinn. It's always a thrill to watch a game on television and see one of "our" guys on the screen.

There are always a few players who hang around the entire season and become fan favorites: Larry Courville (who played his last professional game as a Royal then returned to coach), Dany Roussin, Brock Hooten, Joe Zappala, Jon Francisco, and goaltender Cody Rudkowsky, just to name a few.

Then there are the guys who play for a few weeks, some only for a few days. Not even long enough to memorize their names and numbers. The next week, they're playing for the opposition.

There's no other game that's as fast-paced or as exciting as hockey, and even when I'm shivering under my Royal purple blanket in an ice hockey arena in the dead of winter, there's no other place I'd rather be than by my husband's side cheering on our guys, high-fiving after their goals, and being a member of the Royal's Thrust Crew.

Read on for an excerpt from
Book 1 in the Forgotten Goddesses series

WHAT A GODDESS WANTS

Now available from
Sourcebooks Casablanca

Prologue

THE THIRD BLOW FROM the iron hammer sent Caligo to the ground.

His face hit first, of course, and he spat blood until it pooled on the blacktop beside him. He thought about getting up, but really, why bother? He'd just end up back there again.

Three blows from the pissed-off Roman God of Volcanoes and Blacksmiths were two more than enough to convince Cal that no woman was worth the beating.

Not even Venus.

"Not so pretty now, is he, babe?" Vulcan shook his head, the girly black curls he was so proud of quivering around his ruddy face. "I don't know why you continue to bed these inferior humans. They're weak. And you know they can't satisfy your needs."

Cal couldn't help himself. "Maybe because she knows your dick is no bigger than my thu—"

Vulcan stepped on Cal's neck, effectively cutting off his air supply and his voice with one dainty Italian loafer. "Let's go home, babe. I'm sick of this crap."

"Oh, fine." Venus sighed. "I'm bored now anyway."

The Roman Goddess of Love and Beauty flung flame-red hair over her shoulder and barely glanced down at Cal as she stepped over him to take Vulcan's arm.

Her heel landed mere centimeters from Cal's nose.

He remembered those shoes. She'd worn them the last time they'd fucked. He probably still had the indentations in his thighs from where she'd dug them in, screaming his name as she came.

As Cal watched the deities walk away, Venus turned, her little black dress swinging around her ass, to give him a wink and a little wave.

To which he replied with a time-honored one-finger salute. *Bitch.*

As the couple disappeared down the deserted alley off South Street in Philadelphia, Cal dragged himself to the nearest wall and leaned against it, wiping blood from his chin and his left ear. The ringing in his head sounded like the extended buzz of a heavy-metal guitar, and his face throbbed, though he felt no pain. Probably gonna have a few new scars to add to the collection.

He shook his head, which just made him dizzy, and began assessing the damage. "When are you going to learn, asshole?"

He'd asked himself the question before. But here he was again, wounded and pissed off because he'd gone out of his way to help a pretty woman who obviously hadn't needed his help.

Fucking goddesses. Never a good idea.

As he cataloged the various bruises, cuts, and broken bones, he considered making the trek back to his car on Bainbridge but he figured someone would call the cops at the first sight of him.

Here seemed as good as any place to die. And if, by some miracle, he didn't die, this was the last fucking time he ever took a job for a deity.

They screwed you over every damn time.

Chapter 1

DYING WAS SO BENEATH her.

Of course, she hadn't done much living lately, so if he caught her now... Well, that would just suck. Because she'd recently decided it was time to change her ways. Get out more. Live a little. Get laid.

How pitiful was it that she couldn't remember the last time she'd had sex? Or if it had even been any good.

Pretty freaking pitiful.

Thesan, Etruscan Goddess of the Dawn, Lady of the Golden Light, was sick of being a pretty, useless deity. Much less a pretty, useless one usually just called Tessa.

For centuries... millennia... she'd brought light and beauty to the world. She'd guided the sun into the morning sky. She'd seen the rise and fall of empires. Gods had lusted after her. She'd worn out her share of mortal men in her bed.

She'd been worshipped by millions. Okay, maybe millions was stretching it just a bit. Still, she'd had a following, people who'd adored her and who'd worshipped her.

Now she was being chased by a crazed god intent on consuming her powers and leaving what was left of her soul to rot for all eternity in the dreary Etruscan Underworld of Aitás.

That totally sucked.

So did this. Her lungs heaved as she ran through a dark forest, the night sky black. No moon shone above. No stars twinkled. No reflected sunlight gave her even a hint of power.

Her legs shook like wet noodles, threatening to collapse at any moment. The underbrush swiped at her calves, and tree limbs caught at her hair, yanking and pulling.

Peering over her shoulder, she saw a dark shape weaving through the trees behind her. Her heart hurt as it pounded in her chest. Her bare feet bled and ached as she stumbled along.

Oh, she knew she really wasn't running. She was actually asleep in her lonely bed in her home in the quiet hills of eastern Pennsylvania. She knew that because she'd had the same dream for the past three weeks.

Charun, that blackhearted bastard, was taunting her like a high school bully picking on a weaker kid. But Charun's intent wasn't to merely frighten her, though the bastard did get a kick out of it.

No, he was wearing her down, waiting for her to make a mistake so he could pinpoint her location. So far, she'd been able to keep her whereabouts a secret. But when he broke through her defenses, he'd send one of his demons to drag her down to Aitás. To him.

The bastard couldn't come himself. He was tied to Aitás by bindings even he couldn't break. At least, not now.

But if he found her, if he managed to accomplish what she thought he had planned, then soon, maybe, he would be able to break those bonds. And this world would suffer as the demons and the damned escaped with him.

And she'd never get laid again. Damn it, she'd much rather go out with a literal bang than a figurative one.

With a gasp, she broke free of the dream and sat straight up in her bed, blinking at the bright light even though it was... three o'clock in the morning, according to the clock on the bedside table.

She'd left all the lamps blazing in her bedroom. An infomercial blared from the television, and the stereo on the nightstand blasted Puccini. None of it had been able to keep her awake. Probably because she could count on both hands the number of hours she'd slept in the past three weeks.

Damn it, she needed help.

Her nose wrinkled at the thought. She, a goddess, needed help. Wasn't that a real kick in a perfectly fine ass?

"Which won't mean a damn thing if Charun gets hold of it," she muttered to absolutely no one.

Hell, if she survived Charun, she needed to get out of the house so someone could see her fine ass again. Playing the hermit didn't suit her. She'd been one of the original party girls in her day, playing all night before hurrying off to meet the lovely sun each morning.

But now she was a forgotten goddess, her main reason for being usurped by that bitch of a Roman goddess named Aurora—

She took a deep breath. No, she couldn't think about that. Those thoughts led to teeth gnashing and sore jaws.

Still, she'd become a goddess without a true calling. What should she do with her never-ending life?

Oh, she delivered a baby or ten or twenty every year. In addition to being a sun goddess, she also helped bring new life into the world, one of the more pleasurable aspects of her life.

But that left her with a whole hell of a lot of time to fill. A girl could only do so much shopping and have so much sex before it all became so very… mundane.

She wanted to be useful again. She wanted the remaining Etruscans, those who still followed the old ways, to remember that she even existed. And she most certainly did not want to be eaten by Charun.

She needed help. And she knew just the person to help her find it.

"Hang tight… I'm coming. Just give me a minute."

The voice came from the second floor as Tessa stood in the entry hall of the small townhouse in Reading, Pennsylvania.

In front of her, a stairway led along the right side of the house to the upper floors. To the left of the stairway, a hall led straight down the center of the house. To the far left, a doorway led into the front sitting room.

Every inch of the place looked like it belonged to an inner-city *Brady Bunch*, from the '80s-era paisley wallpaper to the colonial blue paint on the trim. Cream carpet covered every inch of the floor, and an umbrella stood next to the small half-round table in the entry.

It all looked so normal, Tessa thought. So middle class.

Until Salvatorus began to stomp down the stairs. Then what would have seemed completely normal to any *eteri*, any nonmagical human, made a complete left turn into mythology land.

At four foot nothing, Sal had the fully developed upper body of a grown man. Wide shoulders, strong arms, nice pecs.

His face was a true marvel of his Etruscan heritage, handsome and strong. And those brown eyes, so dark they looked almost black, held a knowing warmth that always made Tessa smile.

As did the two shiny black horns sprouting from just above his forehead to peek through his glossy, black, curly hair. On any other man, those horns would have been enough to make a grown man choke on his own breath.

On Sal, well, the goat legs stole the show.

Beginning just below his belly button, those legs were covered with hide, a silky chestnut brown fur that was not a pair of pants. No, Sal had the actual legs of a goat.

"Hey, sweetheart," he said as he clomped down the stairs. "Haven't seen you for a while. What's up?"

His deep Noo Yawk accent made her smile grow. But her fear must have shown in her eyes because Salvatorus's gaze narrowed.

"Are you hurt, Tessa?" He descended the rest of the steps on those small hooves so fast she worried for his safety. But he made it safely to the bottom, took her hand, and began to lead her through the house.

"No." *Not yet, anyway.* "I'm fine."

"Well, you let me be the judge of that."

Salvatorus led her to the kitchen at the very back of the house and pointed her toward a seat at the small table there. He didn't speak, not right away, but set about making her hot chocolate, the rich scent of it making her stomach rumble.

Tessa had been here many times before, mainly for parties. She did love a good party, and Salvatorus threw some of the best. But his home also served as a safe house for anyone of Etruscan descent, including those deities who needed his aid.

She'd never sought aid from Salvatorus before. Really, a goddess who needed help? It sounded ridiculous.

And yet, not so much now.

Sliding into a straight-backed wooden chair, she let her gaze wander out the window over the sink and into the courtyard in the back. The August garden burst with color and fragrance that wafted in through the open window, enticing her to draw a deep breath. Roses, herbs, perennials, bushes, and trees bloomed and thrived in Sal's garden, no bigger than twenty feet by twenty feet.

It was beautiful, a testament to the sun's nurturing power and Salvatorus's skill.

Tears bit at the corners of her eyes. She tried to blink them away before they fell, but one escaped and plopped right into the mug of hot chocolate that appeared in front of her.

"All right, babe." Salvatorus slid into the chair opposite her. "Spill. And I don't mean tears."

She lifted her gaze to his. "Did you know Mlukukh has been missing? For more than a month."

If she'd surprised Salvatorus with her statement about another forgotten Etruscan goddess, he showed no sign of it. "No, I hadn't heard. But then Mel has dropped off the face of the earth for years, sometimes decades. She's always returned."

Tessa shook her head. "I don't think she will this time. In fact, I'm pretty sure I know what happened to her."

Salvatorus's eyelids lifted. "And that is…?"

She took a deep breath before leaving it out on a sigh. "I think Charun had her snatched and taken to Aitás where he consumed her powers and left her shell to rot in the underworld."

Now Salvatorus's eyes narrowed. "And you know this how?"

"Because he told me. He told me that's what he's going to do to me as well."

Acknowledgments

To my husband, David, for putting up with me. To Tay and Josh, for the same (except for the days Mom has to put up with you).

To my editor, Deb Werksman, for pushing me to be better.

To those people who I can call or email when I'm feeling like shit and I know they'll commiserate: Deb, Adele, Marilyn, and Daria.

One last shout-out: To Avenged Sevenfold, who provided much of the soundtrack for this book.

About the Author

Stephanie Julian is the author of *What a Goddess Wants* as well as two erotic romance series with Ellora's Cave: The Magical Seduction (seven books) and Lucani Lovers (second book available). She is a member of RWA and Valley Forge Romance Writers and is an entertainment and lifestyle feature writer for the *Reading Eagle*. Stephanie lives in Shillington, Pennsylvania.

Backstage Pass

SINNERS ON TOUR

By Olivia Cunning

. . . .

FOR HIM, LIFE IS ALL MUSIC AND NO PLAY...
When Brian Sinclair, lead songwriter and guitarist of
the hottest metal band on the scene, loses his creative
spark, it will take nights of downright sinful passion
to release his pent-up genius...

SHE'S THE ONE TO CALL THE TUNE...
When sexy psychologist Myrna Evans goes on tour
with the Sinners, every boy in the band tries to woo
her into his bed. But Brian is the only one she wants
to get her hands on...

Then the two lovers' wildly shocking behavior sparks
the whole band to new heights of glory... and sin...

. . . .

978-1-4022-4442-1 • $14.99 U.S. / £9.99 UK

SINNERS ON TOUR

Rock
HARD

BY OLIVIA CUNNING

{
Trapped together on the Sinners tour bus
for the summer, Sed and Jessica will
rediscover the millions of steamy reasons
they never should have called it
quits in the first place...
}

TOP READS OF 2010 AWARDS
LOVE ROMANCE PASSION ⋆ ALPHA READER
FICTION VIXEN ⋆ LOVES ROMANCES ⋆ SMEXY BOOKS

TOP SEX SCENES OF 2010 AWARDS
GOOD BOOKS, GOOD COFFEE, GOOD LIFE ⋆ SMOKIN'
HOT BOOKS

· ·

Praise for *Backstage Pass*:

"Olivia Cunning's erotic romance debut is
phenomenal."
—*Love Romance Passion*

"A sizzling mix of sex, love, and rock 'n' roll...
The characters are irresistible. Can't wait for the
second book!"
—*DforDarla's Definite Reads, 5 Stars*

978-1-4022-4577-0 • $13.99 U.S./£9.99 UK

WARRIOR

BY CHERYL BROOKS

*"He came to me in the dead of winter,
his body burning with fever."*

EVEN NEAR DEATH, HIS SENSUALITY IS AMAZING...

Leo arrives on Tisana's doorstep a beaten slave from a near extinct race with feline genes. As soon as Leo recovers his strength, he'll use his extraordinary sexual talents to bewitch Tisana and make a bolt for freedom...

PRAISE FOR THE CAT STAR CHRONICLES:

"A compelling tale of danger, intrigue, and sizzling romance!"
—Candace Havens, author of *Charmed & Deadly*

"Hot enough to start a fire. Add in a thrilling new world and my reading experience was complete."
—*Romance Junkies*

978-1-4022-1440-0 • $6.99 U.S. / £3.99 UK

SLAVE

BY CHERYL BROOKS

◇◇◇

"I found him in the slave market on Orpheseus Prime, and even on such a god-forsaken planet as that one, their treatment of him seemed extreme."

◇◇◇

Cat may be the last of a species whose sexual talents were the envy of the galaxy. Even filthy, chained, and beaten, his feline gene gives him a special aura.

Jacinth is on a rescue mission… and she needs a man she can trust with her life.

PRAISE FOR CHERYL BROOKS'S *SLAVE*:

"A sexy adventure with a hero you can't resist!"

> —Candace Havens, author of *Charmed & Deadly*

"Fascinating world customs, a bit of mystery, and the relationship between the hero and heroine make this a very sensual romance."

> —*Romantic Times*

978-1-4022-1192-8 • $7.99 U.S. / £4.99 UK

OUTCAST

BY CHERYL BROOKS

Sold into slavery in a harem, Lynx is a favorite because his feline gene gives him remarkable sexual powers. But after ten years, Lynx is exhausted and is thrown out of the harem without a penny. Then he meets Bonnie, who's determined not to let such a beautiful and sensual young man go to waste...

"Leaves the reader eager for the next story featuring these captivating aliens." —*Romantic Times*

"One of the sweetest love stories...one of the hottest heroes ever conceived and...one of the most exciting and adventurous quests that I have ever had the pleasure of reading." —*Single Titles*

"One of the most sensually imaginative books that I've ever read... A magical story of hope, love and devotion" —*Yankee Romance Reviews*

978-1-4022-1896-5 •$6.99 U.S. / £3.99 UK

ROGUE

BY CHERYL BROOKS

Tychar crawled toward me on his hands and knees like a tiger stalking his prey. "I, for one, am glad you came," he purred. "And I promise you, Kyra, you will never want to leave Darconia."

"Cheryl Brooks knows how to keep the heat on and the reader turning pages!"
—Sydney Croft, author of *Seduced by the Storm*

PRAISE FOR THE CAT STAR CHRONICLES:

"Wow. Just…wow. The romantic chemistry is as close to perfect as you'll find." *—BookFetish.org*

"Will make you purr with delight. Cheryl Brooks has a great talent as a storyteller." *—Cheryl's Book Nook*

978-1-4022-1762-3 •$7.99 U.S. / £4.99 UK

FUGITIVE

BY CHERYL BROOKS

"Really sexy. Sizzling kind of sexy...makes you want to melt in the process." —*Bitten by Books*

A mysterious stranger in danger...

Zetithian warrior Manx, a member of a race hunted to near extinction because of their sexual powers, has done all he can to avoid extermination. But when an uncommon woman enters his jungle lair, the animal inside of him demands he risk it all to have her.

The last thing Drusilla expected to find on vacation was a gorgeous man hiding in the jungle. But what is he running from? And why does she feel so mesmerized that she'll stop at nothing to be near him? Hypnotically attracted, their intense pleasure in each other could destroy them both.

PRAISE FOR THE CAT STAR CHRONICLES:

"Wow. The romantic chemistry is as close to perfect as you'll find." —*BookFetish.org*

"Fabulous off world adventures... Hold on ladies, hot Zetithians are on their way." —*Night Owl Romance*

"Insanely creative... I enjoy this author's voice immensely." —*The Ginger Kids Den of Iniquity*

"I think purring will be on my request list from now on." —*Romance Reader at Heart*

978-1-4022-2940-4 •$6.99 U.S. / £3.99 UK

VIRGIN

BY CHERYL BROOKS

**"Cheryl Books takes readers on an intergalactic
venture that they won't soon forget."**
—*Romance Junkies*

He's never met anyone who made him purr...

Starship pilot Dax never encountered a woman he wanted
badly enough. Until he met Ava Karon...

And he'll never give his body without giving his heart...

Dax is happy to take Ava back to her home planet,
until he finds out she's returning to an old boyfriend...

As their journey together turns into a quest neither expected, Ava would give herself to Dax in a heartbeat. Except he
doesn't know the first thing about seducing a woman...

PRAISE FOR THE CAT STAR CHRONICLES:

"You will laugh, fall in love with an alien or two, and be truly
agog at the richness Ms. Brooks brings to her worlds."
—*The Long and the Short of It*

"Really sexy. A sizzling kind of sexy."
—*Bitten by Books*

"A world of fantasy that will stretch the reader's imagination"
—*The Romance Studio*

978-1-4022-5165-8 •$7.99 U.S. / £4.99 UK

TOUCH IF YOU DARE

STEPHANIE ROWE

✦✦✦

HE'S JUST ABOUT THE HOTTEST WARRIOR SHE'S EVER SEEN...

Reina Fleming really appreciates a man who's on a mission—especially when he's a badass warrior doing his best to impress her. And Jarvis is charmed by the way Reina's magic touch can soothe his dark side.

But when Jarvis's attention puts her job, her home, and her family in danger, Reina has to decide whether love is worth the price...

Enter the nonstop, action-packed world of Stephanie Rowe's love stories—you'll never think of the manly arts in the same way again.

"ROWE IS A PARANORMAL STAR!"

—JR Ward, #1 *New York Times* bestselling author of Black Dagger Brotherhood Series

978-1-4022-4196-3 • $6.99 U.S./£4.99 UK

HOLD ME IF YOU CAN

STEPHANIE ROWE

✦✦✦

ESCAPING HELL WAS THE EASY PART...

Nigel Aquarian finally escaped from hell—now he wants to go back. After losing his best strategy for controlling his all-consuming rage, he'll need to find something—or someone—to keep his inner demons under control long enough to strike back at the maniacal witch who has captured his comrades.

NOT KILLING EACH OTHER'S GOING TO BE THE REAL CHALLENGE...

Enter Natalie Fleming. She is supposed to be able to bend anyone to her will, but since her own brush with death, she's been just a little off. The only way she can kick-start her powers is by giving free rein to her sensual side, and while that didn't go so well last time, the tortured warrior who needs her help is making quite a convincing case for losing control...

When these two fiery, passionate souls cross paths, they discover they are each other's best chance to defeat the hell that haunts them...if, of course, they don't destroy each other first.

978-1-4022-4197-0 • $6.99 U.S./£4.99 UK

DEMONS ARE A GIRL'S BEST FRIEND

BY LINDA WISDOM

A BEWITCHING WOMAN ON A MISSION...

Feisty witch Maggie enjoys her work as a paranormal law enforcement officer—that is, until she's assigned to protect a teenager with major attitude and plenty of Mayan enemies. Maggie's never going to survive this assignment without the help of a half-fire demon who makes her smolder...

Praise for Linda Wisdom

"Hot talent Wisdom does a truly wonderful job mixing passion, danger, and outrageous antics into a tasty blend that's sure to satisfy."
—RT Book Reviews

"Entertaining and sexy... Ms. Wisdom's stories have something for everyone." —Night Owl Romance

"Wickedly captivating... wildly entertaining... full of magical zest and unrivaled witty prose."
—Suite 101

978-1-4022-5439-0 • $7.99 U.S./£4.99 UK